Printed in the United States of America

First Printing, 2016

ISBN: 1530270987
EAN: 978-1530270987

Publishers: CAM Publishing

Other Books by Craig Mullins

Novels
Available in Paperback or Amazon Kindle

Hard Candy

Short Stories
Available on Amazon Kindle only

57
Unplanned Journey

In memory of Guinness

NO REFUNDS

By Craig Mullins

Prologue

Wednesday May 5 1982

She watches as they wheel him away, her beautiful baby boy, the six pound five ounce bundle she held for all of five minutes now going forever, as the tears roll down her cheek and the sobbing increases, she has never felt so alone. All she hears are the creaking wheels of the trolley as she realises that with every second her baby is getting further away, not just physically but emotionally—will she ever be able to forget about him? The smell—she will never forget his scent when she held him, and the taste of her own salt tears as with each sob the droplets become a stream become a torrent.

Left alone in the sterile delivery room of the NHS, Nicola Anderson knows she has no choice, adoption is the only one. Her parents have disowned her and friends shun her since the announcement of her pregnancy five and a half months ago. She denied it to herself for as long as possible but eventually nature took over. With her hormones imbalanced and her parents becoming more and more suspicious of her moods before insisting on seeing the family doctor. Virtually dragging her there, only for him to tell her the shocking news that she was nearly three months pregnant, his condescension was bad enough, but nothing compared to when she told her parents. She initially lied to herself and her parents, convincing them and her that she had a stomach bug and nothing more.

As the enormity of the situation hits her, lying on the hospital issue maternity bed, on her own—a terrified sixteen-year-old girl. The artificial light from the overhead fluorescents flood the delivery room, she thinks back over the events that have led her to this point in time. The ruination of her life, she should write a book—how to screw up your life in one easy step. She is still wearing the Winnie the Pooh pyjamas she had on when she went in to labour, over these she wears the hospital issue gown. She realises that her parents were serious about not wanting her or her bastard child back in the house as she is all alone in the sterile room, with its white walls, and grey trunking circling it.

With the floodgates fully open, she is unsure whether she will have the strength or will to stop, knowing that everything that is happening is her fault, nobody else's.

She lays there thinking back to the moment of her arrival; they brought her to this very room, in pain and screaming, her only concern to have the thing out of her and for the pain to be gone. A midwife attended to her, a rather plump woman, with kind eyes, but a sharp tongue, after a quick examination she told Nicola that she was nowhere near ready to introduce her baby to the world and that she would check back with her every half an hour or so. Within minutes of being left the loneliness too control. Lying on the bed, a pretty sixteen-year-old, with deep green eyes and olive complexion, dark brown hair in ringlets, she has lost the only people in her life who love her.

From the day she told her parents about her real condition she was no longer their daughter, she was a dirty little secret for them to bury away, and keep from 'all decent folk' as her mum is apt to recite to her whenever she opens her mouth. Nicola's belief is that once the baby is gone, they will welcome her back. She can see now that it's not going to happen, she is on her own, her friend Becky's parents are expecting her once she leaves the hospital, they will put her up until she starts her new life in London—alone. They disagree with the way her parents are treating her, but there is only so much they can do, and feel that for her own sake she needs to start afresh where she can lead a normal life without the stigma of a teenage pregnancy hanging around her neck.

As the tears continue to fall, stinging her eyes as they go, she struggles for breath as the snot builds in her nose, with nothing to blow it on she resorts to the sleeve of her pyjamas to wipe it away, smearing Winnie with tears and snot, Eeyore escapes by the narrowest of margins. She feels complete loneliness take over her body, overwhelming even the pain of the childbirth—that was forgotten the moment she held her beautiful baby boy—if she could choose to live or die at this exact second; she would choose the latter without hesitation. The opportunity for her and her son to be together in heaven has gone; she almost has a feeling of regret that she was not strong enough to take that option while she had the chance. Though now that he is here she is glad she has given him the opportunity to have a life, a life that she hopes will be amazing, a life she knows she will never have nor deserve.

Curling up in the foetal position, she closes her eyes and lets the sobs shake her body, how did she go from being a carefree sixteen-year-old to a woman with a baby, one that she gave away. How can her parents be so callous towards her, the time in her life when she needs them the most and where are they? Sitting at home, watching some game show on the telly, her mum shouting at the screen every time a contestant gets the answer wrong, her dad agreeing with her knowing she didn't know the answer either, but anything to keep his wife happy. They will sit there with a cup of tea—just like all English people do, after all tea can solve all the world's problems—and a packet of rich tea biscuits to share, their usual ritual of an evening, her mum will be wearing one of her floral nightdresses, with a flannel dressing gown over the top. Her dad on the other hand will still be wearing his trousers, shirt and tie; he does concede and remove his jacket in the evening.

Nicola misses them more than she can imagine, she longs to be back there with them now, as mundane as the evenings were, she craves the warmth and love that was on offer before she found herself in the predicament she now faces.

She recalls once more the earlier events, barely two hours since her arrival. A nurse pops her head round the door, "Are you okay pet?" in a thick Geordie accent, she repeats the question when she gets no reply, moving over to Nicola she touches her shoulder. "Ken I help pet?"

“Please just leave me alone,” She doesn’t bother to turn around and see who is asking the question. All she knows is that she wants to be left alone until her baby is ready, then it hits her, *this is my baby, why shouldn’t I keep it? Who’s to say I can’t be a mum? People do it all the time, get pregnant at fifteen and sixteen and keep their babies, why can’t I?* Then all the doubts envelop her, where will she live, she can’t take it with her to London, she doesn’t have the first idea about bringing up a baby, this is when she realises she needs her mum. Her sobs get louder, she doesn’t realise the nurse still has her hand on her shoulder, thankful to her for staying but even more thankful for not saying anything—just being there for her—more than she can say for her family.

Her last waking thought before all the exertion and the days emotions finally take its toll is of her perfect little boy, heading for his new life, with a family that will never judge him, will never be disappointed in him and will love him with all their hearts. She falls asleep with a smile on her tear-streaked face, dreaming of the life her little bundle will have, a better one than the one she could ever give him.

1

Friday May 26, 2000

80..90..100mph, at this speed the result should be instant death, body and car as one, unrecognisable, not that it will matter, no one notices him in his short life so surely no one will note his passing. The twelve-foot perimeter wall surrounding this modern industrial park gets ever closer as the car speeds towards it with reckless abandon, though the wall is not approaching at the rate it should be in relation to the speed of his car.

As the car approaches a hundred feet from the wall and seconds from impact and certain death, the wall appears to move away into the distance. 100...110...120mph the faster he drives the faster the wall retreats, his foot now presses hard on the accelerator, almost pushing it through the floor with his aggression. Adrenaline pumps through his veins, sweat drips from his brow and stings his eyes, but still the inevitable will not come. Still the wall retreats almost disappearing over the horizon, nothing else now visible just the wall far off in the distance, the sky a non-descript grey, not a single cloud, then silence, not even the sound of the engine growling, only his own heartbeat in his ears, and then… nothing.

"Beep beep"

"Beep beep"

Waking with a start Anthony bolts upright in bed as the early morning sun streams through the slat blinds burning his eyes. His pillow is soaking wet with sweat, his heart still pounds in his chest, for a moment he is still back in the car with the grey sky around him. This is the third time on three successive mornings he has had the same recurring dream, lately his thoughts are more and more suicidal, he only wishes he had the guts to do it. Maybe that is what the dream is trying to tell him, that he is too much of a coward to go all the way, that one day the wall will not retreat from him and he will be ready to do what has to be done.

He tosses off the sweat soaked quilt and makes his way to the bathroom, stepping over last night's clothes. The flat is small but it suits him, his boss owns it and deducts the rent from his wages. It's comfortable enough and convenient for work and most of the local amenities. It sits above the barbers at the bottom end of the small village high street, there is always a lingering smell of cologne, and hair treatment products as they drift up from below, far from unpleasant.

In the bathroom he starts the shower running, while it heats up he heads to the kitchen where he starts the coffee brewing. He has two indulgences in life, good coffee freshly ground and cigarettes, both of which he inherited from his father who drank a dozen cups and smoked forty Marlboro a day. While the coffee is brewing, a Colombian blend, he heads back to the bathroom and strips off; he has a reasonably toned body, not from working out but from working in the patisserie. The steam makes it impossible to see anything, he jumps in the shower hoping the lashings of steaming water will wash away the remnants of the dream and set him up for the rest of the day. The water is hot enough to strip flesh from the bone. He stands there for almost ten minutes just letting it hit his face, relishing the intense heat of the water—his penchant for pain evident.

Last night's dream still whirring in his head, a few tears seep from the corner of his eyes, in his heart he knows he has a lot to live for, but his head keeps telling him the opposite. Nobody will notice if he just disappears one day, a couple of people would miss him for a day or two, but even they would move on and forget about him—what contribution has he ever made to this planet? And what contribution is he ever likely to make. In all honesty, he knows that the world's resources are better spent on someone else other than him; he is only taking away from those that deserve it more than him.

Hearing a loud knock on the door brings him out of his reverie, he quickly turns off the shower in time to hear a further loud knock—at least he's not hearing things. He grabs a towel from the rail by the sink, now more grey than white and has seen better days, but at least it's clean, wrapping it around his waist he heads for the door dripping water as he goes. Another loud crack on the door and Anthony looks at the clock on the wall as he approaches the front door, seven o'clock, only one person knocks at this hour of the morning. Anna and he have been friends since they were eight, their parents were neighbours and consequently the two of them became friends. The bond they formed all those years ago connects them for life, they are family, she is the main reason he finds it so hard to end it all, if his life didn't have her in it, he believes he would have no hesitation in suicide, but the thought of leaving Anna scares him more than the idea of taking his own life.

He opens the door, "What do you want at this hour of the morning?"

"I thought you might want a bacon sandwich before you head off to work—but in future I won't bother" The hurt look on her face makes her look cute, the banter between the two is always like this. Neither wanting the other to know just how much they need each other, both scared of showing any true emotions, whether it is love, hate or indifference. A coping mechanism, but deep down they both know that without each other they would be the loneliest people on the planet.

"Well now that you're here—make yourself useful and pour the coffee, it's on the side and should have brewed by now, and is there brown sauce in the sandwich? I'll go and get dressed."

"I've known you long enough to know what you like and that you won't eat a bacon sandwich without brown sauce" she snaps back. "And don't get dressed on my account; you know that's how I like my men—all hot and wet and wearing very little" she adds with a glint in her eye. The two of them have an air of sexual tension between them, each of them knowing that there'll never be anything between them, so it is safe to flirt, they're more like brother and sister. Anthony holds a well-hidden torch for Anna, he would like nothing more than for them to be a couple, he has done since they were eight years old but he's never had the confidence to do anything about it. A decision he regrets, he has left it too long and now she sees him only as a friend, he is happy with that as having her as a friend is better than not having her at all.

Five minutes later, they're sat at the breakfast bar in the small but well-designed kitchen, both eating bacon sandwiches as if their lives depend on it and gulping down large mugs of the freshly brewed coffee. After eating in silence they both move to the terrace—for terrace read fire escape—to have a cigarette, Anthony hates smoking indoors and even in the depths of winter chooses to smoke out on the fire escape. An old style metal grill type construction with the littered alleyway below them with piles of black sacks next to the industrial waste bin, there are no steps down as a ladder has to be engaged to reach the ground. A flight of stairs do go up, this gives access to the roof a favourite spot of Anthony's during the summer.

"Have you heard anything back from social services yet?" Anna tentatively asks. Depending on Anthony's mood depends on the sort of answer she'll get. It's the one subject, regardless of how long they've been friends for, it's the thing that can cause tension between them. Fortunately, today seems to be a good day.

"Nothing, although the post hasn't arrived yet." No hint of sadness in his voice as can often be the case. What he's waiting for are the details about his birth mother from social services, he applied for them a couple of days after his eighteenth birthday and was told it could take a few weeks for the information to be delivered—that was two weeks ago today. For a split second he is transported back to his dream, maybe that is why the wall keeps receding, he has unfinished business. The seconds of silence and the glazed eyes do not go unnoticed with Anna, but she doesn't push it, choosing to let it slide for the time being. She knows that he is going to need her more than ever very soon, good or bad, the news from social services is going to change his life forever. For as long as she has known him, the idea of his mother has fixated in his mind. She can't help but feel that whatever the outcome it will never be what his mind has conjured up, she doesn't believe he has any illusions about her, that she will come into his life and be everything that he ever dreamed of, but on the other hand she doesn't believe he is ready is she outright rejects him.

"Are you coming round later for pizza and DVD night?" He quickly asks, changing the subject, aware that he had disappeared in his own little world for a second. The sounds of cars driving up the high street, people going about their daily lives, while the pair of them oblivious to anything but each other.

"Sure, what time are you finishing?"

"Should be home by about six, I'll pick the pizza up on the way home, the key will be in the usual place if you wanna get here earlier." Knowing she'll come here straight from work.

By the time they've finished their coffee and cigarette it's nearly seven-thirty, another day when they're both going to be late for work. Anthony is supposed to start at seven-thirty at the local patisserie a bit further up the high street; he's been working there since his parents died when he was sixteen years old. Although his eighteen-year-old sister took responsibility of him after the tragic car crash that took the lives of his parents, he moved out at his first opportunity, much to her relief. The thought of living with his sister was not an option so he found a job working in a patisserie in a nearby village, a couple of miles from the house he'd lived in his entire life, a place that had never been a home. After a couple of months of working for Mike at his patisserie, he offered Anthony a flat he had above the barbers further down the high street on the condition that he would take the rent from his wages each week before he paid him, ensuring that the rent was paid on time all the time. This arrangement suited Anthony, he had somewhere he could call his own and finally get away from his bitch of a sister. She's the one person he can't see any good in, which is unusual for him as he was born to believe that however despicable or nasty someone is, there's always a good person trying to get out. His sister, he believes that the good person that may have been in her up and left realising she was a lost cause.

She still lives in the family house on a local council estate. Since he has left, she's popped out two brats by two different blokes, neither of whom have stuck around long enough to witness the fruits of their loins being bought forth into this pathetic world, a world of misery they will undoubtedly have to endure with the bitch from hell if his own childhood is anything to go by. Even though she's only two years older than him, from the age of four all he remembers is the constant bullying, both physical and mental. With his parents always siding with his sister, she had a way of winding them round her little finger and giving them the look she had, as though butter wouldn't melt, god he hated her.

Bitterness and resentment is not naturally part of his genetic code, but where his sister is concerned he's prepared to make an exception, he had a certain resentment to his parents as well but also a sense of gratitude for at least pretending they wanted him around. He always had a strange feeling around his parents, whether it was in his mind, or something within their tone or body language that made him think they would rather have traded him in for another model given the chance. They had at least stuck with him and tried to love him, as he had tried to love them. Anthony knew in himself that he wasn't the easiest person to love; he could be stubborn and moody even from an early age. Nevertheless, parents were supposed to see beyond this and love you, deep down he knew it was because he was not part of them unlike his sister who was truly their daughter, his mum had been told after giving birth to Tracey that she would not be able to have any more children of her own. He believed that his parents' belligerence towards him was because he was the unwanted product of some teenage slut's desire for a quick fuck and to hell with the consequences—which as luck would have it, happened to be him. Anthony saw it a different way, that his parents should be grateful that the said slut had the foresight to offer him for adoption rather than the alternative. To reinforce his theory he never forgot that whenever his mother met someone new he was always introduced 'and this is Anthony he's our adopted son' always said in her sickly sweet voice as though she must be a saint for taking in this unwanted by product of some sluts quick fuck.

2

Friday May 26, 2000

"Hey sleepy head, if you don't get a move on your going to be late, aren't you supposed to be meeting the girls at Rico's", Paul gives his wife a playful dig in the ribs until she reluctantly acknowledges that she is awake.

"What time is it? I didn't hear the alarm go off," Nikki questions through half closed eyes, head barely lifting from the pillow.

"Just gone seven thirty, I've got to run, or I'll be late for my meeting" he leans over his wife removing the half eaten slice of toast from his mouth before giving her a kiss on the top of her head, before resuming his breakfast. Mornings are pretty much the same in their household, Paul is always up and out before Nikki drags herself from bed, "I'll pick up a couple of bottles of red on my way home for tonight", it is their turn as hosts for their weekly dinner party with the neighbours. Though these are not ordinary neighbours, Neptune Wharf is a converted warehouse south of the Thames with fantastic views overlooking Canary Wharf. The warehouse, arranged over three storeys, and converted into three luxury apartments each with about four thousand square feet of living space. Paul Pope and his wife Nikki live on the first floor, Paul is a graphic designer working for one of the large advertising agencies in the city—he can see his office block in Canary Wharf from their window. Hayley Carter, Nikki's friend since they were about twenty years old, occupies the ground floor. Hayley is currently single although she likes it that way, her philosophy is why eat the same thing every night when there is so much more on the menu. Her idea is to sample as much of the menu as possible before deciding what her favourite dish is, then maybe, just maybe she will be happy eating the same day in day out knowing that there is nothing better.

The best apartment—the penthouse—is owned by Aimee and Steve Stark, Aimee is Nikki's partner at the beauty salon, and Steve has known Paul since their school days, their apartment is something else as thy have the roof terrace and the views across London are spectacular.

Nikki crawls out of bed and heads straight for the shower. She has a habit of sleeping in the nude; the walk to the bathroom would be daunting for most people, as she has to walk down the stairs from the mezzanine level and across the open expanse of their living area—complete with floor to ceiling picture windows overlooking the Thames—to the main bathroom. They have an en-suite on the mezzanine with a roll top bath, but Nikki prefers the main bathroom with its power shower first thing in the morning to wake her up. Walking across the living space, she is a thing of beauty, with her olive skin tone; she stands about five foot seven, her dark brown hair in ringlets half the way down her back, startling green eyes, the perkiest small breasts and a perfectly rounded bum. She walks with an air of confidence, proud of whom she is, and her life is perfect, she doesn't believe it could be any better. It takes Nikki about forty-five minutes to get ready in the morning; she should be able to make it to the coffee shop on time for a change. The girls meet there most mornings before work, sometimes Hayley cannot make it due to her job as a lawyer, but Monday to Friday, both Nikki and Aimee meet up before heading across the road to the salon. A small boutique style salon south of the river, Aimee has her assistant open up every morning, which means the girls get to have their coffee and danish fix before work, this is a new trend since the amazing success of an American sitcom called Friends based around a coffee shop in New York called Central Perk. It took a while for the trendy coffee bars to establish themselves over here but they have caught on well.

Nikki runs the beauty side of the salon, while Aimee dedicates her time to the hairstyling. Aimee's reputation as the stylist brings the customers through the doors. Once in, Nikki can then offer a range of services including nails, waxing, and beauty treatments and tanning. Nikki met Aimee about twelve years ago when Paul invited his best friend and then girlfriend over to their old flat for dinner. They had an instant chemistry right from the off, Aimee was explaining how her parents had just bought her a hair salon south of the river, and that she was looking for someone to run the beauty side of it. She said that Paul thought she might be interested in coming on board as a partner. Since that night, they had become close and their business could not have been going better.

Standing under the intense heat and pressure of the shower, Nikki knows she has a good life, though from time to time she has a tendency to dwell on the past, this morning is one of them, more melancholic than anything else, a deep regret over things past and forgotten—though forgotten is never really true. Ten minutes under the water and the moment passes, she knows that decisions were made for the right reasons, and the best of intentions now cannot change mistakes of the past. She reminds herself constantly that she could not have handled it.

She steps from the shower, a pristine white towel wrapped around her body and one around her hair, the thoughts of the last five minutes now consigned to the back of her mind.

3

Arriving at the patisserie, ten minutes late as usual, Anthony shouts across to Mike who is just transferring the croissants from the proving oven to the main baking oven "sorry I'm late Mike it won't happen again".

"Like I haven't heard that one before, if I had a pound for every day you were late I'd be retired in the South of France by now" with this, Mike gives out a great big belly laugh. Over the last two years, Mike has become like a father to him. Mike has no kids of his own, he and his wife decided on no kids at an early age, but since Anthony came to work for him, he took an instant liking to him. Mike and his wife are in their forties, and already have a couple of patisseries and half a dozen flats, which they rent out.

"Tony, can you go and make a start on the Danish pastries ready for that order this afternoon?" now Mikes stopped laughing at his own joke he instructs Anthony in his first job of the day. Mike is the only one that has ever called him Tony, and the only reason he does is he knows it winds him up.

"Will do, what time are they picking them up?"

"Around two thirty, hey how's that girl of yours doing?" Mike looks at him and winks.

"You know very well she ain't my girl, we've been mates for too long" Anthony going slightly red in the face, as Mike knew he would.

"Well you should make her your girl before she gets snapped up by someone else, besides looking the way you look I'm not even sure she'd have you" with that he's cracking up with laughter again. Mike knows Anthony and Anna should be together, unfortunately, neither of them can see it. Anthony with his Romany features and olive skin looks like he has stepped straight from a travelling fairground. His deep brown eyes seem to reach into your soul and see the truest form of anyone he looks at—he has the ability of measuring someone up within a few minutes of meeting them, and decides there and then whether he likes and trusts them. It can be quite cold to watch when he meets someone that he doesn't like, no second chances, he just takes on a vacant look as though he's seen enough and is not interested in them anymore. Most people don't notice, but in the two years or so that Mike has known him he has witnessed it first hand on many occasions. In complete contrast if he sees something in someone that interests him, there is a certain spark in his eyes, they could be his friend for life, he would lay down his life for them.

Mike remembers that look the first time this sad looking travelling gypsy came into his patisserie asking for a job, for the first time in his life Mike said yes without even giving it a second thought. It was something in the eyes that told him he would not regret it. Although when he walked in, all six foot of him, wearing stonewashed ripped jeans with a black t-shirt and mop of unruly curly black hair, he was not the sort of person you would expect to employ in a fancy patisserie. As it is Anthony's turned out to be the best decision Mike's made, not only was Anthony a very attentive student and eager to learn, he also seemed to have a very natural ability with pastry work and the customers loved him, he would swear some of the old ladies only came in because Anthony works there.

"Anthony, would you be able to lock up for me tonight, the wife wants us to go out for a meal?" Mike asks.

"Sure, not a problem Mike." He's beginning to feel one of his moods coming on, so it will be a relief to be on his own later.

The day passes uneventfully; Mike's noticed that Anthony seems to be a bit upset and out of sorts today, he knows that when Anthony's in this kind of mood he is best left alone. He makes it clear to him that he is there if he needs him, but doesn't press him on the subject. He knows he's anxious about finding his birth mum, but he thought he was getting better, he hasn't seen him this down in a while, he was full of the joys of spring when he came into work this morning. He has to leave if he is going to make his dinner date with his wife.

"Are you sure you'll be okay?" Mike asks one last time.

"Yes, I'll be fine, you get off." Anthony insists, just wanting to be on his own now. With that, Mike walks out the door leaving Anthony alone. With the shop shut, all Anthony has to do is tidy up the kitchen and lock up, about half an hours work. As the day's gone on, Anthony has been thinking more and more about his birth mum, alternating between loving and hating her. He has days like this, he can't seem to stop them. Standing there in front of the six-burner stainless steel stove, he thinks about why his mum gave him away, he can feel the tears welling up in his eyes, the tears beginning to sting the more he thinks about her not wanting him. What is wrong with him, there must have been some reason for her not to want him.

Sitting now on the floor with his back to the oven, the tears now freely flowing, wiping them away with the sleeve of his chef whites. His mind starts drifting into the darker areas he tries to hide, thoughts turning to ways of hurting himself. Lost in his own world he goes into a place inhabited by demons wanting him to inflict pain, in the past he's cut himself, though his preferred method of torture is burning. The pain always makes him feel better, in some twisted area of his mind it makes him flawed, a legitimate reason why his mum never wanted him, he can tell himself that she gave him away because he isn't perfect, he is faulty. Ultimately, he knows that when she gave him up for adoption he was perfect, but by inflicting these wounds he can justify why she had to get rid of him. Standing up now, and reaching for one of the old kitchen knives (he never uses the good chef knives as Mike would notice if there were scorch marks on them). Knowing that he has securely locked all the doors, he lights one of the gas burners, tears still falling from his eyes, the saltiness running down his cheek into his mouth, the taste reminding him how stupid he is being, he just wants the pain to go away. Rolling his chef jacket sleeve up as far as it will go, wiping away yet more tears, holding the tip of the knife over the blue flame of the gas, mesmerised by the dancing flames and the knife beginning to glow. Going through shades of oranges and reds before eventually glowing white, oblivious to the pain he is about to inflict on his body.

With the white hot blade he places it against the skin of his outer forearm about six inches from his wrist—this is so his chef whites will keep it hidden—rocking the blade he makes one continuous mark about an inch and a half long at a slight angle. The skin sizzling as the blade touches, causing the skin to instantly blister along the line with the area around it reddening. Placing the blade over the flame once more, openly sobbing now, and talking to himself 'What is so wrong with me that she couldn't bear to keep me', the second mark joins the other one creating and upside down 'V' shape. Repeating the process time after time, the pain not registering, his sobbing subsiding and the tears drying up, he doesn't know why but a sense of calm comes over him, a kind of serenity. For a while he knows he will be at peace with himself, he can take anything that the world can throw at him. Knowing it makes no sense, inflicting pain on your self should not make you euphoric, but it does, he just can't explain why.

No one has ever known what he does to himself; he has managed to hide it from the people he cares about most, knowing that they would feel a sense of guilt for not stopping him. Unlike most people that cut themselves or inflict pain, his is not done for attention; he would be devastated if anyone knew what he does to himself. After hiding the knife at the back of one of the drawers, he runs his arm under cold water, with his adrenaline levels now regaining normality, he can feel the heat building within his arm, there is still no pain, the heat of the blade seems to numb the area burned. After patting his arm dry, he looks down at his handiwork, realising how stupid he's been, for there on his arm clearly visible even with all the redness he sees 'ANNA' burned into his skin, he's now become a branded animal. The property of Anna, not that it would bother him being hers, what does bother him is that the weather is warm and he usually wears t-shirts, he should have done the branding further up his arm where a t-shirt could have covered it. There is nothing he can do about it. He finishes cleaning up the kitchen before changing out of his work clothes and locking up before making his way home. His mood lighter now and looking forward to the evening planned with Anna, his fix of pain once more making the world and his life a little more bearable. It's nearly quarter to six by the time he leaves and he has to pick up a DVD and a pizza, the DVD will be of his choosing, however the pizza always has to be pepperoni—Anna's favourite.

Walking down the high street, already feeling better, and his mood has lifted; suddenly things don't seem so bad. He doesn't know why he gets like he does, all he knows is he can't stop it. He's hoping that if he can resolve the issues with his birth mum, get answers to the questions spinning around his head, then he can move on. Whether he has any kind of relationship with her is another story, in his ideal world she will be the mum he didn't get the first time around. At times he feels cheated that he has missed eighteen years of her. Coming to the pizza place first he goes in and orders their pepperoni pizza, while he's waiting he pops two doors down to the video rental place. He knows which film he wants to see, hopefully they will have it in stock, he's decided on Breakfast At

Tiffany's, they both love watching the old films more than the modern ones. After picking the film, which they have in stock, he heads back to pick up the pizza before heading home.

Arriving at his front door, he checks himself over, once more wiping his eyes, just in case, the warmth of his arm reminds him of how stupid he has been. Turning the key in the lock he enters his flat.

4

As she arrives at Rico's she spots Aimee and Hayley at a table by the window, the walk here was glorious, the sun was beating down even this early in the morning. She goes over to the table where Hayley already has her usual waiting for her—Latte and a blueberry danish, "I'm not late am I?" Nikki asks, knowing full well that she is, punctuality has never been a priority for Nikki.

"The day you are the first one here, I will buy breakfast for a month" Hayley laughs, knowing there is not a cat in hells chance of Nikki being here first. She knows that Nikki has a profound dislike of getting up in the morning; she has been the same for as long as she's known her.

"Are we still all on for dinner tonight?" Nikki asks.

"Looking forward to it, although Steve said he may be running a bit late as he has a meeting straight after work, but he has assured me he will be there. Besides, he knows if he lets me down there will be no special treat for him when we leave yours later. And believe me he does not want to miss tonight's treat, all I will say is that it involves whipped cream" Aimee shares with her two closest friends.

"I should be there early as my last client is coming in at three-thirty and he is only booked in for an hour, so it should give me time to get home, get dressed up and be at yours by about six. I can give you a hand then if you like." Hayley offers.

"That would be great, thanks Hales."

They discuss the evening a bit more, Hayley and Nikki attempt to get more details from Aimee about what exactly is in store for Steve after the evening has ended. All Aimee gives them is that it involves a purchase of lingerie and the aforementioned whipped cream. Hayley is the first to leave, heading to work where she has a client booked in for eight-thirty, less than five minutes later Nikki and Aimee head just across the road to the salon. The girls have a very close relationship, yes they have their falling outs, but things always get patched up in the end. The salon is neither small nor large, it has the main reception area, divided into two—a waiting area and the main salon area with three chairs and sinks, although Aimee is the only stylist, she has another girl that helps, and two days a week she rents a chair to another hairdresser. Off the main area are three doors, one leading to the staff area, a cramped room for making tea and coffee, and the door to the toilet, then there is a door to a small stock room, and a door to Nikki's treatment room. This room is about the size of the haircutting area of the salon, it has a treatment couch, table for doing nails, a tanning booth, and a booth for Nikki to do spray tans, she like to think of the room as cosy rather than cramped.

The setup works for both of them, yes they would like larger premises, but they are content where they are, their clientele like them the way they are, and besides larger premises come with larger bills, and with both their husbands in well paid employment, it is not about the money for them. They enjoy what they do, they love working with each other—even if they do drive each other crazy occasionally—they have discussed expanding but neither has the drive or ambition to become beauty moguls, they like the personal touch they have with their clients.

5

Friday May 26, 2000

Anna gets to Anthony's flat just after five thirty, she retrieves the key from under the mat—no one would ever think to look for a key under a mat she thinks to herself. Letting herself in, this is like a home from home for her, she spends more time here than at her parents' house. Anthony has even given her space in his wardrobe and her own drawer for when she stays over.

Knowing she has time before Anthony gets home with the pizza, she walks down the hall shedding her clothes as she heads for the shower, once in the bathroom she turns the shower on, and while waiting for it to heat up she stares at herself in the mirror. Thinking that she needs to tone up and maybe lose a little weight, when in reality she was the fantasy of most men. The reflection staring back standing there in bra and knickers is five foot six, curvy figure, definitely not overweight, none of that wafer thin model look that is so popular these days. Long naturally blonde hair reaching just below her shoulder blades, striking ‘doe caught in the headlights’ azure blue eyes, porcelain smooth skin, firm—not overly large breasts and legs that seem to go on forever promising untold riches for anyone lucky enough to reach their summit.

The bathroom has begun steaming up; she unclips the front of the bra and lets it fall to the ground, stepping out of her knickers she steps into the shower letting her worries wash away from her. She is fearful at the prospect of Anthony getting in touch with his birth mother. Although he acts as if it doesn’t bother him, she knows deep down it terrifies him she will reject him, as everyone else in his life has done over the years. Although ‘reject’ probably is not the right word, indifference is closer to the truth, both his adoptive mother and father—mum and dad would mean they loved him unconditionally—and his self-serving, selfish bitch of a sister could not have cared whether he was there or not. Anna had been round to his parents’ house on many occasions, while they were still alive, to see Anthony and had seen first-hand what they were like; Anna knew that the house was always very welcoming to outsiders. His mother always made you feel most welcome but underlying this there was coldness, a kind of sterility where love and affection had never been. Anna feels that this is partly the reason Anthony is the way he is, she knows he is capable of great love for the right person—he radiates love whenever he’s around her, but she has witnessed times during social interaction with others where he comes across as cold and unfeeling towards anyone in his vicinity. She attributes this to his upbringing in a loveless family.

Anna fears for Anthony and what he might do if his birth mother rejects him without a thought, she knows that in his eyes this will be the ultimate rejection. He could cope with his adoptive family being the way they were, by telling himself that they were not really his family, not his blood, different genetic code, you can't put a stranger into a family—even if it is a new born baby—and expect it to work out perfectly every time. However, when it comes to his birth mother, if she rejects him, does it mean that he has a fatal flaw, she should have destroyed him before inflicting him onto the world. After all, what is the point if the woman who carried him for nine months and went through the agony of childbirth just to bring him to life says she has no interest and wants nothing to do with him?

Now these thoughts keep running around in her head all day every day. She has not mentioned any of this to Anthony. As she stands there under the steaming running water, hair plastered to her head with the force of the jets she can feel the tension beginning to leave her muscles, she just stands there for a couple more minutes letting all the soap wash away before turning the shower to cold only. She lets the freezing water hit her body, bringing her out in goose bumps and making her nipples as hard as bullets, she does this because she believes it will tighten her skin and stop her from ageing too quickly. Turning off the shower, she hops out and quickly wraps a towel around her and another around her hair like a turban.

She crosses the small hallway to Anthony's bedroom, where she goes to her drawer for some clean underwear, then to his wardrobe grabbing his baggiest Miami dolphins football jersey, she puts this on over her knickers, she's all ready for a night of pizza and DVD.

Going into the cosy lounge come kitchen come dining area she puts some music on—John Coltrane's 'Best Of' Album, Anna and Anthony both share a love of Jazz, although they don't always agree on who's the greatest.

It's nearly six now so Anthony should be home relatively soon, Anna goes into the kitchen area and grabs a couple of cans of Carlsberg from the fridge—noticing that there's not much else in there apart from the dozen cans of lager, some cooked chicken, half a dozen eggs and some milk. She pours the lager into a couple of glasses, one thing Anna has noticed about Anthony since he has been living on his own, he keeps the flat remarkably clean and tidy for a guy, he does have a habit of leaving clothes lying about—just like her.

The flat is open plan with the kitchen and lounge one large open space, with a breakfast bar separating the two. Then there is a small hallway leading to the one and only bedroom and bathroom. Mike had the flat refurbished just before Anthony moved in; nothing is too much trouble where Anthony is concerned. She likes the way Mike seems to look out for him, he is the father figure that he never had and Anthony seems to genuinely like and trust him, even love him in the way that he can love. There is an old television in the corner with a DVD player, the television is Mike's but the DVD player Anthony bought as a moving in present to himself. Then there is a two-seat sofa and a single chair, again it came with the flat. The open fireplace is Anthony's favourite thing about the flat; he loves the winter evenings when he can put some wood in the fire and just chill out.

Just as Anna is settling into the sofa, she hears Anthony's key in the lock, the time is about ten past six and true to his word; he is carrying a pizza box and a DVD rental from the shop down the road. One of the great things about living above a shop in the high street is everything being close at hand, which is just as well as Anthony doesn't have a car.

"Hi, what time did you get here?" Anthony enquires.

"About half five, hope you don't mind but I grabbed a quick shower and one of your t-shirts" she replies.

"I can see that from the trail of clothes you've left across the floor"

"Don't worry I'll pick them up later, ooh what pizza did you get? It'd better be pepperoni or you're in big trouble mister"

"I'm shaking in my boots, of course its pepperoni; do we ever eat any other type? Could you dish it up and I'll jump in the shower quickly"

"Sure, then I'll come and give your back a scrub" Anna says looking over her shoulder and winking.

"Looking like you do, you can scrub my back anytime" with that, they both burst out laughing. Standing in the shower with the steaming water hitting his body, he becomes conscious of his arm which is beginning to sting a bit under the hot water, looking at it he can't believe he wrote Anna's name on his arm, how is he going to keep it from her, she often sees him with his top off. The heat is making his arm redder by the minute. After getting out of the shower, he puts on a clean long sleeved t-shirt and a pair of jogging bottoms. Anthony always has two showers a day, one to set him up for the day ahead and one to wash away the sweat and toil. His parents were always complaining about the amount of hot water he used. Anna is sitting on the sofa legs curled underneath her, plate in one hand and a slice of pizza in the other, "you'd better hurry up before I finish it all".

"Move over then so I can sit down" he says at the same time nudging her across the sofa.

"So what film did you get—hope it's an oldie?"

"Breakfast at Tiffany's, It's a film I've always wanted to see"

"Me too, I saw it years ago when my parents watched it but I was only about nine so I don't remember it that well, I do remember at the time that I wanted to grow up to be as beautiful and sophisticated as Audrey Hepburn" Anna reminisces.

"Well I suppose there's still time" Anthony gives her a quick poke in the ribs.

After putting the DVD in the player and getting them both another couple of drinks from the fridge, Anna settles back down on the sofa and snuggles up under Anthony's arm. She loves the smell of him when he is fresh out of the shower, he has his arm around her shoulder draping across her chest. She always feels safe and secure when they're like this, just the two of them as if no one else exists. At times Anna wonders what it would be like if they were more than just friends, but Anthony has always said that she is like his family, the one he never had. There have been moments between them when she has thought, it might lead to more, they will be sitting like this and his arm will brush across her breast, she'll feel her nipples getting hard then realise that he was just getting comfortable and it had just been what it was, his arm accidentally brushing her breast.

Anthony uses the remote to start the film playing, and then his mind is wandering back to what Mike said earlier about Anna being snapped up by some lucky guy, that would mean the end of evenings like this, snuggled up on the sofa watching old movies, eating pizza. He doesn't know what he would do if he didn't have Anna in his life. He's always thought of Anna as more than a friend, but he thinks she feels differently, she was amazingly beautiful, the one fact she couldn't see. She could have any guy she wanted, and it still amazed him that she wanted to hang out with him, he wasn't used to people actually wanting to be in his company out of choice. He had always found it easy to open up to Anna and he could pretty much tell her anything, certain things he did keep from her, and he had to admit that he thinks he has always loved her; these feelings have gotten stronger over the last couple of weeks almost becoming unbearable.

It seemed the closer he got to finding out about his birth mother the more he wanted Anna, whether it was just a defence mechanism to ensure he wasn't left completely alone when his mother ignored his pleas for contact. He did not think this was the case because recently he has been noticing things about Anna that he never had before—like her top two front teeth were slightly longer than the rest of the teeth, which is what made her smile so sexy. The way she would flirt with him, and like tonight wearing his Miami Dolphins t-shirt with no bra underneath—if he didn't know better he would think she was interested in him. However, he knew she was only like this with him because they had been friends for so long and that she felt at ease in his company, that she just acts as she would at home.

He will keep his thoughts to himself, the last thing he wants to do is get his wires crossed, and lose the one constant in his life that he would die without—he truly believes life with no Anna is a life not worth living.

After the film finishes Anthony looks over at Anna, "do you fancy a cigarette?"

"As long as you don't mind me having one of yours" She never buys cigarettes as she only smokes at Anthony's and usually only when they have had a drink.

"I don't know why you ask, you know what's mine is yours" he gets up and walks over to the door leading to the fire escape, closely followed by Anna. The night has turned a bit chilly and Anna shivers as they step into the cold night air, cooler than it should be for a May evening. Anthony has an old baked bean can that he uses as an ashtray. They both light up their cigarettes.

"You will tell me when you hear from Social Services won't you?" Anna asks starring out into the night sky at the big dipper constellation—the one she thinks looks like a big saucepan. The cool night air whips around them, the hustle and bustle below them carries on oblivious to them sitting there. What seems like a millennia passes before Anthony replies.

"I was hoping you'd be with me when I open it" he gives a nervous laugh, "besides it will only be the details about who she is. So no big deal, but will you come round when it arrives?" there is almost a pleading in his voice, he puts his arm around her as she shudders with the cold—he can't help noticing the hardness of her nipples. They stand there side by side leaning on the cold steel of the fire escape railings both drawing on their cigarettes at the same time, neither saying a word just staring straight ahead at the multi storey car park which is directly behind the high street—no one ever said the flat came with fantastic views. He pulls her closer enjoying her fresh smell and the warmth of her body against his, she in turn slides her arm around his waist and squeezes.

“I’m here whenever you need me, never forget that.” out of the corner of her eye, she sees a single tear roll down his cheek, this single tear makes her sadder and makes her want him more than she thought possible.

6

Friday May 26, 2000

“Come in, come in” Nikki ushers Hayley in, at just gone six Hayley is true to her word about getting here early to help.

“Is Paul not home from work yet” Hayley asks, not seeing any sign of him in the apartment.

“No, he rang about ten minutes ago to say he would be home around seven, something about a deadline that had to be met for one of the big clients, apparently they are busting his balls on this one” Nikki informs her.

“Well in that case let’s crack open this bottle” handing her the Pinot Grigio she bought in with her for Nikki to open.

“I’ve got to say Hales you look gorgeous tonight” Nikki compliments her, and she did, Hayley was the shortest of the three of them at only five foot three, with her slight frame and fiery red hair, dressed all in black she looks stunning. Her temper was her downfall socially but her biggest asset professionally, as a solicitor it was what gave her the edge over her male colleagues. She could argue night is day and black is white if the mood took her. As friends they have had their difficulties, at one time they didn't speak for nearly a year, all because Nikki commented that she did not like Hayley's new boyfriend. Hayley broke up with him a week after, because she found out he was cheating on her. It then took a year for her to start speaking to Nikki; Hayley has a tendency to be stubborn, she will never admit to being wrong.

"So what's on the menu tonight?" Hayley asks taking a sip of her wine, a fruity Californian Pinot.

"Well for starter we have Parma ham wrapped melon with a balsamic vinegar dressing. For main, we have pan-fried duck breast with Port and damson sauce on a bed of braised red cabbage, served with sauté potatoes. Finally, for dessert we have chocolate mousse in a brandy snap basket with raspberry coulis. Does that sound alright?" Nikki smiles, as she knows her friends love it when they hold the dinner party here. Nikki is the only one that does the cooking herself, Aimee and Steve usually use a catering company, with Hayley it is normally Indian or Chinese takeaway.

"I suppose that will have to do, I thought you might have made a bit more effort for your friends" Laughing as she says this. "Right, so what can I help with?" she thinks she should offer as she did say she would help.

"Nothing thanks, it's all in hand I think, what you can do though is fill up the wine glasses, they're looking a bit empty" Nikki says.

“Any more wine and I dread to think what the meal is going to taste like” Hayley laughs. She is sitting on one of the bar stools at the breakfast bar, watching as Nikki juggles half a dozen tasks with ease. Shaking a stainless steel sauté pan with a reduction of port and damson jam bubbling away, while getting the braised red cabbage out of the oven, she is just a natural in the kitchen. Turning back to her friend, Nikki picks up her refilled glass of wine, taking a large sip asks, “So how is your love life going?” Picking up a large cook’s knife, she starts to slice the potatoes, “so come on, spill, who is this week’s conquest?”

“No one this week, it has now been nearly a month since the last one, and he was a big disappointment, or should I say little disappointment. I think I might try celibacy for a while, to be honest my battery powered friends has been more satisfying lately” Hayley laughs.

“Do you ever think about settling down and having a family, you can’t keep having one night stands or being the other woman” Nikki says with a hint of sadness in her voice, she thinks her friend is unhappy with her personal life, although she jokes about all her conquests it never seems genuine.

“I would love to meet someone and settle down, but I never seem to meet the right one, maybe I should get to know them before taking them to bed” another laugh, this time tinged with regret. “Why can’t I find someone like your Paul or Aimee’s Steve?”

“You will meet someone in time; you are young, beautiful and intelligent. What man wouldn’t want you? You just need to find the right one and keep your knees together at least until after the first date” Nikki turns to add the sauce to the port and damson reduction, and boil the potatoes on the state of the art cooking range. Apart from at the salon, she is most comfortable in her Kitchen, and it is her kitchen, as Paul doesn't know the difference between a frying pan and a saucepan. The occasions when he has helped his wife in the kitchen, they have a habit of skipping the food and going straight to dessert. Looking at the clock on the wall, Nikki sees that she has about ten minutes until Aimee arrives. Tasting the sauce she decides it just needs a touch of salt, tasting again, she pulls the pan to one side ready for later. She has already prepared the starter, which is sitting in their American style refrigerator, plated and ready to serve. The components for the dessert ready and just need assembling prior to serving, all she will have left to do when her guests are here is to pan fry the duck, and sauté the potatoes. As Nikki turns back to grab her glass, she hears Paul's key in the front door, this makes a change, he's earlier than expected.

Walking through the door, he is quite a sight. Standing at six foot two, toned muscular frame, courtesy of the gym they have installed in one of the bedrooms. Short-cropped black hair, chiselled Italian features, strong square jaw and beautiful bronzed skin. The killer smile he has when he sees Nikki in the kitchen, enough to melt any woman's heart, he heads straight for the kitchen. Grabbing hold of his wife round her waist, hands cupping her bum, lifting her clean off the floor; he plants a sensuous kiss on her lips. Reluctantly pulling away, "You look gorgeous babe, and the food smells amazing, I'm just going to grab a quick shower, Hales you can come and scrub my back—just don't tell my wife" with this they're all laughing as he heads off to the bathroom. "I'll be ten minutes, Hales you couldn't pour me a beer could you?"

"Of course I can handsome, I'll bring it in when I come and scrub your back" Hayley winks at him and flutters her eyelashes. She can be a terrible flirt, especially with her friends' husbands.

Just as Paul vanishes into the bathroom, the doorbell goes. "Could you get that Hales, it should be Aimee," Nikki asks,

"Sure" Hayley hops off her stool, heads from the kitchen, past the impressive antique oak dining table with its high back chairs. She opens the front door; Aimee is standing there in a breath-taking black cocktail dress. Hayley thinks that Aimee is far too thin; she has a figure like Victoria Beckham. That is where the similarity ends, at five foot eight, with natural platinum blonde hair down to the small of her back and the deepest blue eyes. She has legs that seem impossibly long for her height, emphasised by her incredibly short dress, barely covering her modesty. To finish off the ensemble, black leather wrist cuffs. She likes to remind people of her younger Goth days. Stepping through the door, she kisses Hayley on both cheeks, "You look gorgeous babe, have you been here long?"

"I look gorgeous, look at you and that dress you're nearly wearing. I've got belts that cover more than that dress" Hayley jokes, she knows that Aimee looks stunning in anything she wears. At times, she is jealous of her, though she would never admit it; she barely admits it to herself. Hayley has a tendency to see other people's lives as better than hers, whereas most people would kill for her life. She has a great career, fantastic home and an amazing social life, but still she sees her friends and how happy they are within their own bodies and they have a contentment within that radiates to all around them. She thinks that is her problem, she isn't content with her life, in particular her lack of a solid relationship.

"So how much help have you given Nikki with dinner," Aimee asks, knowing the answer.

"Well more than usual, we've nearly finished off the first bottle of the night, talking of which you're lagging behind. Come on we had better get you sorted with a drink," Hayley says.

With everything ready for dinner, Nikki grabs a glass and a fresh bottle of wine, meeting up with the other two in the living area. Hayley and Aimee having already made themselves comfortable on the white leather corner sofa.

"I don't know how you do it Nikki, a couple of hours in the kitchen, and you still look great" Aimee compliments her friend.

"You've got to be joking, I'm just going to go and freshen up a bit. You too put me to shame, sitting there looking gorgeous." Nikki laughs, "Here I bought you a glass and here's the bottle, you need to catch up". She heads to the bathroom, where she finds Paul just stepping out of the shower, standing there glistening with water dripping off his naked body. Rubbing a towel over his head, his perfect abs taut and chiselled, he spots her entering the bathroom and smiles, he makes no attempt to cover up. "God, if we didn't have guests less than twenty feet away, I'd let you have me right here, right now on the floor"

"If we didn't have guests I'd have had you in the shower with me" walking to her he cups his hands around her face and places his lips on hers, slowly parting her lips with his tongue and probing the depths of her mouth, She responds in kind, before pulling away. "Spoilsport" he laughs.

"Get dressed and go and entertain our guests, I'll be out in five minutes, I just wanna freshen up quickly", she ushers him out of the bathroom in just a towel.

As he walks across from the bathroom to the master bedroom on the mezzanine floor a chorus of wolf whistles from the sofa greets him. Confidently he carries on strutting across the living space, and says "I'll be with you in two minutes ladies, be patient" with that he bounds up the stairs and disappears from view. Although the mezzanine overlooks the living area, it goes far enough back to afford some privacy for such moments as this. True to his word, two minutes later he is walking back down the stairs in pressed Chinos and a plain white t-shirt. "Right ladies, can I top up your wine for you?" he offers,

"Always the perfect gentleman Paul" Aimee says.

"So what are you two talking about, or should I say who are you talking about?"

"You know us, we never gossip", Hayley offers.

"We were just discussing finding Hayley her perfect man to settle down with" Aimee reveals.

"Well that should be easy, I thought the only requirement was a pulse" Paul jokes, with that Hayley gives him a sharp dig to the ribs, "Ouch that hurt".

"Seriously Paul, do you have anyone you work with that might be suitable?" Aimee asks.

"There's maybe one, Stuart, I could invite him over the next time we have dinner here if you want" Paul suggests.

"What's he like, is he a keeper, because I think I'm ready for a serious relationship?" Hayley asks.

"Am I hearing right, Hayley ready to settle down, how much have you had to drink?" Paul says laughing. This gets him another dig in the ribs. With that, Nikki wanders in, dressed in an emerald green and black corset, and a plain black pair of trousers. The corset accentuates her curves, and the green brings out the colour in her eyes, giving them a sexy glint.

Nikki reclaims her glass of wine from the kitchen counter before joining her friends on the sofa, "What time is Steve hoping to get here?" Nikki asks Aimee.

"He's hoping to be here about seven-thirty," Aimee tells her.

"In that case we'll have dinner about seven-forty-five if that's OK with everyone?" Nikki asks, not expecting an answer, as she knows they wouldn't start without Steve.

"Are you sure we can't help with anything for dinner" Aimee offers this time, knowing Nikki won't let anyone in her kitchen, safe in the knowledge that her offer of help will be declined. Aimee is the complete opposite to Nikki in the domesticity stakes. She and Steve have a cleaner that comes in three times a week, a Polish girl who does the cleaning, washing and ironing, and occasionally goes grocery shopping for them. They live on pre-prepared meals or takeaways; they have the largest collection of takeaway menus, from Indian and Chinese to Vietnamese and Ethiopian. Aimee's idea of cooking is taking the wrapper off a ready meal and popping it in the oven. It's amazing how they both manage to stay so trim and fit with the amount of rubbish they eat.

"No, you're fine, I'm just going to go and start the duck and potatoes, I'll leave you in Paul's capable hands, just make sure I get him back in one piece" Nikki laughs, seeing the look of apprehension on Paul's face.

"Please don't leave me with them Nik" Paul says in a mock pleading tone.

"Don't worry Nikki, we won't play too rough" spoke in unison by both Aimee and Hayley, with devilish grins on their faces.

"Just remember I'm only going to be over there" she says pointing over to the kitchen, with that she heads over to start pan-frying the duck breasts, she'll part fry them, then leave them in the oven to finish off while they have their starters. In the kitchen, she can overhear her friends beginning to tease Paul. To look at Paul you wouldn't believe that he is actually very shy, if it hadn't been for Nikki they would never have got together. Paul would never have got up the nerve to ask her out, if she had not asked him out on a date all those years ago, they would not be here today, enjoying the wonderful life they have together. With that, the doorbell goes once more, this must be Steve, he's early too, it's only seven-fifteen. She sees Paul get up to go and answer the door.

True enough it is Steve standing there, Paul puts his arm around his shoulder, "Thank god you're here mate, Nik's in the kitchen and she fed me to the lions, otherwise known as Hayley and your wife" Paul says with an over exaggerated sigh of relief. Steve is dressed in a casual ivory linen suit, which looks impressive on his six foot four frame; the suit hides his muscular body. Originally coming from the Gambia, his rich chocolate skin highlights his huge white smile with two rows of perfect white teeth, and hazel eyes.

"Grab me a beer and I'll go and sort the pair of them out for you," Steve says laughing, walking over to his wife his gives her a kiss on the lips and whispers in her ear how gorgeous she looks and that he can't wait to get her home. Then leaning over to Hayley, gives her a peck on the cheek, "What's this I've been hearing about the two of you ganging up on Paul. Remember neither of you are too big for me to put over my knee and give you a spank" he says trying to keep a straight face.

"Yes please" Hayley responds as quick as a flash with her hand raised in the air like a naughty schoolgirl, everyone bursts out laughing, including Nikki who is making her way across from the kitchen.

On reaching Steve, he leans in to her and gives her a peck on the cheek. "The food smells fantastic as always Nik" Steve compliments her, "When do we eat?" Steve's first thought is always his stomach. He loves his food.

"Well now that our guest of honour has deigned to grant us with his company, we can now proceed to partake in festivities," Nikki informs him in her best servant voice. They all make their way to the dining area, while Nikki and Paul go to retrieve the starters from the fridge. With the starters out of the fridge, Nikki drizzles the balsamic dressing around the plate. Carrying them to the table, she places them in front of her guests. She and Paul sit at either end of the table, with Steve and Aimee on one side, leaving Hayley on the other side. The table looks stunning as usual, with all the right cutlery, glasses and linen napkins in napkin rings. She gets a kick going all out with her dinner parties. As they are only once a month or so she makes every effort to ensure everything is perfect.

Her insecurities dictate the effort she goes to, not that anyone would realise. She has a deep-seated fear that without making the effort her friends may not want to come to dinner anymore. She knows this is an irrational thought, but some switch inside her tells her to make the most of her friends while she has them. To some extent, this applies to Paul too. Every day she wakes up thinking is this the last day of her life, as she knows it. This thinking stems back to her youth when a life-changing event altered her parents perception of her, they stopped loving her, and viewed her differently. That is what she is afraid of everyday, that people would see her differently somehow. It is not something she constantly thinks about, it seems to be hard-wired into her. She enjoys doing things like the dinner parties, but somewhere in her subconscious, she knows she has to.

7

Around eleven-thirty their guests leave, after wishing them a goodnight and thanking them for their company. Nikki heads back to the kitchen where Paul is putting the last of the crockery away. She walks up behind him and puts her arms around his waist and kissing the nape of his neck "Well I think that went well," she says.

"Everything was great babe, they all cleared their plates, including Hayley, and you know what a fussy bugger she can be at times. Come on let's go and sit down and finish this bottle," he offers.

"That sounds like a plan," she says, grabbing the glasses. Paul puts on some music, something to chill out to, a bit of Ella Fitzgerald, and turns the lights down. As he sits down, Nikki lies down with her head in his lap, looking up into his hazel eyes. "You do still love me, don't you?" she often asks him this, with all her outer confidence she still needs reassurance from those closest to her.

“More than anything babe” he says, his arm across her stomach giving a slight squeeze, triggering a soft moan from her. He leans down as she lifts her head, their lips meet, and their tongues fighting each other to go even deeper. She gets up and manoeuvres herself so that she is straddling his lap. She resumes kissing him. His arms are now around her waist, his hand lightly caressing her back from the base of her neck to the bottom of her spine. He knows she loves the sensation. With their lips still locked, he picks her up; she wraps her legs around his waist. Their hunger now building for each other, Paul carries her like this to the bedroom, their lips never once leaving the others.

In the bedroom, he gently lowers her on to the bed, supporting his weight with his arms. Now kissing her neck, Nikki arches her back, and pulls his t-shirt from his trousers and pulls it over his head. Luckily for Paul the corset is front fastening, he deftly undoes the hooks, kissing the swell of her bosom as he does, kissing lower with each successful unhooking. As he gets to the last one he lets the corset fall away, now making small circular motions with his tongue on her stomach, then blowing gently across the dampness sending chills through her entire body. She grabs at his trousers, releasing the button; she can feel his hardness straining against the fabric. With one fluid movement, she removes both the trousers and the boxers. She then removes her own trousers and panties, both now entwined in each other’s bodies. The raw animal passion now taking over, he is deep inside her with one swift movement, both in a state of frenzy now it’s not long before they are both reaching the point of no return.

Afterwards they both just lay in each other’s arms; Paul doesn’t see the single tear roll down her cheek, Nikki is like this every time, it is part happiness, part sorrow and part regret. The happiness is just for being here with Paul. The sorrow is that one day this will all be taken away from her and the regret is the sacrifices she has made to be here.

8

Monday June 5 2000

"That was a busy day," Mike says to Anthony, over a cup of coffee. This is their first break of the day, at nearly four-thirty it has to be a record. Sitting outside in the small courtyard behind the patisserie, a pleasant space about fifteen feet by twenty feet, there's a gate along the back wall where the deliveries arrive. The walls, six feet high, painted in white, making the space appear bigger than it is, a great space to escape from the mayhem of the kitchen. A cheap white plastic patio set with four chairs, its seen better days, but does the job; Mike and Anthony are occupying two of the chairs right now.

“I know, and we’re not even finished yet, hasn’t the birthday cake got to be finished yet?” Anthony asks, lighting a cigarette and offering one to Mike.

“I‘m going to finish it off when we head back in, but first we’re going to enjoy our well-deserved coffee and cigarette.” Mike tells him, “Have you heard anything from social services yet?” he asks.

“No, though it is due any day, might even be there when I get home.” Anthony says.

“Remember, when you have it, give me the details and I’ll get my mate to find out what he can. He says he should be able to get a current address, whether she’s married, if she has any kids, stuff like that. He says once he has the information it should take him about five days to get the info and verify it.” Mike offers, taking a drag on his cigarette, and blowing the smoke into the clear blue sky. “How’s Anna these days? She hasn’t been in lately.” He asks.

“She’s good, thanks. I was gonna ask your advice about her actually,” Anthony says.

“Finally, the penny drops, you like her don’t you?” he says with the biggest grin forming on his face. Mike is not your typical pastry chef, ex-army, he still has that swagger about him that says ‘I’m in charge’ and he has the lightest touch when it comes to creating desserts and pastries for the shop. Slightly taller than Anthony, and close cropped hair in contrast to Anthony’s curly locks, he has the chiselled features of a Scandinavian.

“I think so, after what you said the other day, about her getting snapped up by some lucky guy, it got me thinking. I’ve started seeing her differently; it’s the little things that I’ve always taken for granted. She’s always been there for me, even when I'm at my lowest and not much fun to be around, she's there. She has this way about her, just being near her makes me feel better about myself, it's as if she brings out all the best qualities in me. Why haven't I noticed all this before?"

"Because you're a pratt" Mike points out. "She's good for you, and believe it or not, I think you're good for her. I've always felt that Anna doesn't value herself highly enough, most men will take advantage of her, you won't. She needs you as much as you need her, do you know how she feels about you?" Mike asks.

"No, at times I think she might like me, but at other times it's as if we're just friends, and I don't want to say anything in case it ruins the friendship." He says.

"A bit of friendly advice for you, say something, or you may end up regretting it for the rest of your life. I admit if she doesn't feel the same it could be awkward, but I think the two of you have known each other for long enough that you will get over it. From what I know of Anna, I think she probably feels the same as you, she is deeply insecure, I know I've only known her a couple of years, but she is always quick to put herself down, she obviously thinks you can do better than her. Believe me though, you could do a lot worse, and so could she. Tell her before it's too late." He says before adding, "And today's relationship advice is courtesy of Dr. Mike, PhD. in bullshit."

Both of them erupt into hysterics, laughing until their sides ache.

"I think I'll get all this business with my birth mother sorted out first and then have a serious chat with Anna." Anthony says.

"Just make sure you do, now the kitchen isn't going to clean itself is it?" Mike says putting out his cigarette and swallowing the last of his coffee.

"Thanks Mike, I'm gonna have another quick smoke before making a start if that's okay?"

"No problem, I'll just dock your wages" he says, prompting more laughter from the pair.

Anthony takes another cigarette from the packet, lighting it, he thinks back to the years he has known Anna. After initially meeting her when they were both eight, instantly they became best friends, unusual for a girl and boy of that age. They seemed to recognise something in each other, a sense of loneliness, even helplessness. Finishing the last of his cigarette he spots a pigeon staring at him from atop the wall, thinking how easy the birds have it, not having to worry about relationships, or work or whether anyone loves you, they can just fly around all day, eat when they want and do whatever they want. With the bird still staring he is drawn once more to thoughts of Anna.

Anna is an only child; Anthony always has the impression that her parents see her as a big disappointment. The early years as friends, her parents tried to discourage her from hanging around with him, claiming that it was his influence turning their little princess into a tomboy. She would have climbed trees, and swung on tyre swings without his help. On a number of occasions, her parents had gone to see his parents, to ask if they could keep him away from her. During the worst of it, when they were nine or so, they kept their friendship secret, she made up an imaginary friend from school and told her parents she was her new best friend. Her parents never once met her, Anna used to make up story's about where they had been and what they had done, even going so far as to invent an imaginary set of parents for this non-existent friend. All the time they would meet up around the corner of their road, and then head off over the recreation field, where they could spend hours in each other's company—no-one any the wiser. The recreation field, which led down to the old disused railway line, the railway line in which the two of them would walk along for hours. Sometimes, they would walk as far as the bridge, about a mile from the bottom of the field—if their parents knew they ventured this far from home there would be hell to pay, but what they didn't know didn't hurt them. Anthony's parents couldn't have cared, as long as he made it back for tea, usually around five-thirty, which gave them almost ten hours together during school holidays and weekends. At the bridge they would sit for hours, Anthony usually smuggled drink and food out of the house for the two of them, carried in an old satchel, it had seen better days, but it served its purpose. They would sit, sometimes chucking stones into the river below, sometimes just sitting talking. Anna would tell him what her parents were like, sometimes he thought to himself that maybe he didn't have it too bad at home. They put immense pressure on her to succeed, even at eleven, they could see her as a doctor or lawyer, when in reality Anna had no intention of going into either of those professions. Not because she wasn't smart enough, she just didn't have the self-belief to do it, if only her parents could have seen that all the pressure and bullying for her to do exceptional work at school, had led to her self-doubt and insecurity. They were to blame for their daughter not becoming what they wanted her to be.

When they found out she wanted to draw or paint for a living, they were not happy. Telling her that painting and drawing is a hobby and not a career, and that she could do it in her spare time. Some of Anna's drawings were stunning, but like Anna herself, she never sees them as good enough. Always the first to criticise her own work, she is definitely her own worst critic. Eventually leaving school with eight GCSE's, she found work in a local art gallery, a small independently run family establishment, Anna helps in all aspects of the running of the place. The owner saw a passion in her for art that no other applicant had shown, and realised that he could work with her and mould her. She still does her art, mainly charcoal or pastels in her spare time, hoping one day to have her own exhibition. Until that day arrives, she is thrilled to be working in an industry she loves. She gets to meet up and coming artists, often quizzing them for ideas and techniques, some of them even showing an interest in her work, she has had many compliments regarding her pastel work depicting nudes.

Anthony can't remember the number of times they sat on that bridge, moaning to each other about who has the hardest life, most times agreeing that they probably had it as bad as each other. It is on that bridge that Anthony first told Anna about his adoption, they were eleven at the time, and his parents inadvertently told him a few days before. Anthony always knew something wasn't right with his family, for starters, it hadn't gone unnoticed that he looked like neither of his parents, and his sister was a different species altogether. The fact that they once told him they were going to take him back for a refund should have given him an idea. This particular night though, he can't remember why they were mad at him, it didn't take them a lot, they could lose their temper with him just for looking at them in the wrong way, so it really could have been anything. Well his parents started arguing about him, and his mother said they should never have gone through with the adoption and that she always knew he would be trouble. With that, Anthony asked what an adoption was. The look on his parents face when they realised what they had said was a picture, a moment he will never forget. It's the first and only time he saw genuine guilt and regret in their eyes, the first true emotion he had ever had directed at him, apart from anger, which always seemed genuine.

The tension immediately changed, and they sat him down and proceeded to explain about his adoption. They explained how his real mum didn't want him, said in exactly those words, not why, or if there were any good reasons, just 'she didn't want him' and they were good enough to offer him a home. They explained, it's good people like them that take in unwanted children. Anthony remembers crying after hearing this, and being told that it isn't anything to get upset about as there is nothing he could do about it. Telling him, they were stuck with each other, as there are no refunds—that they can't just give him back. They left him crying, before going about their business.

Over the years, he tried asking them questions about his real mum—as he likes to call her—knowing it upsets his mother. He gets the same answer repeatedly, just that she didn't want him and what else is there to know. He tries asking who she is, but is told they were never given that information, the subject of his dad never came up. Anthony remembers when he was telling Anna all this, even at eleven years old she got upset.

He can visualise it, as if it was yesterday, she took his hand in hers and told him that he would always have her.

*

Finishing his cigarette, he returns to the kitchen to finish cleaning up.

"It looks good Mike" Anthony comments on the cake Mike's working on, "and thanks again for the advice, I will tell her, when the time is right."

"Don't wait too long." Mike insists.

*

Anthony arrives home at just gone six, picking up his mail from inside the door downstairs, walking up the flight of stairs flicking through his mail. Most of which is junk, but one catches his eye, stamped social services, the one he is waiting for. Anna rang him at work earlier and told him that she would be a bit late tonight, probably closer to seven, as the gallery had an exhibition, which they were setting up. Knowing he promised Anna, he wouldn't open the letter until she is with him, he decides to have a quick shower and cook dinner for the two of them. Nothing adventurous, just some chicken breast in a white wine and mushroom sauce, some sauté potatoes and carrots. Anthony has discovered he enjoys cooking, not just the pastry and desserts side, but also meals. He bought himself a couple of decent French cook books and is teaching himself the basics, not that he wants to work in a restaurant or hotel, but he likes the idea of being able to cook for himself—and Anna.

He pan-fries the chicken breasts before putting them in the oven, preparing the potatoes and carrots, trying to get as much ready before jumping in the shower. Having a quick shower, he's back in the kitchen in no time, preparing his masterpiece. By six forty-five, he has everything ready, even opening a bottle of white wine for the occasion. Fifteen minutes until Anna is due to arrive, Anthony picks up the letter, looking it over, front, back, tempted to open it. But he promised Anna he'd wait until she was here. Pouring himself a glass of wine, he puts the stereo on, picking an Etta James CD, putting it in the tray and hitting play. Relishing the soothing voice and familiar sound of 'At Last', finishing the glass of wine in a couple of mouthfuls, he hasn't realised how nervous he is. It's just a letter, it doesn't mean anything, it's just words on a sheet of paper. Maybe if he keeps telling himself that, he'll start believing it. He knows though that the words in the envelope are more than just words, they spell the beginning or the end of what could be the singular most important event in his life.

Hearing the key in the lock, Anna's five minutes early, Anthony heads back to the kitchen to check on dinner.

"Honey, I'm home."

"Hi, how was your day babe?"

"Really good thanks; have I got time to have a shower before dinner?"

"As long as you're not too long, dinner will be ruined in fifteen minutes." He lets her know, he's decided to wait until after the meal before opening the letter. He hears her turn the shower on, pouring himself his second glass of wine of the evening. For some reason, while he's cooking the sauté potatoes, he begins thinking about Anna in the shower, a thought that makes him want her even more than he realised. As he starts plating up dinner, he sees Anna out of the corner of his eye, wearing her pyjamas, a pair of black satin shorts, with a matching camisole, her midriff exposed. Noticing the absence of a bra, he knows he wants her more than ever.

Sitting down on the sofa, Anna starts eating her dinner, "This is lovely" she says after the first mouthful.

"Glad you like it, it was just something I threw together at the last minute," he says modestly, "the letter arrived today" he tries to slip in without drawing attention to it.

"That's great, why didn't you tell me?" she wants to know.

"I thought we'd have dinner first, and a few drinks for Dutch courage"

"I can't believe you didn't open it the second you got home"

"I promised you that when it arrived, I'd wait for you before I opened it." He says.

Fifteen minutes later, Anna is taking the plates over to the sink, telling Anthony to get the cigarettes, refill the glasses and she'll meet him on the fire escape, and not to forget the letter. When she gets out there, Anthony's sitting with his back to the door, the letter sitting in his lap.

"Right I'm here now, are you gonna open it, or stare at it all night." She says.

"You open it," he says handing her the letter.

"Are you sure?"

"Yes"

"Right then, here goes," she says carefully opening the envelope, inside there are three sheets of paper, one's a letter from the social worker, one's his original birth certificate and the last one is a brief synopsis of his birth mothers life. Handing them to Anthony, "here, you should be the first to read them."

Taking the papers from Anna, he shuffles closer to her, their bodies now touching, "We'll read them together." Starting with the letter from the social worker, it's just a letter stating what documents are enclosed and wishing him all the best with the information he now has, and if there is any more they can do, just get in touch.

Then his original birth certificate, Anthony gets a sudden weird sensation, the feeling that whom he has been for the last eighteen years is a lie. That this single piece of paper is the truth, he knows it's absurd, but somehow what is written here is who he is, or more to the point it's who he is supposed to be. In the space where child's name is input, in clear black typed letters is Mark Anderson, so all these years he has been Anthony Allen, he should have been Mark Anderson. The next line reveals his birth mothers name, Nicola Louise Anderson, the space available for fathers name simply has written 'unknown'. The social worker did explain that this could be the case, as it takes away the need for both parents to consent to the adoption; the father waives the right to any say in the adoption process.

Seeing this information in black and white, brings it home to Anthony—Mark—that he knows even less about himself then he initially thought. He knows that the life he is leading right at this minute is his life, but somehow he can't help feeling that he's living someone else's life. It's a stupid thing to think, and he knows it.

"Are you all right?" Anna asks him, a concerned look on her face, taking his hand in hers, “Remember I’m here, that’s all that matters.”

“I’m fine; it’s a strange sensation, finding out after eighteen years, what your real name is. It’s surreal, all these years I’ve been Anthony to everyone, except Mike, who insists on calling me Tony—I swear it’s because he knows I hate it. Then you find out when you were born your mum thinks you look like a Mark—not an Anthony, I wonder if the name had any significance for her, or whether she just liked the name” he says.

“Well to me, you’ll always be my Anthony,” she leans over and gives him a kiss on the cheek. “So, are you ready for the last piece of the puzzle.”

“We’ve come this far, why not,” he says, lighting up two cigarettes, one for him and one for Anna. He’ll be glad when this is all over, he’s been smoking far too much of late. Reading the third page, it starts off with his mum’s name, and that she was born in Oxford, she was sixteen at the time of giving birth to her son. Her parents were not supportive of the baby and had refused to accept the child into their house, they had even refused to accept their own daughter back into their home after she had given birth. It stated that after the birth she was going to be staying with a friend and her parents.

One paragraph is all that they had on his mum, one paragraph, eight lines. He wonders if everyone’s life could be condensed down to eight lines. Reading the passage for the third time, it still doesn’t make sense that this is all there is. He doesn’t know what he was expecting, more, or at least more than this. Looking at Anna, she is looking as confused as he is.

“What do you make of this?” he says, waving the piece of paper about.

“I don’t know, I thought there would be more”

“It’s not just me then, I thought there would be more to,”

“It sounds like she didn’t have much choice though” Anna tries to find a positive.

“Do you remember years ago when I told you about me being adopted” he asks.

“We used to make up stories where we thought you came from,” she remembers with a smile. “My favourite one, when we decided that you were the love child of a famous rock star and a gypsy from a travelling fair, it was after we watched the film ‘That’ll be the day’ with David Essex in, you sneaked me into your house to watch it when your parents took your sister shopping.” She says.

“If they had known we watched that film, they would have killed us.” He jokes. “My favourite, we thought I had been born to a famous movie star, who couldn’t keep me because of the scandal it would’ve caused.”

Both of them laughing now, Anna is relieved the opening of the letter hasn’t sent him into a mood, she’s impressed with how well he’s handling it. She knows it may not last, when he finally digests the information he has. She knows he has varying images of his birth mum, sometimes he is angry with her for giving him away, and other times he is accepting of the fact that she may not have had a choice.

“Do you want another glass of wine?” she asks him.

“I’ll go and get them, you’re supposed to be my guest,” he says pulling himself off the floor with the help of the railings, “be back in a second".

After Anthony goes back inside to get the wine, Anna gets up, walking up the fire escape, she decides on such a lovely evening they should enjoy it from the roof. A couple of minutes later, Anthony returns, carrying the two glasses of wine, and the bottle. Lying on her back, eyes closed, legs dangling over the edge, she senses Anthony's presence before he speaks.

"I'm gone for two minutes and you fall asleep on me," he says, admiring her body while she's not looking.

"I'm not asleep, and stop looking at me." She says, opening one eye, watching him quickly avert his eyes, "see I knew you were looking at me, so do you like what you see?"

"Of course, what's not to like," he says, starting to get that rosy glow around the cheek area.

"Come and join me down here, and bring the wine," More an order than a request.

Lying down next to her, they both spark up yet another cigarette, side by side, their arms touching; Anthony loves the feel of her skin on his. Pushing these thoughts to the back of his mind, knowing he will have to revisit them in the not too distant future, almost relishing the thought of telling Anna how he feels towards her, he just has to work out the best way to go about it. Now, his main thoughts are about the documents he has just read.

"I'll take the details into Mike tomorrow; he said his friend will probably take about five days, and then I should have an address, know if she's married and has any children." He says, "I was thinking I would start by writing a letter to her, I don't want to just go to see her, I think it maybe too much of a shock if I just turn up on her doorstep, don't you?"

"I wouldn't just go there, writing is probably the best way to go, she'll be able to process it in her own time without any pressure, and if she has got a family, they may not know about you, this way she has the chance to explain it all to them. If you just turn up, it could seriously damage her family, and possibly ruin any relationship you may have with her. What do you think you will do if she wants to get to know you?" Anna asks.

"I don't know, first I just want to know the truth, about my dad, what exactly happened, why her parents were so against her having a child, and I want to know about her life since she gave me up. Hopefully she'll want to know about my life." He answers, the sun is beginning to fade now, the sky a burnt orange colour, and he looks over at Anna, the evening sky making her skin glow with a bronze hue. His mind conflicted, he has dreamt of this moment, finding out about his birth mother for years. But all he can think about now is Anna, what she truly means to him, not just the physical presence of her but the emotional impact she has on his life. Without her the last ten years of his life, he doesn't know where he would be now, he certainly wouldn't be as calm about the possibility of meeting his mum as he is at this precise moment. He remembers some of the dark days when he has tried to hide his moods from Anna. Even going back to the days when they used to sit on the bridge of the disused railway line, they would be talking about the adoption and his mood would change, he'd know it was happening, he would go very quiet. Luckily Anna wouldn't think anything of it, she just thought he was thinking, which in truth he was, what she never guessed was what he was thinking. Even as young as twelve or thirteen he thought about killing himself, thought of just leaning forward and falling off the edge, into oblivion, all the hurt and anger disappearing into the murky waters below. The thing that stopped him every time—Anna—she is his guardian angel, she doesn't know it, but without her, he knows he wouldn't be here now. Even when they would joke and make up stories about his origins, hidden behind the laughter, were the dark thoughts of suicide. As he got older though he realised these thoughts were just that.

The possibility of him taking his own life diminished. The feelings were still as strong, just his will to survive had grown stronger, his own mortality, what once never entered his mind, now played a huge part. The thought that should he go ahead and take his own life, taking your own life sounds better than suicide, it implies that you have a right to do it and it is not merely a selfish act. The thought of it all being over for ever scared him, the realisation that once you were gone, wiped from the face of the earth, there is no coming back, no second chance.

No do over.

Ever.

The end.

The thought that the world would still go on, people living their lives, only the very few even realising he had existed—eventually they would get over it and go about living again. His mind couldn't comprehend years, let alone millions or even billions of years of his body as dust. His soul on the other hand is a different matter, not that he is religious, but he couldn't help but wonder what happened to his soul. Is it just a series of electrical impulses which make up the soul of a person or is it eternally sent to heaven or hell, could he take the chance of the latter. For taking one's own life would surely have meant eternal damnation in the bowels of hell. When in his younger teens, these thoughts of his own mortality never entered his mind, his just wanted out, out of his life, out of his family.

Anna would never know how many times she had saved his life, even now lying here next to her, having dark thoughts—not as dark anymore as the possibility of his origin gets closer, but still dark. Anna his saviour, Anna the one he now knows he loves, loves with all his being. Yes he wants her physically as much as emotionally now, though physically in the way he hopes it will bond them together stronger, more resilient to whatever the world has to throw at them. Hoping that she feels the same as he does about her, lying here next to her, wanting to touch, wanting to kiss, wanting to caress, but scared—no terrified—of the rejection that would surely follow. He will talk to her, find out how she feels about him.

"You seem miles away" Anna says "anywhere nice?"

"Not really, just thinking and hoping that my mum will want to know me" he answers, for once one of his most honest answers, trying to be more open and honest with Anna, he trusts Anna, which for him is very hard. Of all the people in the world there are two people he can trust and depend on—Anna and Mike. Out of more than six billion people on the planet, he has two. What does that say about his life, in over eighteen years, to forge only two friendships, two people that care about him. At his lowest points, he doubts even these, his mind telling him, they put up with him; they couldn't care if he is there or not. He knows this is utter nonsense, but his mind plays tricks on him, trying to make him give up and just do it, just end it, rid the world of one more worthless soul. How many people have been where he has been, been tempted by the devil to do it—and then have. In his mind, he has considered every conceivable method, thinking of the pain involved with each method. His favoured is to drive a car extremely fast into something solid; with no seat belt, it should be fairly quick and painless. His one concern with any method is how quick is quick, do the last few seconds, or even hundredths of a second last a lifetime, will the pain be so intense as to make him wish it wasn't too late and that he could go on living. Will he have regrets in those last few nanoseconds, when altering the course of events is not an option, his life at an end, no chance of a reprise? Worse still, he doesn't die, lying in a hospital bed, unable to communicate, people poking and probing him. Concerned friends would probably visit at the beginning, but for how long, a week, a month, a year at most. Then he can be filed away as some whack job that couldn't see that life still had a lot to offer, receiving his food through tubes, still aware of all his surroundings, though no one realising it. People talking to him, hoping he can hear them but not knowing, saying to each other 'what a waste of such a young life, he had so much to live for', what a load of shit, how can anyone know how much another person has to live for. What they mean is the selfish bastard didn't give a toss about the people he left behind, the least he could have done was finish the job properly—whoever heard of someone taking half their life? Anthony believes that euthanasia should be made legal, to avoid the countless people incompetent enough not to fully kill themselves taking up hospital beds.

"How are things at home with your parents?" Anthony asks Anna out of the blue.

"Same as usual, not interested in what I'm doing, because I'm not doing what they think I should be. They live their lives and I live mine, as soon as I can afford to move out I will, but until then I'll make do." She says.

"You know the offers always there for you to move in here," he says, rather hoping that one day she will take him up on his offer.

"Thanks, but I think I need to make my own way, besides you only have one bedroom, so unless you're offering to give up your bed and sleep on the couch?" she offers, secretly loving the prospect of sharing the flat—even sharing his bed.

"If that's what it would take you can have the bed, I'll be quite happy on the couch." He says, relishing the thought of having her to himself twenty-four seven. "Do your parents know how much time you spend here, do they even know we're still friends?" he asks.

"They couldn't care anymore, ever since I took the job at the gallery. They made it quite clear that it was up to me how I lived my life. But not to expect any help from them." She answers.

The sun just barely visible, the street lights just beginning to blink on, taking it in turns as the light fades around them. Both sitting up, looking out over the rooftops and car park, listening to the sounds of the people below going about their lives, oblivious to the two of them perched up here. There's a couple of young boys over on the top level of the car park playing football, trying their best not to hit the few cars that remain, not doing a good job of it judging by the frequency of the car alarms going off. Anthony moves his hand to intertwine with Anna's, she freely takes hold of his, not a word spoken, each knowing that the other is there for them whatever they need. Neither knowing the true feelings of the other, neither wanting to explore that opportunity with the current state of things.

9

Tuesday June 27 2000

"Tony, my mates just emailed across the details, do you want me to print them off before you leave?" Mike's says knowing Anthony's been waiting on tenterhooks for the information since the moment he handed the social services letter to him with his birth mum's name and some family history on it.

"Are you kidding, has he really sent it?"

"I wouldn't kid about something like this—not even with you, I know what it means to you. So I assume that's a yes for printing it off."

"If you don't mind, I can't wait to show Anna." The joy in his voice evident at the development in tracking down his mum.

"Have you had the talk with Anna yet? No of course you haven't, or I would have heard all about it by now."

"I will, once this is over I will talk to her, I'll tell her it's all your idea." Laughing at the look of incredulity on Mike's face.

Mike hands him a single piece of paper as he leaves for the day. "Is that it? I thought there would have been more, I don't know why, it makes sense that it would fit on a single sheet."

"My mate did say one other thing in the email, now I don't want you making more out of it then there is. Apparently, the only thing he can't find out is if she is still alive, that's only because death records aren't in the public domain for two years after a death. Basically all it means is that two years ago she was alive and kicking, but until you contact her there is no way of knowing for certain if she has died in the last two years."

"Don't worry I'm gonna stay positive—she is still alive, I wonder if what you read about twins is true and if it applies to parents—that I would instinctively know if she was no longer living, would I have felt a loss or something?"

"I have no idea, but the sooner you contact her the sooner you'll know."

Leaving the patisserie with a spring in his step, he can't wait to see Anna when he gets home and tell her the good news. The wait has been agonising, with each day and week passing with no news, thinking that Mike's friend can't find anything out about her. He's reading the piece of paper as he's walking along, taking no notice of his surroundings, somehow avoiding bumping into people and things along his route home. The page is simple with just facts, it lists her name, date of birth, and the last listing entered in to the electoral role. This address is hopefully where she is currently living; it's an address in London, south of the river. It also tells him that she is married to a Paul Pope and that her name is now Nicola Pope, they have no children. The only other information is her parents name and last known address. At least now, he has somewhere to start his search for his mum. He's already decided that his best move is to write her a letter.

Picking up some fried chicken and chips on the way home for himself and Anna, she told him she would be at his after he finished work as she only had a half day today. Finding the flat empty, but with obvious signs that Anna is about he grabs a couple of plates and cutlery and heads up to the roof—on a sunny day like today she isn't going to pass up the opportunity to do some sunbathing. True enough, as he climbs the stairs to the roof he sees Anna lying there in her bikini—nothing like coming prepared. Laying on her front, with the bikini un-clasped to avoid the tell-tale white line, she hears his footsteps on the ladder and sitting up with her arm across her chest to stop her bikini falling. With one hand, she grabs hold of one end of the clasp and then carefully with the other manages to redo the top up keeping her modesty intact.

"Hi, no need to ask how long you've been up here judging by your colour, Mike's friend sent through the information; I now know where my mum lives." The excitement in his voice evident, he can hardly contain his pleasure.

Anna is so pleased for him, his moods lately have been all over the place, not that he ever lets them show. She occasionally catches glimpses of the many facades that make up Anthony, she knows that at times when he is quietest is when he's suffering emotionally, trying to keep a lid on it. Afraid that if speaks he will erupt, hence the silences and broodiness, in his mind by not speaking, his emotions will remain hidden from the world and the people he cares about most—Anna and Mike. Yet over the years, Anna has sensed these emotions, if he's quiet but angry then his jaw muscles twitch where he's gritting and grinding his teeth. If he's quiet and upset, then his mouth becomes contorted where he bites the inside of his lip and cheek, his way of stemming the tears by inflicting pain on himself. Anthony would be horrified if he suspected she knew what he was going through, which is why she doesn't say anything to him, she just lets him be.

"So, come on then where does she live?"

"London, just south of the river." He tells her this titbit of information as he's laying the food out and handing Anna a plate with knife and fork. "She's married to a guy named Paul Pope, they have no children, her name is now Nicola Pope. So all I have to do is write her a letter and wait to see if I hear from her." The words tumbling from his lips, afraid that if he keeps them in any longer they may not be true, by telling Anna they must be. He hands her the piece of paper Mike gave him, to verify that the facts he has just told her are in fact true and he isn't making them up.

"Have you decided what to put in the letter yet?"

"No, I was hoping you might help me after we've eaten, I'd like to get the letter in the post tomorrow if we can."

"Right, let's eat this lovely meal you've prepared and then we can get writing." Even with all that is going on in Anthony's head at the moment, with the imminent prospect of contacting his mum, it is not lost on her the way he looks at her, when he thinks she's not looking he steals glances at her body, averting his eyes whenever she looks his way. Sometimes the focus is on her breasts, and the faintness of her raised nipples, other times she catches his eye wandering to the triangular patch of material between her legs. If only he realised how she felt about him, and that they could have so much more together if that is what he wants. She fears though that it isn't, that he is just a man and men are interested in certain parts of female anatomy regardless of whether they fancy them or not.

Having cleared away the remains of dinner, and Anthony returning with a pen and notepad, the two of them set about trying to write a letter to his birth mum.

"I don't know where to start, do I start it with 'Hi Mum' or do I stick with the more formal 'Dear Nicola Pope', I think the first one's being a bit to forward, I don't want to scare her off before I've even got to meet her."

"I think you should start it with 'Dear Nicola Anderson' using her unmarried name should give some indication that you are who you say you are, the fact that you have used her name at the time she gave you up for adoption. I think you should just tell her the facts, keep it simple and don't put too much emotion into it; you don't want her thinking that you're angry with her." Lighting the cigarette that Anthony's just handed her, catching him again looking at her breasts, secretly she likes it when he looks at her this way. Laying back down to catch the last of the sun's rays, leaving Anthony writing his letter, she feels that the actual writing of the letter is something he needs to do on his own, she will help him where she can, but the words have to be his own. The letter will be more sincere if he writes it rather than someone else, and is more likely to get her attention, in the same way that she has told him a hand written letter will be better than a typed one—more personal.

After several more cigarettes and just as the sun is beginning to set, the temperature still high though, Anthony announces that he has finished the letter. Handing it to Anna, almost not wanting to, but wanting a second opinion to see if he has gone too far, he relinquishes the piece of paper. Sitting there biting the inside of his cheek, he does this when he's nervous as well as upset or hurt, waiting for Anna to comment. She must have read it half a dozen times by now, it must be bad if she can't tell him what she thinks, then he sees a tear fall from her eye.

"It's beautiful, if she doesn't get in touch with you after reading that, then there must be something wrong with her. It's perfect, just the right amount of insight into who you are and enough reasons for you to want to meet her. Now put it in the envelope before you have any more time to think about it and change it. I don't think it could be any better." Handing him the letter back she gives him a hug, more to hide the tears she can feel running down her face than to comfort him. Enjoying the firmness of his body against hers, not wanting to let him go, realising that there is definitely more to their relationship than either of them are prepared to admit to.

The following morning on his way to work, clutching the envelope in his hand, placing it gently in the post box he passes every day, hoping that in a short time his mum will contact him. His whole world now hinging on the Royal mail postal service safely delivering the letter to his mum.

10

Friday June 30 2000

"See you Monday Aimee," Nikki says as she's walking out the salon door, "Same time at the coffee shop?" she asks at the last minute. The walk home is fantastic, the early evening sun is warm on her back, Nikki realises what a fantastic life she has, she spends all day doing what she loves, with one of her closest friends. Then she goes home to her gorgeous apartment and even more gorgeous husband. Walking along she appreciates everything she passes from smells coming from the various bistro's, she can almost taste the Bolognese—the garlic and rich beef— to the bustling traffic clogging up the streets, she often imagines the lives these people have, and wonders if it is a patch on hers. She thinks about whistling as she walks, then realises she can't whistle.

The short walk takes about five minutes, she can always tell when she's nearly home, the smell of the Thames drifts through the narrow alleyway, an acquired smell, but a reassuring one and one she wouldn't be without. This particular corner of London has a touch of openness about it, the street she walks along—tree lined—many of the streets cobbled, the buildings architecture breath-taking. The sight as she turns the last corner always makes her realise how lucky she is.

What was once an old print factory, is now three luxury apartments courtesy of Steve Stark's Architect's. The buildings character hasn't changed since it was built, Steve did a fantastic job, sympathetically restoring the exterior, the interior however was a different story. Many of the original features are still visible, many of the internal steel joists cleaned, the exposed brickwork remains in many areas. However, the work Steve had done making the run down factory into apartments is exquisite, from the hand crafted bespoke kitchens, with the best fixtures and fittings, to the Italian marble worktops. The best products used throughout the refurbishment, meaning the three apartments did not come cheap. Steve could easily have made the factory into six luxury apartments, but instead decided on just the three extravagant abodes.

Nikki places her key in the lock, opening the door she enters the lobby, with its marble floors, each floor has its own landing. Just inside the lobby are the mailboxes, she uses her key to open hers and Paul's box, grabbing the mail—half a dozen letters—making her way up the stairs to the first floor, their apartment. She still finds it hard to believe that she lives in this place, growing up in the tree lined suburban streets of Oxfordshire, she had always dreamt of living in the hustle and bustle of a metropolitan city.

With its diverse cultures, the closeness and proximity of fellow city dwellers, she loves nothing more on a weekend than trekking up to Camden with Paul, to browse the market with its quirky stalls and even quirkier traders. She loved the choices of all the ethnic food on offer, they spend hours just wandering from stall to stall. Hand in hand, they stop when something catches their eye, she loves chatting with the traders, getting the history of the things they are selling, buying things if there is a great story attached to it. One time buying a vase, they didn't particularly like it, but because it had been a prop in a film both of them loved, they bought it. It is moments like this that Nikki loves, the romance of it, like living in their own world, where nothing matters apart from them, and their destiny in their own hands. The thought of it ever ending was inevitable; she knew she didn't deserve this life.

Entering the apartment, she puts her bag and keys, along with the mail on the rustic oak side table just inside the door. The apartment was an eclectic mix of modern, vintage, with a touch of chic and a hint of kitsch. Leaving her shoes by the door, she heads across to the kitchen, tonight was their takeaway night, it was a rare occurrence but it meant that she had no cooking to do. She takes a bottle of red Burgundy from the wine rack, opening it to let it breath, grabbing a couple of glasses to sit next to it. At just before six, Paul should be home in about thirty minutes, heading back to the lounge switching the Bose stereo on as she goes. She grabs the best of Blondie album from the shelf, putting it in the machine and turning the volume up.

Retrieving the post, she sits down on the sofa tucking her legs underneath her. Starting with the post, she opens the first one addressed to both her and Paul, looks like a bill, sure enough it's their television licence renewal. Putting this to one side to deal with another day, the second is addressed to the occupier, meaning whoever sent it doesn't have a clue who lives here but expects them to buy something, if you want someone to buy from you, at least find out their names, that's her philosophy. Looking at the third envelope certain it's another bill, she goes to put it to one side when someone puts their hands over her eyes. "Who's that?" she asks knowing full well it's Paul.

Lowering his hands to cup her breasts and kissing the back of her neck.

"We'd better be quick, my husband's due home anytime" she whispers playfully.

"I don't do quick" he responds, gently massaging her breasts.

Softly moaning she turns her head to meet his lips, gently biting his upper lip, raising her arm to the back of his neck and running her fingers through his hair. He places his hand inside her blouse, tracing his finger slowly along the lacy edge of her bra. She responds by running her tongue over his teeth, feeling his tongue probing her mouth. He slips his finger under the silky fabric, seeking the hardness of her nipple, finding it; she arches her back and nips his lip with her teeth. Breaking away, he comes around the sofa, kneeling in front of her now. Putting his hands on her hips and pulling her forward, her legs either side of his. Hitching her skirt up to allow him closer, she can feel his hardness pressing against her, separated now only by fabric. He leans forward, kissing the space to the side of throat, while unbuttoning her blouse. Planting light kisses all over her throat, inching ever lower. He loves the scent of her skin, drinking in the aroma, alternating between light kisses, slow licks and sharp bites. He knows how much she likes the sensation; he can feel the thrust of her hips grinding against him, making him harder.

She leans forward unbuttoning his shirt, pulling it from him; she makes small bite marks in his shoulder. He takes the opportunity to remove her blouse and unclasp her bra, slowly pulling at the straps he lets the bra fall letting her breasts spill out, gently squeezing her nipple; she bites down hard onto his shoulder. Pushing her back onto the sofa, lowering his mouth to her breast, he sucks gently at the flesh around the nipple, hearing her soft moans getting louder the closer he gets. Taking her nipple between his teeth, her hips arch upwards, she fumbles for his button to his trousers. Finding it she pulls it clean off and rips open the zip, pulling his trousers down, she can see his erect member straining at the thin cotton of his boxers. Reaching inside she grabs hold of his balls and gently squeezes, making him in turn suck harder on her nipple. Gently pulling on his member, he's harder than ever, she pushes him off her onto the rug behind him. Standing over him she removes her lace panties, leaving her skirt hitched up she climbs on top of him. Leaning forward to kiss him, she rubs herself against his hardness. Their breathing becoming laboured, not able to take it any longer, she reaches down and guides him into her. Slowly lowering herself until he's fully inside her. Sitting upright on him, both moving in sync with each other, he massages her breasts while she's riding him. Within minutes, they're both at the point of climax, one final burst of energy. Rolling off him, Nikki lies next to her husband, both spent, she leans over to him "I love you Paul".

Both lying side by side on their backs, Nikki turns onto her side laying her hand across his chest, "I wish we could stay like this forever," she whispers.

"Why can't we, I'd be more than happy doing this all day, every day." Paul says.

"How was I so lucky to find you?"

"Just lucky I guess" he jokes. This earns him a poke in the ribs, they're both still sweating, and their breathing is still laboured from the exertion. "I'm gonna grab a shower, you joining me?" he asks, running a finger along from her shoulder, down her side and across her stomach.

"You go and start it off and I'll join you in a second," she says getting up, still with her skirt hitched up, she walks across to the kitchen. Paul stays where he is for a second admiring the view.

"You should lose the skirt," he says. With that she looks over her shoulder, grinning she undoes her skirt and lets it fall to the ground. Stepping out of it, she is now as naked as the day she was born, reaching the marble-topped breakfast bar; she provocatively reaches across grabbing a bottle of red and two glasses. Knowing Paul is still lying there watching her, she stays leaning over the counter longer than she needs to. Standing up straight and turning around she notices Paul getting aroused again.

"I see you're ready for round two, are we having this shower or not?" she asks, walking towards him with the bottle and glasses. "I thought we might need refreshment, I'll bring this with us" walking over to him, grabs hold of his hand and pulls him up. He puts his arm around her waist and they walk to the shower. Once in there he turns the shower on, while Nikki pours them both a glass of wine. He grabs her round the waist; she can feel him pressing into her. She loves him so much, at times it hurts, no one has ever made her feel so safe. Never in her life has she ever felt needed, with Paul she feels that he wants her as well as needs her. It is more than sexual between them, he is her soul mate, from the first moment she saw him she knew he was the one.

"Come on, lets grab that shower" he says.

*

Laying on the sofa, Paul with just his towel, Nikki in a towelling robe, "We are going to grow old and grey together aren't we" she asks, out of the blue.

"What's bought this on? And besides I'm not gonna go grey" he says.

"I don't know, at times I just think this is all a dream, and one day I'll wake up and it will all be gone" she says.

"Nothing will tear me away from you babe" he reassures her.

She smiles at him, and he gives her a gentle squeeze.

11

July 1 2000

With the Gaggia espresso maker gurgling away, making its two shots, Nikki puts some milk in a jug to make the frothy milk to finish off the cappuccinos. A Saturday when neither of them has to work is a rare occurrence, making the most of it, Paul is still in bed, at ten in the morning this is a real indulgence. While Nikki drew the short straw and got up to go and make the coffee, standing in the kitchen, at thirty-four she still has the body she had at twenty. She has lucky genes that allow her to keep her youthful looks. With the steam infused milk now light and frothy, she proceeds to make the cappuccinos. Carrying them back to the bedroom, she stops at the large picture window to look out at the Thames, not at all self-conscious at not having a stitch on. She loves the view across the river at Canary Wharf.

"Are you growing the beans for the coffee?" she hears Paul shout from the bedroom.

"I'm on my way" she replies, she walks up the stairs and into the bedroom "I was just admiring the view out over the river."

"Well I much prefer the view from here," he says looking her over from top to toe.

Handing him his coffee, climbing back into bed next to him, they both sip their coffees, savoury the strong rich flavour. "What do you fancy for breakfast?" she asks him.

"It's your day off too, you're not cooking today, I'll pop down to the bakery and pick us up some pastries after I finish my coffee," he tells her.

"You don't have to do that"

"I know, I want to"

"Don't be gone too long, 'cos I get lonely all by myself" she says in her best pout.

"I'll be there and back in no time, is there anything you want me to get while I'm out?" he asks.

"No thanks, I've got all I need right here" she says putting her arm across his chest.

After finishing their coffee, Paul gets out of bed, Nikki trying to pull him back telling him not to go, putting on a pair of jogging bottoms and a t-shirt. "I won't be long babe," he says leaning over and kissing her lips. "You just stay right there and I'll join you when I get back".

She hears the door shut behind him, grabbing the two empty coffee cups, she puts on the black silk robe she keeps by the bed, heading to the kitchen, she remembers yesterday's post that she never finished opening.

Flashbacks to why she never read the letters make her smile. After depositing the cups in the sink she goes over to the coffee table where she left the letters, picking up the unopened ones, three of them left. Heading back up to bed, she can't resist another look out at the Thames and the boats going about their business, this time though her modesty is covered, not to say if anyone could see in they would still be pleased with what they saw. Once in the bedroom she climbs under the duvet and quickly flicks through the remaining letters, her heart sinks seeing the front of one of the letters.

Her pulse quickens, with fear but also with a sense of longing. A day she knew would come eventually; she thought she had time though. The remaining letters now tossed to one side, this one now held in both hands, just starring at it, part of her willing it to vanish into thin air. For eighteen years, she has thought about this moment, for eighteen years not a day has gone past when she has not thought about him. This can't be happening now, she is not prepared, how can she tell Paul, will she tell Paul, she knows she has to, but how. Have eighteen years really gone by this quickly, in her mind she recalls the day as if it was yesterday. The day in the hospital, barely out of school, having to say goodbye, thinking it will be last time she ever sees him. In some deep place in her mind, hoping it would be the last time. Staring at the letter, it's not going to vanish, she can't bring herself to open it. With her heart still racing, mind buzzing, a thousand thoughts blurring into one. Paul will be back soon.

Why didn't she tell Paul years ago? She thought about it when he asked her to marry him twelve years ago. Then she thought she would wait until they were married, then once they were she realised she should of told him before the big day. Then as the days turned into years it became harder and harder. She realises she is crying, tears rolling down both cheeks, dripping off her chin onto the satin bed sheets, forming dark spots.

Both she and Paul decided before they were married that they did not want children, this was probably more Paul's decision than hers. She was happy to go along with it, if it meant spending the rest of her life with him. Having children is not a lifelong dream of hers, she knows for many women life isn't complete without them. She has never had a desire to be a mother, not to say, if Paul suddenly said he wanted a baby, she would be more than happy to bear his child. Her life is Paul and all that it entails, although being strong willed herself, she loves the way they both seem to gel together. When together they are as one, rarely arguing, thinking the same thoughts, each able to complete the others' sentences. They are soul mates, so why has she never told him, deep down it's because she is ashamed, she has never forgiven herself, how can she expect anyone else to forgive her.

Will Paul leave her?

Will he be able to look at her anymore; the way he looks at her now is with a sense of desire. Will he see her now as second hand goods? Why didn't she tell him she had a son?

Still not able to bring herself to open the letter, she gets out of bed, going to the en-suite still carrying the letter. She goes over to the mango wood storage unit where the towels are all neatly stacked and places the letter under the bottom one. Going to the sink she fills it with cold water, splashing her face washing away the tears, Paul can't see her like this.

Somehow the letter has made her feel dirty, letting the water run away down the plug hole, feeling this is where her life is heading too. She begins filling the bath, hoping this will make things better, knowing deep down that nothing is ever going to make her feel better again.

She sits on the edge of the bath, pours some camomile bubble bath into the stream of fast flowing water, immediately the bath water begins to froth. Feeling the temperature of the water, she removes her silk robe and tentatively puts her toe in the water, before lowering herself all the way in. With the water still flowing, she lets it get to within a couple of inches of the top. Turning the taps off, she lays back, her body physically shaking, not from cold but from terror. The last time she felt this scared and alone was when she realised she had done something unbelievably stupid, she was sixteen at the time. The aftermath of that mistake had been her son, born nearly nine months later. The son she had held once, before what she hoped would be the loss of him forever. She would move on as if it had never happened, unfortunately nothing had prepared her for what was to come. Even though her son was not with her, she still felt a strange bond to him, a bond that had lasted for eighteen years. For eighteen long years, not a day has passed without a thought for the little bundle she handed over like a child's discarded toy.

Immersing her whole body under water, holding her breath for as long as possible, thinking if she holds it long enough, she may never have to come up for air again. Self-preservation gets the better of her, pushing herself up through the foaming water, gasping for air. Brushing the suds away from her face, mixed with fresh tears, her body has stopped shaking. She closes her eyes, placing a flannel over them to block out the light, she begins replaying in her mind the night that changed her life, and bought with it a new one.

*

That night is still so vivid in her mind; she can still taste and smell the memories. A warm, humid August night in nineteen eighty-one, barely a month since her sixteenth birthday and she is heading off to her friend Leigh's party. She is round her best friends' house getting ready to go to Leigh's; Becky's parents are out for the evening. She has bought a bottle of vodka with her, one she liberated from her mum's drink's cabinet. Becky has her stereo blaring out Soft Cell's Tainted Love; they each take turns swigging the vodka straight from the bottle. Becky tries on five outfits before deciding on the first one she tried, a red low cut top with a black mini skirt, being top heavy she is almost bursting out of the top. She is wearing a pink mini skirt with a brown and pink top. They both do their make-up, looking older than they are; at this point the bottle of vodka is half-empty. She remembers thinking at the time how bad the vodka tasted, even now she can taste the sharp tang on her tongue and the burning as it went down.

She recalls they decide to walk to Leigh's, about half a mile away; the party would have started by the time they left. Getting to Leigh's about fifteen minutes later, the party is in full swing, it's not really Leigh's party, it's her brother Neil's. Neil is three years older than they are at nineteen; most of the people are his friends. He told Leigh she could invite two friends, in return she wouldn't tell their parents about the party. Knocking on the door Neil invites them in, greeting Nikki with a big smile, she has always had a thing for Neil, and he is sophisticated and intellectual. He points them in the direction of Leigh, and tells them where the drinks are, she remembers feeling incredibly grown up, treated as an adult. With hindsight, she knows now that she was not acting like an adult. She remembers the first hour or so of the party. She, Leigh and Becky dancing, they were attracting the attention of some of the older boys, getting dirty looks from some of the older girls. She remembers later on in the evening Neil coming up to her and asking her if she was okay, she vaguely recollects telling him that she felt a bit sick. He took her upstairs to lie on his bed, he left her there and said he would check back on her in a little while, she has no idea where Leigh or Becky were.

The next thing she remembers is Neil leaning over her, smelling his sour breath from the alcohol and cigarettes, asking her if she felt better, and she did. He then leans in and kisses her on the lips, she doesn't pull away. Her head is still spinning but she doesn't feel sick anymore, she feels his hand going up under her top and squeezing her breast hard. Still kissing her, he pulls her forward up from the bed and fumbles with her bra strap. He takes her top off and removes her bra. She instinctively crosses her arms over her exposed breasts; Neil pulls them away and begins roughly chewing at her nipples as if he's a dog with a bone. While doing this he starts removing his trousers and underpants, then he asks her if she is a virgin. She tells him that she is, he carries on alternating between chewing and sucking, she grimaces in pain at the roughness. With his hand up her skirt, he pulls hard on her knickers until they are off. He gets off her and walks over to a chair in the corner with carrier bags on, she can see he is hard; this is the first one she has seen. Grabbing a couple of the carrier bags, bringing them back, tells her to roll over and puts the carrier bags underneath her. He tells her that she may bleed, as this is her first time, she remembers feeling scared and embarrassed and just wanting to go home. Lying there now on a couple of carrier bags, he climbs on top of her, pushing her legs apart with his knees. After a couple of unsuccessful attempts to penetrate her, he adjusts his position, this time he is in and the pain hits her, she lets out a pitiful scream. Not deterred, Neil carries on vigorously thrusting in and out, thankfully within a dozen strokes it is all over. Neil rolls off her and pulling on his jeans and t-shirt disappears back downstairs to the party. Nikki just lies there; a tear rolling down her face, putting her hand between her legs, feeling moisture, and the smell of iron, she sees the blood. Quickly retrieving her clothes, she gets dressed, grabbing the carrier bags, she screws them up and puts them in the bin by his bed. Almost running from the room she bumps into one of the older girls, who stares at her, looks her up and down and calls her a slut. Running now down the stairs and out the front door, she carries on running until she can't run anymore. Stopping to sit on someone's front garden wall, she leans over and wretches, the vomit just missing her shoes, tasting the sourness of the alcohol mixed with the stale sweat from Neil. She carries on vomiting until just bile comes out, standing up she tries to work out where she is, she just ran from the house aimlessly. Now she didn't recognise where she was, none of the houses looked familiar, she couldn't ring her parents, where was she going to go? She was supposed to be staying at Becky's tonight, but she'd left Becky at the party.

She decided to walk back the way she had come to see if anything looked familiar. She had no idea what the time was, or where she was going to stay, she didn't want to see Becky tonight, what would she say to her? Trying to trace her steps she thought one of the roads looked familiar, she remembered walking along this road on the way to Leigh's. Getting her bearings now, the effects of the alcohol wearing off helping, she decided she would go home. She would wait until all the lights were off, and then sneak in, her mum would probably be two sheets to the wind, and her dad wouldn't be much better. An hour later she was standing outside her front door, she had been sick again about five minutes ago, she hated to think what a state she looked, her make-up had probably all run, her clothes had been pulled on in a hurry, she just hoped her parents didn't catch her sneaking in. All the lights were off, but she thought she would give it about half an hour just to be sure.

Slowly putting her key in the lock, trying her hardest not to make a sound, The click of the lock sounding like a gunshot to her ears, certain that it would wake her parents, waiting to hear movement from within. After what seemed an eternity, she pushes the door forward, inch by inch, every one seeming to create its own squeak, once inside she pushes the door closed, carefully releasing the catch and locking it. Tiptoeing up the stairs, she never knew there were so many creaking floorboards, past her parents' room, them silently into her own. Safe now in her room, she undresses, removing her skirt she sees the bloodstained knickers and the dried blood that must have trickled down her leg, now a dark brown. She screws up her skirt and knickers, hiding them away, ready to dispose of them tomorrow. With the effects of the drink wearing off, she begins to get pain from down below, and her nipples are extremely tender; they hurt as she removes her top and bra. Luckily, she has a bathroom attached to her room, running the tap and wetting a flannel she begins to wash herself from head to toe. Already she regrets going to the party, deciding she is never drinking again, she swears to herself she is never going to be this stupid again.

The worst is the feeling of dirtiness and shame, she can't believe after what they did, Neil just got dressed and went back to the party, leaving her there alone, crying and feeling dirty. She always thought that her first time would be special, with somebody she loved and who loved her back. Now all that was gone, her lifelong memory of her first time would be this, pawed at like a piece of meat, and tossed aside like yesterday's garbage. She hated Neil. She would never forgive him.

*

"Breakfast is served" Paul announces, bringing her back to reality, removing the flannel from her eyes, plastering a smile on her face she replies,

"Sorry I was miles away" trying her best to appear jolly, maybe even overdoing it, she looks at the tray of food he has prepared. Fresh Pain au chocolat, her favourite, a cup of steaming coffee, and a single red rose in a vase, "That looks fantastic; you shouldn't have gone to that much trouble" she says wiping a tear from her eye.

"There's no need to cry, it's only breakfast."

"Oh, it's just me being stupid, I love you so much," she responds. "Do you wanna take it back to bed and I'll join you in a couple of minutes," she asks.

"Sure don't be long or I might have it."

As he leaves the bathroom, she submerges herself once more before surfacing and getting out of the bath. Standing on the tiled floor dripping water everywhere, she tries to relax before leaving the confines of her sanctuary. She dries her hair and body, leaving the towel wrapped round her head, putting the robe back on, still feeling dirty even after the bubble bath. At least the shakes have stopped; she just needs to get through today and tomorrow, then she can decide what to do. Walking out of the bathroom with a big smile on her face, she sees Paul sitting up in bed with his cup of coffee; he's already eaten his breakfast. Getting in bed beside him, she starts eating hers.

"Are you alright babe, you look a bit pale" he asks, with concern in his voice.

"I'm fine, just starving," she says, carrying on eating, no appetite really, while trying to put the letter sitting under the towels out of her mind, if only hiding her son could be that easy.

12

July 1 2000

With no work and no Anna today, Anthony decides on a nostalgia trip. Mike is making him take a well-earned day off, with a slower than usual day in the patisserie, Mike told him to take the time to decide what he wants to do about his relationship with Anna. So that he what he decides to do, a trip down memory lane, he will decide the pros and cons of telling Anna how he feels, as an added bonus it will distract his mind from his birth mum.

He's made himself a packed lunch, packed plenty to drink, including a couple of cans of lager, and sets of, it's only a five minute walk to the old disused railway line, the same one he and Anna would walk as kids. His starting point is about two miles further up the track to where he and Anna used to join it. He walks along the high street, cutting through an alley to the main road, from there he hops between the traffic and down an embankment to the canal. Walking along passing the occasional angler, and moving out of the way of impatient cyclists, he decides to take a slight detour, rather than crossing the canal at the lock and up the flight of wooden sleepers set into the bank up to the tracks, he decides to carry on along the canal. This will add about half a mile to his journey, but this way is more scenic, with the array of brightly coloured narrowboats moored along the banks.

With his backpack slung over his shoulder, he reaches in and grabs a bottle of water, flipping the cap he takes a mouthful of water, the early morning sun is already warm on his back. He smiles to himself as he passes a narrowboat with the name 'Anna's Delight', *is this a sign?* He wonders to himself. Up ahead he can see an angler wrestling with a fish, drawing closer he realises just what a mismatched battle it had been, for the monster fish in question is a five inch Perch, hardly Jaws, he stops long enough to watch the youngster take the hook from the mouth and toss it back, before placing another poor unsuspecting maggot on the end of the hook—the circle of life in action.

Before too long he comes to where he has to part ways with the canal, crossing at the lock, careful as he goes, he stops midway, looking back at the way he has come, the angler still sitting there watching his float—he will probable stare at that thing for the next six hours and not get another bite. He watches a flotilla of moorhens paddle their way across from one side to the safety of the overhanging trees on the far bank. Saying goodbye to the canal he begins his trek across the moors to the disused railway track awaiting on the other side.

The moors aren't exactly Dartmoor or Exmoor, less than a square mile of wasteland separating the industrial estate one side from the Grand Union canal the other, but a lovely spot nonetheless. When he was very young he vaguely remembers family trips here, as it was such a short walk from the council estate where he grew up, he parents would sometimes bring them here, he and his sister would paddle in the little river next to the canal, the little minnows would swim around his feet and make him laugh. He smiles as he reminisces one of the few happy memories he has of his childhood. At the same time he recalls that most of the happiest memories are of him on his own, even this memory, his sister and parents were further up the river, they were trying to catch fish in a net they had bought for Tracey. He remembers they had told him he was too young to have a net and that he should go and explore by himself.

Watching where he places his feet, the moor littered with cowpats, the culprits currently grazing at the far end by the tree-line. As he walks, he turns his attention back to the matter at hand—Anna—Deep down he knows he has to tell her, this was a foregone conclusion before he even set out this morning, he thinks all he wants from today is a distraction, and he can think of no better distraction than Anna. What he has to decide is how to tell her and when to tell her.

In his heart he wants to tell her now, right this second, but his head tells him that as soon as he does he will lose his best friend. Nearing the far side of the moor, he recognises the break in the trees leading to the disused railway, stepping onto the tracks he is transported into the film 'Stand By Me' with a group of kids doing exactly what he is now. He walks down the centre of the tracks, his stride the perfect length to coincide with the space between sleepers. His mind distracted he returns to the matter in hand, when to tell her, as he's mulling this question over in his head a muntjac runs across his path less than ten feet ahead.

Less than a mile down the track he passes the bottom of the recreation field at the end of his old house where he lived with his 'family', the place his sister still lives with her two brats. This area of track rises above the level of the field, though still tree lined it is hidden from view. He stops by an old felled oak, a good four feet in diameter he decides this will be a good spot to stop for a bite to eat. Perching himself on the trunk, his feet not reaching the floor, the rough bark not making the most comfortable of seats, but good enough. Opening his bag, he pulls out one round of his chicken and mayonnaise on rye sandwiches. Taking the first bite, realising just how hungry he is, he watches as a group of kids about halfway across the field kick a ball about, with a couple of jumpers for goalposts, why they aren't in school he has no idea, they can only be about thirteen, and there must be half a dozen of them. He watches as one of them scores a goal and goes on to raise his shirt over his head and arms aloft runs around like a thing possessed. Fifteen minutes of watching and reminiscing all the times he played on this same field with Anna, he hops from the trunk, back to the track, if he remembers correctly just past the next bend, a hundred metres or so of the track is missing. He never knew why, but he and Anna used to think that aliens came one night and took it away to study it. He can't help but smile to himself at the random memories that keep flashing before him—he is so glad he came today –if nothing else it is helping to clarify in his mind that he has the two most important events in his life coming up. One of which he has no control over, the second he does, and win her or lose her he knows he has to tell Anna how he feels, for the first time in his life he thinks he knows what love is like.

He arrives at their bridge a little before midday, just as the sun is at its highest and hottest. The bridge is just as it was all those years ago, only now he sits here with answers, or at least some of them. The times he and Anna sat here making up stories about where he came from, now he has some idea, and it appears he isn't the spawn of some rock star. He thinks back to the times here with Anna—did he love her even back then? Maybe?

He lays on his back staring up at the sky, not a cloud in sight, he wishes Anna was with him, she would have liked this trip down memory lane, maybe if she was here he would be able to talk to her about them, or more to the point if there is a them. He can't believe that after all these years he leaves it until he finds his mum to decide he has fallen for her.

He breaks the seal on one of the cans of lager, a sort of celebration to himself for deciding that he wants Anna, as much as he loves her as his friend, he realises that will no longer be enough, he wants to spend the rest of his life with her. He can't envisage anyone else coming along that could even come close to her. And for the first time he realises that it is not even about what she looks like, he would want her no matter what package she came in, the fact that she is wrapped the way she is, that's a bonus.

As he takes a drink from the can he mulls over what it is to be in love—at least he thinks that that is what he feels for her, he can't imagine what else it could be. As a side line to his current thoughts he has the sudden realisation that he has more feelings for Nicola Anderson—his mum—than he ever had for his parents or sister. The thought scares him, he has never met her, has no idea if she will even want to know him, yet the feelings grow stronger each day towards her, he knows that is a mistake, that it could all come tumbling down around him. If she rejects him, if Anna rejects him, where will he be left.

On such a beautiful day he is left lying there wondering how in the space of thirty seconds he has gone from one of his highest of highs to where he is now, with thoughts he can't push from the forefront of his mind, back to his dream and the car heading towards the wall. Not wanting to fight it anymore he just lets the tears flow, not bothering to wipe them away, relishing the stinging as they pool in his eyes, before overflowing down the side of his cheeks, flowing like the river some twenty feet below him.

He absently rubs at his arm, knowing the scaring is still there, probably will be for the foreseeable future, he has managed so far to avoid Anna seeing it, a couple of times she has questioned why he always wears long sleeves lately, he told her he thought he may be coming down with something.

13

July 3 2000

She hears Paul shut the door on his way out to work, she managed to get through the weekend without losing it, and she thinks without Paul realising anything is wrong. He commented a couple of times while they were in Camden that she was quiet, but apart from that nothing. She just told him she hadn't slept very well, when all the time her mind kept going back to the letter.

She phoned Aimee to ask her if she could cope without her today, as she was feeling a bit under the weather. She hated lying to her friend, she had decided she would tell both Aimee and Hayley as soon as she got the chance. In fact, once she had read the letter she was going to ring Aimee back and ask her if she could meet her for lunch to explain things. Not able to put it off any longer, she goes to the bathroom where the hidden letter still resides, retrieving it she takes it back downstairs, sitting in the chair overlooking the Thames, once again in the familiar position of holding the letter in front of her with both hands. Looking at the postmark, seeing it's from a town north-west of London, probably twenty or thirty miles away. She opens the letter carefully, as if expecting it to explode in her hands at any moment. Unfolding the letter, she sees a neatly written page.

Dear Nicola Anderson,

I don't quite know how to begin writing this letter; I have gone over it a thousand times in my head, all the things I want to ask, all the things I need to know, but in the end I guess it all comes down to this—why? I don't have any ulterior motives, I would just like to meet you and if possible get to know you, and at the same time, I may be able to understand who I am.

I am sure that you will need time to think about this, all I am asking is that you do think about it, I am not trying to intrude in your life or family—if you have one. If you do decide you would be willing to meet with me, I have included my contact details.

For eighteen years I have not known who I am, wondering on a daily basis, where did I come from? Who do I look like? Did you ever love me? Plus, a thousand other questions. Maybe there was a good reason you didn't want me, I need to know what it is that made you give me to someone else. As I have said there is no other reason for me getting in touch, I don't want money, I just need to meet you.

I really hope that you reply to my letter, if for no other reason than to find out how I turned out. Have you thought about me at all in the last eighteen years?

Anthony Allen

Nikki sits there having read the letter at least a dozen times, her heart breaking, what has she done? She can feel the tears stinging her eyes, before long they'll carve their own groove down her cheeks, it's all she seems to be doing lately. A couple of the tears land on the letter, blurring some of the words. Staring across at Canary Wharf, picturing Paul over there working, oblivious to the secrets she holds, secrets that will make their world come tumbling down around them. Nikki has thought of doing nothing and hoping it will all go away, then remembers that he has her address and could just turn up if she ignores him. Sitting there drifting off into her own world again, she is taken back to the birth of her son.

Late on a balmy May evening, Nikki started getting contractions while watching Coronation Street, after ignoring them long enough to see the end of the programme, she went to tell her mum. Her mum instantly called Nikki's dad, told him they had to go to the hospital. They have not been supportive, or understanding, as soon as she has had the baby they've told her they want her out, although nearly seventeen, she was terrified about making her own way in the world. She remembers when she first broke the news to them that she was pregnant. Her mum didn't speak to her for a week, even now it's only to admonish her, and her dad threatened to beat the little bastard who had done this to a pulp. When her mum did speak to her, she called her a slut, a whore, a slag who thought of nobody but herself, she asked her how she was supposed to hold her head up in the street when everyone knew what a slapper she had for a daughter. Her mum told her there was no way she was keeping the baby, that no bastard was living under her roof. Since telling her parents neither one of them wanted anything to do with her, they ignored her at home, so she spent most of her time at Becky's, her parents had been fantastic, it was with their help she had sorted out the adoption. Nikki knew her parents were slagging her off to anyone that would listen; they had made it quite clear that she was no daughter of theirs. She had endured months of hell with her parents, the snide comments when they thought she wasn't listening, or maybe because she was listening, she couldn't wait to get the baby out of her. Months of her family telling her how worthless she was, her world falling apart around her, most of her friends avoiding her at every chance—except Becky. Friends who had been over the moon when she had told them about the pregnancy, suddenly stopped calling or visiting, she knows it had to be her mum poisoning them against her, but what could she do. She knew that as soon as the baby was born, she was on her own; Becky's mum had arranged for her to go to London. A good friend of Becky's mum's owned a salon in the west end, she offered her the flat above rent free in exchange for working in the salon and being trained. Her plan, once the baby had been born, after a few days stay in hospital, she stays at Becky's for the next few days before going to her new life in London. She would never set foot in her parents' house again, Becky's mum and dad offered to collect her stuff from the house and take her to London; she would have been lost without them.

She remembers driving through the streets of Oxford, in too much pain to notice anything going on around her, her mum and dad sitting in the front of their Peugeot 405 completely ignoring her discomfort in the back seat. The one thing they did say to her when she got in the car 'don't you dare make a mess in the back—or you will be cleaning it up', this hurt her more than anything they had said previously, obviously caring more for the car than their daughter. The car journey took them about twenty minutes, her dad not rushing, not wanting to get a speeding ticket, pulling up at the hospital's emergency entrance her mum got out of the car. Walking around the car, she opens the door for her daughter to get out, not bothering to help, just standing there watching her daughter struggle to remove herself from their car. A nurse appears with a wheelchair, helping her in, as the nurse wheels her off, her mum calls after her "We'll pack your things up ready for them to be collected." These are the last words she would hear from her mum or dad.

Alone in the delivery room, she remembers being terrified, she gets chills down her spine even now thinking back to that moment, sitting there looking out on the tranquil Thames, a barge trudging past down below her, the delivery could've been yesterday the images are so vivid. The stark white delivery room, the grey plastic trunking encircling the room, the overhead fluorescents shrouding the room in an artificial glow, the antiseptic hospital smell, the machines and tools all on hand should they be needed. She doesn't know what any of them are for, and that scares her even more, after being put in here a midwife gave a cursory assessment of her condition, obviously deciding she warranted no further attention left saying someone would pop back in a while, and to relax. Lying there not knowing what was going on, Becky didn't know she was here, she decided the next person that came in, she would ask if they could ring her.

A sailboat is sailing up the Thames on its way out to sea no doubt, Nikki doesn't know how long she has been sitting here, could be five minutes, could be five hours. At this precise moment, she couldn't care less, reading the letter once again, the guilt and shame once again washing over her. What life could she have given him; he is better off without her, if only he knew that, then maybe he would leave her alone. She knew she was asking for a miracle, if she were in his position, she would want to meet her. Getting out of the chair leaving the letter behind, subconsciously trying to distance herself from it, knowing she could be a hundred miles from it and it would still be with her, eating away at her. Walking in to the kitchen, she makes herself a cup of strong black coffee, puts a couple of slices of bread in the toaster in the hope of settling her stomach. She can't recall the last time she felt this nauseous.

After a couple of visits from the nurses, over several hours, and the odd visit from the midwife they decided it was time, as she had dilated enough. Her contractions were now coming at short regular intervals. The pain was indescribable, her body no longer felt as if it were her own, the sweat pouring out of every pore, saturating the sheets. With her legs apart for the entire world to see, the midwife with her hands on her, telling her to push and breathe, oblivious now to the pain, she just wanted to die. She remembers feeling alone, either the nurse hasn't phoned Becky or it's taking them a long time to get here, she didn't even consider the possibility that they hadn't been allowed in with her. At one point she recalls shouting at the midwife to 'get the little bastard out of her' regretting it immediately and apologising profusely ignoring the pain and the fact that the baby had popped itself into the world during these apologies. The next part is a blur and to this day she doesn't remember what happened, the next thing she remembers is waking up with Becky and her parents at her bedside, explaining the staff had not allowed them into the delivery room while she had the baby. She didn't know why but she wanted to see the baby, she didn't know if it was a boy or girl, healthy, nothing. She asked Becky's mum and dad to find out for her. They came back five minutes later and told her that the baby had had trouble breathing but was okay now and that she would bring him to her in a few minutes, so it was a boy. Then the bad news, the social worker was waiting to see Nikki, she knew this time would arrive, and in some ways, she welcomed it. She knew the baby had to go; she couldn't keep it, could she?

The best thing for her son, she thought of him as her son, is for the adoption to go as planned. He would be handed to foster parents, she understood, in the interim, as there was a six-week period where she could change her mind. After this time if both parties agreed, she could meet the adoptive parents, Nikki knew she didn't want to meet them, and she didn't want the updates each year either. The best for her son is to forget she ever existed and make his own way in the world, with a family that loves him. She resigned herself that she would not be a fit mother to him, reinforcement from her parents confirmed that she could not look after herself, let alone care for a baby. What could she, a sixteen-year-old girl, hope to accomplish looking after a baby? The prospect of looking after herself scared the shit out of her, no, the best thing all round is to have him bought up in a loving and caring environment with his new family.

Wiping away the tears from the recollection of all those years ago, Nikki takes the toast from the toaster and begins buttering; not realising that the toast is cold, time just seems to keep disappearing today into an abyss. Looking at the clock she sees that's it's eleven-thirty. She puts the toast straight in the bin, her stomach rebelling at the thought of food in it. Nikki decides to take a shower before ringing Aimee back; she needs to speak to someone.

*

An hour later, walking through the streets to the coffee shop, Nikki wonders if she is doing the right thing. At the moment no one knows her dirty little secret, that's not what she thinks of her son, just her part in it, the getting pregnant the way she did, the getting rid of him, the complete disregard for his life. What is Aimee likely to make of the situation, Nikki is terrified that she will judge her for what she has done, she feels as if she is about to go on trial for the crime of the century, standing in the dock at the Old Bailey, accused of crimes against humanity. The worst crime, a mother giving away her flesh and blood, her first born, for what could be seen as purely selfish reasons, she just didn't want him—

though that's not entirely the truth.

Getting closer to the coffee shop, Nikki decides on a slight detour to make the trip that tiny bit longer, putting off the inevitable moment of trying to offload her guilt to her best friend. Running five minutes late, she can't put off the inevitable any longer, entering the coffee shop, she sees Aimee wave her over to the table, where there are two steaming coffee's waiting along with two, what look like smoked salmon bagels.

"Hi, I thought you'd got lost" Aimee greets her, a worried look on her face, telling Nikki that she knows something is wrong.

"Sorry, but I didn't feel too good" Nikki explains, the redness around her eyes still visible.

"Have you been crying?" Aimee asks, seeing the redness and puffiness now she's up close. With that, Nikki bursts into uncontrollable sobs, attracting the attention of what is becoming a full coffee shop. Aimee puts her arms around her, as Rico, the coffee shop owner comes over and tells her to take Nikki into the back room, the one where the staff take their tea breaks. He promises they can have it for as long as they need it and that they won't be disturbed.

In the back room, Aimee tries to console Nikki, telling her that everything is going to be all right.

"It can't be," Nikki tries to tell her between sobs.

"What do you mean? You're not making much sense," Aimee asks, confused now, this is not at all like Nikki, she is normally a strong person, and she has been ever since the first time she met her, all those years ago. "Start from the beginning, and tell me everything, don't leave anything out. I've cleared my diary for the rest of the day, after your phone call, you sounded desperate." She adds.

"You shouldn't have done that." Nikki says. With that she opens her bag, retrieving the letter, now neatly back in its envelope. Handing it to Aimee, "This arrived Friday, I didn't read it until this morning, although I knew what it was. Don't ask me how I knew, I just did." The sobbing had now subsided, "read it and then I'll explain".

Aimee takes the letter, noticing it is to Nicola Anderson, Aimee knows she hasn't been Nicola Anderson for nearly eleven years. Intrigued now, Aimee removes the letter and starts to read, Nikki can see the confusion on her friends face, buts lets her carry on. Aimee rereads the letter what must be four or five times, before placing it on the table in front of her.

"I don't understand, you don't have a son. Even if it's true, you'd only have been sixteen, you would have mentioned something this big," Aimee states, more confused than ever now.

"It is true, I've never told anyone, not even Paul," The tears are rolling freely down her face again, "I should have told Paul when I met him." Composing herself, wiping away the tears, "I'll start at the beginning." Nikki then proceeds to tell Aimee about the night she got pregnant, the nine months of hell living at home with her parents, and culminating in the birth and the giving away of her baby.

Aimee just sits there for nearly an hour, not saying a word, not interrupting, and just sitting with her mouth agape. Finding it hard to believe the story coming from Nikki's mouth, this is not the Nikki she knows and loves.

"So, now you know, call me what you want—a heartless bitch, a selfish cunt, go on do your worst" Nikki taunts her.

With that, Aimee stands up, walks to the door and goes out to the coffee shop, without saying a word. Nikki is heartbroken, her friend couldn't look her in the eye, Putting her face in her hands, she can feel her body going into convulsions, her chest heaving, the feeling that she is going to vomit, when the door opens and in walks Aimee with a bottle of Brandy and two glasses, courtesy of Rico.

"Here, I think we need one of these," she says while pouring a couple of liberal measures of the brandy. "We'll work this out, together."

"How can we sort it out, I can't tell Paul, he'll leave me. Why have I been so stupid?" She asks.

"If I know Paul, he won't leave you; he might be hurt that you didn't trust him enough to tell him sooner. However, he won't leave you. Why have you kept this to yourself all these years?" Aimee asks.

"I was ashamed, thinking about it made me feel dirty, the thought of how he was conceived, the way my family disowned me, I hoped that when he was adopted that would be the end of it and I could get on with living my life." She pauses to take a sip of her brandy, "I know it sounds selfish, but I believed he would have a better life without me, I was on my own after the baby was born, my parents wouldn't have me back in the house when I came out of hospital. I stayed with a friend for a about a week after, then her parents had set me up with a job and accommodation in London, working in a salon. I think they wanted me out of their house, thinking I would be a bad influence on their daughter. Don't get me wrong, they were fantastic, supportive, they helped me through every step of the way, from sorting out the adoption, they were there after I had the baby, but in the end, they saw me for what I was. A cheap dirty little slut, who couldn't keep her legs closed." As she says this, Aimee pulls her close to her; she too now has tears streaming down her face.

"It's okay babe, I can't believe you have been through all this on your own. How are your parents with you now?" she wants to know.

"The day they dropped me at the hospital, and told me they wanted nothing more to do with me. That is the last time I had any contact with them. Becky, she was my best friend whom I stayed with, she kept in touch for about six months after I left for London. The salon I worked in were friends of her parents, they used to let them know how I was getting on, but the day I left Oxford was the last day I ever saw the place, I never went back." She says this in a matter of fact tone, like it is just one of those things that happen to you, your parents disown you, you're dumped in a city where you know no one, all this a week after giving birth to a baby you gave away.

Not saying anything, Aimee holds on to her tightly, not wanting to let her go, Nikki seems calm, although Aimee's body is shaking, not for Nikki, but anger at her family and so called friends, for putting her through all that pain and torment. A sixteen-year-old girl, who's just had a baby, should be cared for and loved, not punished in this cruel and vindictive way. She hopes she never has the opportunity to meet any of them.

"Does Hayley know any of this?" She asks Nikki.

"No, you're the only one I've told so far. I'm not sure what to do, I was hoping I could ignore the letter and see what happens, before telling anyone else." Knowing as she is saying it, that it isn't an option.

"I think you should tell Paul as soon as possible," Aimee suggests, "If you want me to be there with you when you tell him, I'm quite happy to do that." She offers.

"Thank you, but no, I think when I tell Paul it should just be me and him, I don't want him to feel ambushed, If you're there he will feel obliged to be supportive. I don't want that, I want a true reaction from him, I can't live a life not knowing what his true feelings are. I would rather he hated, and left me, than stay with me out of some kind of obligation or pity." She says, meaning every word she's saying. Looking at nothing in particular, she suddenly says, "You know, I've thought about him every day since I left him at the hospital, sometimes with regret, but mostly with the hope that I did the right thing and he's having a good life. I won't be able to handle the guilt if I find out he is not part of a loving family."

"I'm sure he is being bought up well, and is happy, contacting you is probably just his curiosity getting the better of him." Aimee tries to reassure her.

14

Sunday July 16 2000

"How much time are you going to give her to reply." Anna asks Anthony, it has been nearly three weeks since Anthony sent the letter to his birth mum. They're sitting on the sofa in Anthony's flat, both still in their pyjamas, even though it has gone one o'clock. Anthony has just cooked them a fried lunch of bacon, eggs, sausage and mushrooms. Now they're just chilling out watching an old carry on movie—the one where Dr. Nookie is sent to a tropical island and discovers the secret to weight loss. The two of them love days like this, Sundays, neither of them have to work, Anna stayed over last night, meaning Anthony slept on the sofa, he seems to be doing this more and more these days.

"I was thinking of going to see her, not to talk to her, just to get an idea of who she is. I was thinking of going tomorrow, I was going to ring Mike and see if he is okay with me taking the day off tomorrow. He has told me to take anytime I need at the moment—he has been so understanding, I can't thank him enough—I don't suppose there is any way you could get the time off tomorrow too is there?" he asks. He knows it's short notice but he wants Anna to be there with him, especially as it could be the first time he sees his mum, the first time of seeing someone with the same genes. Things he may recognise in her that are in him, will she have the same eyes, nose, mouth, or has he inherited more her personality rather than features. In some ways, he's excited about the prospect of meeting her, in others apprehensive.

Ever since he has known he's adopted he has conjured up images of his mum, almost seeing her as his saviour from the family that took him from her. He is worried that in the flesh she may not meet up with his expectations of her. He knows this is unfair of him; she is who she is, all that matters is that she's his mum. The one who gave birth to him, the one with the right to call him her son, he understands that most people don't see it like that, they would say his adoptive parents are the ones with all the rights, they are the ones that loved and cared for him for eighteen years. They are the ones that loved him when no one else did, they would say his birth mum gave up her rights the day she got rid of him. He sees it differently, his adoptive parents never loved him, at least not in the sense that a parent should love their child, he believes whatever the circumstances for his adoption, his mum loves him, whether she knows it now or not, she has to love him.

Eighteen years of pinning his hopes that there is one person in the world who truly loves him, he has gone through his fair share of feelings for her, between love and hate, resentment to understanding, sadness and loneliness, the list goes on, name an emotion and he has felt it towards the person who created him.

"You just try to stop me being there." She tells him with a tone of authority in her voice. "You're not doing this alone, I told you that, I'll ring in sick in the morning, it's not like I have a lot of time off, I can't even remember the last day I took off sick." She adds. She has a look of determination on her face, the one that says 'you don't mess with me'. She can see that he doesn't want to do this on his own, this is one of the things she loves about him, his vulnerability, to look at him you wouldn't believe he could be vulnerable. It's only when you get to know him like she has, there is a tender side to him, at times she sees him as still that little boy she first met. The one, even back then she wanted to take care of; she saw something all those years ago, deep down that told her he needed her in his life. Since that day, she has been there for him every step of the way. Nothing will ever change that.

"That's decided then, we'll head into the city about six-thirty, and hopefully we'll see her leave for work, assuming she works. We just have to hope she doesn't stay at home all day. From what information I have we know it's an apartment, so we'll find somewhere we can watch the front door of the building from." He says, his excitement building at the prospect of it.

"You sound like a private detective, have you got all your surveillance gear ready, the camera, tripod, ooh and don't forget the listening device." She says mocking him.

"Very funny, if you don't want to come you don't have to." He says, feigning hurt. Knowing she will not pass up the chance to be there with him, she is as curious now as he is about the woman that gave birth to him. If they head off at six-thirty, they should arrive at Surrey Quays tube about eight o'clock assuming all the train connections go well, and there are no delays. The thought of getting up any earlier doesn't appeal to either of them.

"How long are you hoping to carry out your surveillance for?" Anna questions him,

"We'll just see how it goes, I don't want to stalk her, and I don't want her to know we're there, I thought we'd watch her come out of the apartment, see where she works, and that will be about it. Do you think we'll recognise her?" he asks.

"I don't know, it depends if you look like her at all, hopefully you'll just know it's her, if not we could be following the wrong woman around the streets of London tomorrow." She laughs. Looking forward to spending another whole day with Anthony, She is hoping that once he has resolved his feelings for his mum, whether meeting her face to face, or her refusing to see him, then she is going to ask him out. Not like they go out together now, but like a date. If he says no, not to be so stupid, then she will laugh it off and tell him she was only joking. She thinks he has feelings for her though; he just keeps it well hidden.

"Well, tomorrow morning we'll find out won't we?" he says, getting up to go and make a cup of coffee, "I suppose you want a cup?" He says walking away, hearing a positive response from her as he gets to the kitchen area.

15

July 17 2000

Six o'clock Monday morning and the alarm is going off, Anna rolls over putting the pillow over her head to blot out the infernal noise. Seconds later the alarm shuts off.

"Come on; time to get up sleepy head." Anthony tells her, he's been up for about an hour, unable to sleep with the anticipation of the day ahead.

"What time is it, it feels like the middle of the night?" Anna says, her voice muffled from beneath the pillow.

"Six o'clock, you've got time to grab a shower if you're quick. I'm doing breakfast, so get a move on." He says.

"Why are you so happy at his hour of the morning? I'll just have another five minutes."

"If you don't get up now, I'm gonna take the quilt, carry you to the shower and turn the cold water on."

"Okay, okay, I'm up." She says, tossing the quilt off, revealing her pyjama clad body, "Do we have to be up this early?" still angling to get an extra five minutes in bed.

Anthony returns to the kitchen, puts the croissants on a tray and pops them in the oven. He hears Anna start the shower running, he starts thinking about the steaming water hitting her perfect body, at least it's perfect in his eyes. He needs to stop thinking of her like that; it's not good for him. His daily thoughts now switch between his mum (he's conscious of the fact that he thinks of Nicola as his mum knowing it's not that healthy) and Anna, some days more about Anna, some more about his mum.

Five minutes later Anna is sat at the breakfast bar with just a towel wrapped around her, her bust straining against the material in a battle to be let loose,

"You could've got dressed you know, you had time." He says.

"What's wrong, don't you like my new dress." Standing up and giving a twirl, the towel showing off her curves.

"You look lovely, but I think we might stand out and attract attention on the underground if you intend to go out like that." He says, laughing.

They eat their breakfast, croissants with jam, and freshly brewed coffee, then Anna gets up to go and get dressed, Anthony puts the dirty dishes in the sink. It's twenty past six when they head out the door to catch their train. They have two changes to make; they get the fast train into Liverpool Street, then change to the Hammersmith and City line for two stops to Whitechapel, site of the infamous Jack The Ripper murders more than a century ago, then the East London Line for four stops, getting off at Surrey Quays. The journey into London, is busy at this time of the morning, commuters on their way to their respective jobs, packed onto the trains as if sardines in a can.

Anna and Anthony are lucky, the train is virtually empty when they get on, within a couple of stops the carriages start filling up rapidly. Men in business suits carrying brief cases, women power dressed for a day at the office, all heading into one of the busiest cities in the world. The two of them along for the ride just this one time, “I couldn’t do this every day, and go and sit in an office, could you?” Anna asks.

“Definitely not, it would drive me nuts, it’s feels as if we’re a herd of animals being led to the slaughter, only these people do this five or six days a week. I bet some of them wish they were heading for the slaughter house, I haven’t seen any happy smiling faces yet.” He says to Anna in a whisper, not wanting to offend anyone.

Pulling into Liverpool Street, Anthony grabs hold of Anna’s hand, so that they aren’t separated. They can’t believe the sheer number of people jostling for position, each in their own little world, focused on one thing and one thing only, being the first to get to the train with the aim of grabbing a seat for a couple of stops. Finding the nearest underground map on the wall, they work out where they need to get to, this also allows the crowd to thin out a little. Heading in the general direction of where they need to be, trying to avoid bumping into other travellers. Finding the platform for Hammersmith and City, the platform is already crowded, the sickly sweet smell of all the perfumes and colognes adulterating their senses, they can’t wait to be out in the open air, still, only two stops on this line. After five minutes they feel the familiar rush of air indicating the approach of the train.

As it pulls into the station, a stampede ensues, everyone trying to get as close to the edge of the platform as is humanly possible without stepping into the path of the train. There has been a time when Anthony has considered just that option, walking out into the path of an oncoming high-speed train. The thought of the instantaneousness of it appeals, the thought of putting the driver through it does not. In some weird macabre way, he would leave a lasting impression of his existence, be it only in the memory of the poor sod driving the train, but a memory none the less, no he couldn't do it. The doors open with the customary stand-off, do people get off first or do people get on first, both camps decide that it is them who move first causing mayhem and confusion every time. With people trying to board while others try to get off, worried that the doors will close leaving them to travel further down the line and then having to return to try their luck a second time. They're on, crammed in like sardines, Anna pressed hard up against Anthony, enjoying the smell of him, his arm around her waist holding her close, the fullness of the train giving him the perfect opportunity to keep her close.

The train stops at the next station, where the same dance happens all over again, some people having to remove themselves from the train in order to let other passengers disembark before quickly jumping back in to their sacred position by the door. Anthony and Anna are in the middle of the train, Anthony decides it's better that way because you never know which side the platform is going to be on, at least in the middle you only have to fight your way across half the train. Unlike the guy standing by the door, if the station he needs is the other side will there be enough time for him to jostle across before the train continues on its journey.

Next station Whitechapel, They start getting ready to make their way across, planning for either outcome, to the left they have a relatively clear path to the door, to the right, a young mum with a pushchair, this could be a bit more tricky, fingers crossed for the platform to be on the left. Pulling into the station, sure enough, it's going to be the hard option, they are going to have to manoeuvre their way around the young mum with her pushchair, Anthony guides Anna past the pushchair, some businessman pushing him in the back thinking this will make him move faster. Instead Anthony stops, takes a small step backwards intentionally steeping on the man's foot, before offering an apology, the businessman in his flash suit gets the hint and moves away, not wanting confrontation this early in the working day. Getting out unscathed they look for directions to the East London Line, knowing that four more stops and they will be at their destination, or rather Anthony's destination.

Getting out into the fresh air of Surrey Quays, the sun creating a haze over the city skyline, having just gone seven-thirty, hoping they're not too late. The day promises to be very hot judging by the temperature, out in the sunlight Anthony unfolds the map he bought with them, finding the tube they decide on the general direction they should be heading.

"It should take us about fifteen minutes to walk there." Anthony tells Anna.

"What if she's already left for work?"

"I haven't thought that far ahead."

"If you see her will you not be tempted to talk to her?"

"Of course, but we agreed today is just about looking, I think I should give her a bit more time to come to terms with me. I don't want to scare her before I've got to know her."

"Right, just looking it is, did you bring anything to eat or drink, I'm starving."

"Anna, you're always hungry, we'll get a drink if we pass a shop, and then we'll get something to eat after we've seen her." He tells her.

"I could waste away by then."

"There's a shop just up ahead, will a packet of biscuits do for now? We can have a picnic while we stake her out." He says laughing. They both run towards the shop, the front of it not very inviting, urine up the walls where somebody has spent the night in the doorway, faded notices in the window of rooms to rent, cars to buy, all probably long gone now. A sign informing that the lottery can be played here, Anthony and Anna have spent the money in their heads should they ever win, both agreeing that if either wins the other will get half. Anna true to her word did give him a fiver a couple of weeks ago when she won a tenner, he did try to tell her to keep it but she insisted a deal is a deal. Spending the minimum amount of time in the shop, the smell of urine, sweat and curry overpowering, they quickly purchase two bottles of water and a packet of chocolate biscuits. Leaving the shop, Anna lets out an exaggerated breath, indicating she had not breathed the whole time in the shop.

"Thank god we're out of there." She says.

"It did smell a bit didn't it," Anthony being the usual diplomat, when he knows it smelled awful.

"Come on I think we're nearly there." She says pointing at a large building at the end where the road goes round the bend. Almost running now, they rush up to the door of the building, sure enough the address matches, this one time factory or warehouse is now three apartments. Anna looks at Anthony, "Are you telling me this whole building is just three apartments, and that your mum lives in the middle one?"

"I guess so, I wouldn't have cared if we got here and it was a little tin shack." He says, for him it is about finding out who he is, not about what she's got, he never gave it a second thought that she may be looking at his letter thinking 'what does he want from me'. When he wrote the letter, it didn't occur to him that he may be getting in touch with her in the hope of getting money from her. He voices these concerns to Anna, all the while they are stood outside what looks like the only door in and out of the building, and the chance that his mum could be coming through it at any moment and walk right in to them.

"Come on, let's go over and sit in the gardens, we can see this door from there, and hopefully she won't see us, and if she does she'll think we're just a couple of kids making out." He laughs.

"So we're going to be making out are we?" Anna says looking all innocent and shocked.

"How else do you propose we pass the time while we're waiting?" He says laughing louder now as they head across the road to the gardens, a nice clean area, with a few benches, well maintained flowerbeds with an avalanche of colour this time of year. Finding the bench that will give them the best view of the front door, they sit and both stare at it. It's now a couple of minute to eight

*

At five past eight, Nikki is putting the finishing touches to her make-up, Paul has gone to work, he didn't even say goodbye. She knows it's her fault, she has been pushing him away the last couple of weeks, she's preparing herself for when he leaves her. Knowing it is just a matter of time, Aimee keeps telling her to tell him the truth and get it all out in the open. The thing that's scares her the most is if she tells him and he has a look of revulsion on his face—how could they ever come back from that. Looks like she could be early for a change, this has been happening a lot lately, she is always awake before the alarm, she's lucky if she gets more than five or six hours sleep, lying awake, looking at Paul sleeping, thinking he shouldn't have to go through this. It is her mess, not his. Locking the door as she leaves the apartment, just in time to see Aimee coming down the stairs.

"Am I seeing things? Is this Nikki early again?" Aimee jokes, then seeing the look on Nikki's face realising now isn't a good time to be making jokes. "What's wrong, you look shattered."

"I'm not sleeping too well; I've got to tell him, I can't carry on like this. I feel sick all the time, tired, anxious, and I can't bear to see Paul unhappy, I know it's killing him, he thinks it's his fault that things aren't right between us. He's tried talking to me, keeps asking if he's done something wrong, I just tell him I'm tired and that I'll get over it."

"The longer you leave it the harder it's going to be, just get it over with and then we can deal with the aftermath, although you know what I think, I'm sure he will understand." She says, "Do you want to take the day off, I can manage?"

"No thanks, I'm better off working, it helps occupy my mind." Nikki says, making her way down the stairs.

*

"What time is it?" Anna asks.

"Just gone ten past eight." He tells her after looking at his watch, the first time he has taken his eyes from the front door, scared of missing her coming through.

"Anthony, quick, I think someone's about to come out, I'm sure I saw movement inside." She says, barely able to get the words out quick enough.

*

Nikki and Aimee walk over to the post boxes in the entrance, both checking to see if they have any mail, Nikki comes up empty, no mail today, in some ways it's a relief, no mail means no more letters from Anthony, maybe he's given up. She can live in hope. Walking to the door, Aimee grabs hold of Nikki, giving her a hug says, "I'm here for you, don't ever forget that."

Opening the door, stepping out into the bright sunshine, the warmth hitting their skin, the two of them together making quite a sight, for their years they were still both stunning, Nikki with the sun glistening off her olive skin, wearing a red summer dress, flaring out just above the knee, thin shoulder straps leaving exposed arms and shoulders. Aimee, her long blond hair reflecting the sun, wearing faded, ripped jeans with a white t-shirt with one word printed on it—Babe—made up of sparkling rhinestone gems, she knew she looked good, that air of confidence coming off her in waves. Nikki rather more subdued of late, never realising just how beautiful she is.

*

"Is this her?" Anna asks, excitement in her voice, a clear view of the door, they can see two women coming through the entrance, in Anna's opinion both are stunning, sitting some fifty metres away from them the view is excellent.

"The one on the left is her." Anthony says, although he has no idea what his mum looks like some sixth sense tells him that it's her. He is staring straight at her, not knowing how he should be feeling, the urge building inside him to just go up to her. She is talking to the other woman, getting ready to look away should she look over in his direction. In this instance he knows he loves her unconditionally, he can't describe the feeling, he would never be able to explain to another living soul why. He doesn't know whether it is pre-programming in his D.N.A. or just some deep longing within him that makes him want to love her, to love somebody, to love anybody. The feelings he is feeling now are different to the love he knows he feels for Anna, that is a desire love, rather than a bonding love you feel for family, To Anthony the difference is you choose who you desire, the bonded love of family should be there regardless of any other influences. He notices his palms are sweating, he is still staring straight at her, not realising that for a split second she is staring straight at him, he looks away, turning to face Anna, "I think she saw me, what is she doing now?"

"They're both walking away, down the road to the right, what do you want to do now?" She asks.

"I just want to see where they go, if we light a cigarette then we'll follow them, we just need to stay far enough away so they don't see us."

*

"That young couple were staring at us." Nikki remarks to Aimee.

"What young couple?"

"The two over in the gardens, I swear they were staring, they're talking to each other now, but I know they were looking right at me."

"They were probably just admiring how good looking we are."

"You're right; my mind is in a mess recently." She confesses.

"Come on let's go and have breakfast, before you start seeing little green men in spaceships." Aimee jokes, nudging her friend to show that she doesn't mean anything by it. Linking arms they wander off towards Rico's and his fabulous coffee and Danish.

*

"She doesn't look old enough to be your mum." Anna says, making a reasonable observation, "She doesn't look thirty-four."

"I'm sure it's her though, something about looking at her is as if I'm looking in a mirror. I've never experienced anything like it before, whenever I looked at my parents or sister; it was like looking at strangers."

"We'll see where they go; I just hope they're not going to get on the tube."

"First impressions what do you think of her?" Anthony already seeking reassurance from Anna that he's making the right decision wanting to get to know her.

"You obviously got your looks from your dad, because she is gorgeous." She says with a smile on her face, "Being serious, if she is your mum, I can see a lot of you in her, the skin tone and the eyes, especially the eyes. I wonder in what other ways you are like her, maybe you get your stubbornness from her." Anna remarks.

Following them for a hundred metres or so, they see them disappear into a building, not able to make out what the place is from this side of the road, waiting for a gap in the traffic they decide to cross over, hoping to get a better vantage point. Anna is gripping Anthony's hand tightly, surprised she's not cutting off his circulation with the force, trying to re-emphasise that she is here for him. Walking a little further, they can now see the coffee shop.

"It's a shame they went in there, otherwise we could have a proper breakfast, if we stay on this side and carry on walking straight past, then we can stop a little bit further up." He offers. At this time of the morning the streets are bustling, they can easily get lost in the people milling around going about their daily business, two teenagers wandering about aren't going to draw unwanted attention to them. They pass an array of shops, a launderette, a pawnbrokers, and grocers. Coming level with the coffee shop—called Rico's—on their side of the road is a hairdressers and beauty salon—Hair by Aimee—looking over at the coffee shop, they can see three women now sitting at a table by the window, the two from the apartment building and a third has joined them. Not looking where he is going now, Anthony is relying on Anna to steer him in the right direction, part of him wanting his mum to look his way again, the need for her to see him getting ever greater, not just to look at him but to see him for who he is. The person he has turned out to be, the baby she made eighteen years ago, now all grown up. He wants her to see what she gave away all those years ago, not out of revenge or hate, but to make her see that things turned out okay. That she doesn't have to feel guilty for what she did, yes it still hurts him that she gave him away, at times he still feels anger, not necessarily directed at her but at the circumstances of his birth and subsequent life. He knows she is not to blame for the decisions he has made in his life, or for the family that bought him up.

Part of his adoption for him is to think of himself as an outsider, he is an outsider within his family, whether partly of his own making or not, but an outsider never the less. Within his family, he always felt like a second-class citizen, and after a while you accept it, but now with the woman who he thinks is his mum, maybe he no longer needs to think like that. Maybe, just maybe he will have what he's longed for all these years, a family where he is not an accessory to be mocked, not just 'this is Anthony, our adopted son', but a bona fide part of a family. Even if that family just entails him, Anna and his mum, that is enough, to be a part of something other than just himself. He accepts Anna has always been there for him, and he owes her a debt of gratitude for putting up with him all this time. He hopes that he can repay her for the love and kindness she has shown him by taking care of her for the rest of their lives. He can see in the not too distant future his perfect life, the alternative doesn't even bear thinking about, rejection by Anna, following rejection by his mum.

Now a couple of shops past where his mum is enjoying her breakfast, he looks at Anna, "Thank you."

"Thank you for what?"

"For making sure I didn't do anything stupid."

"You wouldn't have done."

"I don't know about that, a part of me wanted to make a break for it and go into the coffee shop."

"She will get in touch, I'm sure of it, she just needs time to come to terms with it."

"I hope you're right."

"I am, I'm always right, I thought you would have learnt that by now."

"We'll see, won't we, I wonder if her friends know about me? How long do you think they will be in there? Do you think they work or just sit in there all day gossiping?" He asks.

*

The three of them are sitting at the table by the window; Nikki staring out into space, not taking any notice of what her friends are talking about, feeling guilty for not taking an interest. After the support she has had from both of them, they are amazing, Hayley didn't take the news as well as Aimee at first but after a few days she has been a rock, her main concern is that she hasn't told Paul yet. Hayley believes she shouldn't have left it this long to tell him, she told Nikki that she should have told him years ago. But what is done is done, you can't change the past, you just have to make the best of the situation as it is, as her mum always told her if life gives you lemons, make lemonade.

Staring out the window, Nikki has to do a double take, is that the same couple she saw watching her earlier in the gardens outside the apartment? She could be wrong, she did only get a brief glimpse of them earlier, just a fleeting glance, but she is sure they're the ones, there is something familiar about them. They are looking in shop windows now, on the opposite side of the road, walking in the direction of the coffee shop, they can't be more than eighteen or so. She goes back to her coffee and Danish, still in her own little world.

"Earth to Nikki, is there anyone there?" Aimee says as a joke, aware that her friend hasn't been listening to a word they've been saying.

"Sorry, what did you say?"

"We were just discussing dinner, Friday night, are you still up for it?" She asks.

"We'll be there, all being well, do you remember the couple I pointed out to you earlier, the ones I thought were staring at me, well I think they've just gone past on the other side of the road." Nikki tells her friends.

"What's this, are you being stalked?" Hayley asks, intrigued, looking for some gossip.

"Nikki, this is the main road, from the gardens there are only two ways they could have gone, so it's not that surprising is it that they should pass by here." Aimee tries to rationalise the situation, she can see her friend falling to pieces before her eyes. She wants her old friend back; secretly she wishes she would just tell Paul and get it over with, though she would never say it to her.

"I know you're right, I'm not in the mood for breakfast, I'm gonna go and make a start over the road, I'll see you tomorrow Hayley, sorry for not being good company." She apologises, getting up and making her way out and across the road.

"I'm worried about her Aimee, she needs to tell Paul." Hayley says.

"Tell me about it; it's been two weeks, if she carries on like this she's going to have a nervous breakdown, have you noticed how much weight she's lost?"

"I know, it's not good for her, she's making herself ill, and I think Paul will be okay once he gets over the initial shock of it. He loves her; nothing is going to change that, certainly not something that happened years before they met. What would Steve be like if you were in Nikki's situation?"

"I know Steve loves me, I think he would be okay, I wouldn't want to be in that situation though—I don't think I would have kept the secret so long." Aimee confides to her friend.

*

Having stopped a couple of shops further up, Anthony and Anna are looking back towards the coffee shop, when they see who they think is his mum coming out through the door, standing at the kerb, looking both ways, she crosses the road, less than fifty feet from them, this is the best view they have had of her. Anthony can't take his eyes off her, he is certain she is his mum, they watch her go into the salon, the salon they were stood outside of a few minutes earlier.

"She didn't look very happy did she?" Anna says.

"She looked sad; I hope that's not because of me." He says, sounding uneasy, the thought that he could be the cause of somebody else's misery. He had hoped that his letter would be viewed as good news by his mum, not a burden for her to carry around with her, maybe his letter isn't the cause of her sadness.

"Can we go and get breakfast now?" Anna says, always thinking of her stomach, “We can go to the coffee shop, you can still keep an eye on the salon she went into. I wonder if she works there or if she’s just having her hair done or something?”

“Sure, why not, it’s the least I can do for dragging you here for the day.” He says, giving in to her need for food. Crossing the road, Anthony is still conscious that his mum’s friends are still sitting in the coffee shop. Walking in the front door, the smell hits them straight away, the aroma of freshly brewed coffee and baked pastries. The place is buzzing, old and young alike, they’ve never seen so much choice of coffee, Anthony tells Anna to grab the last remaining table, which happens to be next to his mum’s friends.

Returning to the table after getting their order, two cappuccino’s and an assortment of pastries, the coffee shop has a retro feel, chrome tables and chairs, stainless steel condiments on the tables, the walls painted in rich browns, coffee artwork adorn the walls.

“I got a selection of pastries, I’m sure you’ll like some of them.” He says placing the tray on the table and taking the seat opposite her, his back to his mum’s friend—the blonde haired one.

“I thought I was hungry, how many did you get?” She laughs. No sooner have they sat down, the two women behind him get up, standing by the table, they are talking about his mum, they call her Nikki, this can’t be coincidence, it confirms what he thinks, that the woman who went into the salon is his mum. The blonde one is saying to the dark haired one that she is worried about Nikki, that they have to find a way to get her to tell Paul (He knows her husband is called Paul) about Anthony. Hearing his name mentioned sends a chill down his spine and the hairs on his arm stand on end, he wants the ground to open up and swallow him, so he is the cause of her sadness. They kiss each other good bye, and Anthony and Anna see them leave the coffee shop, the blonde haired one who apparently is called Aimee heads across the road to the same salon his mum went into, the dark haired one called Hayley turned left and walked down the road.

For several minutes they both sit in silence, sipping their too hot coffee, neither wanting to speak first, after the confirmation that they have been watching his mum, both feeling but not sharing that they have in some way violated her by being here. This is her world and they have no right intruding, Anthony is feeling ashamed that he has dragged Anna into this, it's bad enough that he came, he should never have bought Anna although he is glad she's here with him.

"That explains why you haven't heard from her yet." Anna says, breaking the tension, "Are you all right?"

"It was just a shock to hear them say my name, not knowing that I was sitting right here. We shouldn't have come, I'm sorry for bringing you into this."

"You needed to see her, you've done nothing wrong."

"I know, but I still feel that we've invaded her privacy, walked into a world that she is happy in, or I should say was happy in. I've ruined her safe world, where she exists without a son."

"She seems to have good friends who will see she's all right, and besides you didn't choose to be adopted, she made the decision eighteen years ago and knew that there was always the possibility of you showing up on her doorstep one day." Anna tries to make him see that he shouldn't punish himself for what they are doing. To see that he has every right to find out whom he is and where he came from. "Would you still have looked for her if your parents were still alive?" Anna asks,

"Yes, I decided years ago that as soon as I was eighteen I would try to find her. Don't get me wrong I struggled with the decision for years, thinking how much it could hurt them knowing I wanted to see my birth mum. I don't think I would have told them what I was doing, I could have kept it from them. Then when they died the question became irrelevant." He says with a tinge of regret in his voice.

"Do you miss them?"

"No" he answers straight away with no hesitation. Seeing the look of shock on Anna's face, he decides to explain his answer and the quickness with which he responded. "I think about them occasionally, but I didn't see them as part of my life, if that makes any sense."

"Sort of." She says, kind of understanding where he is coming from, she doesn't get on too well with her parents, but she knows she would miss them if they were no longer around, she finds it hard to understand how someone can be part of your life for sixteen years and then you don't miss them when they're gone.

"For as long as I have known I was adopted I had this dream of one day being with my real family. Making my parents temporary, or 'stand ins' until my real family were available. I know that sounds terrible, and I hate myself for thinking it, I think they saw me as a project they had to complete. A project that came with no instruction manual, what they didn't realise, it's the same manual for me as it was my sister. The fact they adopted me should never have been an issue, but they made it one, not me. I wasn't the one who told all my friends that they were my adoptive parents—you're the only person I ever told that I had been adopted, everyone else found out from my parents or sister. She had great delight in telling all her friends I wasn't her real brother, that her parents were just looking after me as my real mum didn't want me. I would often hear her tell her friends that she wished her parents would take me back and get a refund so that they could spend the money on getting her a puppy." Anthony says, his eyes glossing over with tears forming at the memory, taking a bite from a maple and walnut Danish, and a sip of the cappuccino, trying to hold back the tears he knows are waiting to fall, concentrating hard on keeping the fluid in his eyes. Anna reaches over, taking his hand in hers, not saying a word, letting him know she understands.

"When they died, do you remember what you thought?" saying this without thinking she quickly adds, "You don't have to answer that."

"I don't mind, you might not like the answer though, I've never talked to anyone about it. The truth is nothing, I tried to be sad about it, I even tried to cry, I just couldn't. It was as if I was watching the news and the announcer says that some celebrity or famous person has died, you feel sorry for them, but it doesn't affect you. That's how it felt, no emotion at all, yes I felt sorry they died but what difference would it make to me. They were never there for me while they were alive so what would change now that they weren't there anymore. I feel guilty even saying all this aloud, even to you, I know you won't judge me, at least no more than I judge myself. I'm glad I didn't go to the funeral, it would have meant putting on a front for all the vultures, if I acted how I felt then everyone would have seen what a useless son I was." Now a tear does roll down his cheek, he can't believe he's crying in a coffee shop in south London, Anna's still holding his hand.

"Don't get upset, it's how you feel, there's nothing wrong with that, what's past is past, I never knew that was how you felt about your family. Of course, I knew you never got on with them, but I always thought that deep down there was some kind of love for them. I wish I had known before how alone you must have felt while we were growing up, not that I could have done anything, but you could have talked to me." She tries to comfort him.

"Back then I couldn't talk to anyone, until I met you, I had no one to talk to, I know we were only eight, and at that time I didn't know I had been adopted. Something was wrong even then, I felt isolated, I didn't belong and I didn't know why. That was the worst part, looking at your parents and thinking 'who are you?—Why am I here?' knowing you don't fit in is the worst feeling in the world. That was worse than finding out about the adoption, at least then I had a reason to feel the way I did. In some respects it made it easier, I didn't have to feel guilty anymore, now I had a reason. I always felt bad that Tracey and me didn't have a brother and sister bond, I know it hurt our parents that we didn't. Especially my mother, she longed for the day we would have that kind of relationship with each other, I think my sister resented me for taking our parents attention and focus away from her, she would have preferred to have their love to herself. With Tracey it wasn't only because she wasn't related to me, I just didn't like her, if she had of been my biological sibling I still don't think I would have liked her. You know her, what do you think about her?" he asks, without realising it they have both finished their coffee, and the plate that fifteen minutes ago had six Danish pastries on it, is now spattered with a few flakes of pastry and some crumbs. "While you think about your answer, I'll get us another cup of coffee, are you full up yet, or did you want something else to eat?"

"I'm full up now; I couldn't eat another thing." She tells him. After he gets up, she focuses her attention on the salon she can clearly see from their position at the window. Across the road in between the cars and buses passing by, she can see the blonde woman—Aimee—cutting some young girls hair, she obviously works there. Within a couple of minutes Anthony is back with two more oversized mugs of steaming cappuccino, she points out to him about Aimee working in the salon across the road and points out that maybe his mum works there too.

"So did you think about my question?" he reminds her.

"I never liked your sister and she never liked me. I remember the first time I met her, we were eight and she was ten. You had invited me round to play in the garden, we walked in to the house and she was standing there, she looked me up and down from head to toe and said 'who's this then?' I remember feeling very uncomfortable and wanting to make a run for the door. I thought then that I hated her, even after a few years of getting to know her, I always had to force myself to pretend to like her, I did it hoping she wouldn't take it out on you. I know that if I had been horrible to her, she would have thought you had turned me against her. What she doesn't realise is that she turns people against her, she sees herself as queen bee and no one is better than her, no one has a right to anything that she hasn't. I'm just surprised that you never hit her, if I lived with her I would have ended up punching her. Your parents could never see the evil in her, and that's what it was, pure evil. To them she was the apple of their eye, could do no wrong, you were the bad apple. They didn't appreciate what they had in you, if they had treated you right, treated you the way they treated Tracey, things may have turned out differently for all of you." Anna tells him, she has never been this honest about his family in all the time she has known him. "I know this is going to sound horrible, but I think you are better off without any of them, the way they treated you when it came to their funeral was disgusting. Although they didn't tell you not to go, it was the way they ignored you and treated you like an outcast, as if you would taint the memory of your parents if you were to grace the proceedings with your presence." This last she says in her best posh voice, signifying that his family thought they were so much better than the rest of the peasants around them. When in truth most of the family are the scum of the earth, with his sister leading the pack of rabid animals.

"Do you know why your parents adopted you?" Anna says.

"I do, but only because I overheard a conversation, actually it wasn't long before they died, my mother was talking to her best friend, you know, Marsha from number ten. They were having a drink; they thought Tracey and I were in bed, my father was down the pub as usual. I was trying to sneak down to get something to eat, as you know the stairs creaked so I had to take it slowly. I got about half way down when I heard voices, Marsha couldn't be quiet if her life depended on it, and she was asking my mum if she was seeing someone. I didn't understand what she meant at first, then she said something a bit odd, she said 'did he ever find out about the other one, Tracey's dad?' that was when the penny dropped, my father was not the biological dad to Tracey. Although as far as I know he never knew, then I heard my mum telling Marsha that she was seeing someone else. So I came to the conclusion that my father couldn't have kids, I might be wrong but I can't see any other reason for adopting. I am glad he never knew about Tracey, he worshipped her, it would have killed him if he had known, and no one deserves that, not even him." Anthony says. Recalling memories of his father calling Tracey his little princess, whatever she asked for she got, even if they couldn't afford it. Whereas he would get hand me downs from the older boy who lived up the road. Even his bike was his sisters old one, when he was twelve, his parents had told them both they could have a bike for Christmas, Anthony remembers being so excited at the prospect of getting something new that was his. He remembers hardly sleeping the night before, just wanting to get downstairs to open his knew bike. Christmas morning came, and to give his parents credit, there were two bike shaped presents in the lounge. Both him and his sister went straight to the bikes and started ripping the paper of, Tracey shrieking with glee at the shiny red and silver bike standing before her. He remembers his father watching him rip the paper from his, Anthony trying to hide the look of disappointment as he discovers the bike was Tracey's old pink one. Then his father walking over to him, patting him on the shoulder and saying 'there's plenty of life left in that bike yet'.

Sitting now in silence enjoying their coffee, neither had been expecting this heart to heart in a South London coffee shop watching his birth mothers workplace. It is a strange feeling for Anthony knowing that half an hour ago, his mum sat in a chair not six feet from him, and is now at work across the road

16

Friday July 21 2000

"Happy birthday you" Aimee says, giving her friend a big hug and a kiss, as she hadn't seen her on her birthday which was yesterday. Paul had surprised her with a trip up the west end to take in a show—Mama Mia—followed by a meal at La Gavroche in Upper Brook Street, the Michelin star Restaurant owned and run by Michel Roux. "How was the big night last night," she asks.

"Great" she says.

"You could try sounding a little bit more enthusiastic, what's wrong?"

"Nothing, honestly," Nikki's says, in a mere whisper. Trying her best not to let Paul and Steve overhear them, they're over in the lounge area, laughing about something that's amused them.

"Something is wrong, I know you, has something happened with

Anthony?" she asks.

"Keep your voice down, they're only over there, no nothing's happened, I've tried to tell Paul about him but the words won't come out." She confesses, "I think he's knows something's wrong, we haven't made love in nearly three weeks, I can't bear him to touch me. Not because of him, I just feel dirty, he deserves better, a couple of times I've come close to blurting it all out, but when I try to speak nothing comes out. Even last night, although it was a great evening, the show fantastic, the meal beyond good, all I could think about was Anthony. What is wrong with me?" she asks.

"Nothing babe, but you do need to tell him." Aimee says, trying to convince her friend that it will be for the best.

"I might try talking to him later, when we go home, hopefully a few drinks in me might loosen my tongue." She says, resigned to the thought of actually having to tell Paul her sordid secret "What time is Hayley due to get here? she's normally the first one here to make a start on the wine. What are we eating tonight?" Nikki asks, trying to change the subject and lighten the mood. The last thing she wants to do is spoil the evening for everyone.

"We've ordered Indian, and Hayley rang to say she is stuck at work, and that we should start without her, she has no idea what time she'll get here." She says.

*

"So how are things at work?" Paul asks Steve.

"Not too bad, we're working on a conversion in docklands of an old shipping warehouse, should be good when it's done, not as good as these though." Steve replies, waving his arm around the room showing off his apartment, stunning does not even come close to describing the place. Steve and Aimee's place is pretty much the same layout as the other two except the huge square skylight in the ceiling. The skylight floods the room with daylight, at night it comes into its own, staring up at the night sky, watching the stars twinkling, the moon adding it's glow to the surfaces. The whole apartment painted in shades of white, with the furniture and accessories in whites, silvers and dark greys. Not that there is much of it, Steve likes the minimalist look, even the large canvas paintings on the walls, match the surroundings, the largest and most impressive is a canvas on the feature wall of the main lounge area. An eight by twelve feet canvas, depicting a nude lying on a white leather couch, back to the artist, head and upper body twisted to face the painter. One hand provocatively covering her breast, the other draped, fingers touching the black and white chequerboard floor, the subject of the painting is clearly Aimee. Steve painted the canvas himself.

"Can I ask you something Steve" his voice a mere whisper, "Has Nikki said anything to Aimee the last couple of weeks?"

"Aimee hasn't mentioned anything, why?"

"Nikki's been a bit off for a while, she's very quiet, which as you know isn't like her, and she doesn't seem to want me anywhere near her, she's constantly tired, headaches most evenings this week. I'm worried about her." Paul says.

"Have you asked her what's wrong?

"I've tried, she just says it's tiredness and she'll be fine soon. There's more to it than that though, I just know, Nikki and I talk about everything, no subject has ever been off limits."

"Try asking her again, and make it clear to her that whatever is wrong, you can sort it out, the two of you. I'll ask Aimee later and see if I can get anything out of her, if something's wrong you can bet she would have told her." Steve offers.

"The only thing I can think is, it's something to do with her family, the one subject we have never really spoken about, I've never met her family, and she has no contact with them. I asked about them when we met, she said that they had fallen out years ago, and that there was nothing else to say on the matter. She shut down then, never mentioning them again, no birthday or Christmas cards, nothing. Maybe over the years I should have tried bringing the subject up again. I know whatever happened it affected her deeply, there are times I'll look over at her and she could be a million miles away or another planet, when she's like that I've talked to her and she is oblivious to anything I say, she doesn't even know I'm there when she's like it." He says to his best friend, a sense of sadness in his voice, it kills him that she could be hurting and nothing he can do about it.

"Try bringing her family up again, it could be she's heard from them, something may have happened to one of her parents, does she have any brothers or sisters?" Steve asks.

"As far as I know she is an only child, like you say one of her parents could be ill, or heaven forbid could have died. She hasn't had any contact with then since she moved to London, which was when she was sixteen. She told me that much, about eighteen years of no family interaction, I know she moved to London to work in a salon, as to why, I have no idea. Everything about her since she moved is like an open book, boyfriends she had, jobs she has done, everything. Before London, nothing, apart from she lived in Oxford with her parents." He tells him.

"Well, don't give up mate, I'm sure it will work itself out." With that the doorbell goes. The takeaway has arrived.

Steve goes to the door, and takes the food from the driver, handing him a fiver for his troubles, Steve paid for the meal when he rang up to order it.

*

"Have another glass of wine, try to forget about things for the next couple of hours, and try to enjoy yourself." Aimee tells Nikki. Hearing the doorbell, she starts to gather the plates and cutlery together, heading over to the dining area with Nikki in tow, carrying the wine and their glasses. Setting the plates down she whispers to Nikki "Remember have a good time and forget about everything for now, besides there's nothing you can do tonight."

"Hope you're all hungry?" Steve announces carrying three bags of food and placing them on the table, a smoked glass topped table with chrome frame and eight matching high backed chrome chairs.

"How many people are you expecting tonight? It looks like you're feeding an army." Paul Jokes.

All now sitting around the table, containers all lined up with lids off, everybody tucking into the food, still no sign of Hayley. Nikki is self-conscious of the fact she's not saying much, trying her best to appear happy, even making the odd joke now and then, she knows though that no one is buying her act. Making it even harder, when after they have finished the meal, Aimee appears with a birthday cake, having lit the candles, carrying it through to the dining area, Nikki sees it and bursts into tears. Unable any longer to hold inside what she is feeling, she pushes her chair backwards, "Sorry" she sobs through tears running down her face, mascara already running. She heads for the stairs; make her way up to the landing area with a door leading to the roof terrace. Pushing open the door, gasping for air, she's having trouble catching her breath now, the sobbing getting louder and louder. Completely losing control of herself, she walks over to the edge of the roof terrace, leaning over the railings Steve had installed for safety. Letting it all out now, howling into the night sky like some kind of banshee, "Why I am so stupid." She sits down with her legs through the railings, her arms over the middle railing, still struggling to breath, knowing there is no way back from this. They have all seen her, they know something is up; it's time to tell Paul the truth. She can't live with the guilt any longer, if it's the end of her and Paul then so be it, she couldn't blame him.

*

"What was that all about?" Steve asks of no one in particular.

"I'll go and see if she's okay," Aimee offers.

"No, I'll go, I am so sorry about this, I don't know what's wrong with her." Paul says, "I'll take her home."

"You're fine, take all the time you need, she needs you Paul." Aimee says.

"What do you mean 'she needs me' what do you know?" Paul confronts her.

"Just listen to her, don't make any rash decisions, and don't say anything you might regret. Just listen and hear her out." She tries to convince him.

Paul heads up to the roof terrace, "What the fuck is going on babe?" Steve demands.

"I suppose I can tell you now, though not a word to anyone, just in case she doesn't tell him. Nikki has a son," she says, as if it's the most natural thing to say about your best friend.

"What, you mean she's pregnant, Paul will be thrilled, I know they haven't planned to have kids, but if she is I know he will be overjoyed." Steve says, not quite grasping the gravity of what Aimee has told him.

"No Steve, she's not pregnant, she has an eighteen-year-old son called Anthony." Aimee tries to get him to understand. Steve's face has gone ashen, suddenly realising what she is telling him.

"Fucking hell, how do we not know about it? How long have you known? Why doesn't Paul know?" All the questions coming out at once, taking his glass of beer and downing the contents in one long slow gulp. The look of bewilderment on his face, the last thing he expected to hear tonight is that Nikki has an eighteen-year-old son. Of all people, he wouldn't have thought of Nikki, Hayley he could have understood it from, but not Nikki. Aimee's just watching him, seeing his face trying to process what she has just told him. "The poor thing, carrying this around all this time. Why is this all coming out now?" he says.

"Firstly, I've only known a few weeks. Nikki has never told anyone, including Paul, she hoped it would never be an issue, she thought that once he was adopted that would be the last she would ever hear, but she was wrong. She got a letter three weeks ago today, she didn't open it until the Monday, and she's been a mess ever since. I've tried to get her to tell Paul as soon as possible, I think she regrets not telling him years ago. She wants to ignore it and hopes it will go away, I've told her it's not an option, her son won't give up that easily. If he's gone to the trouble of tracking her down, ignoring his letter is not going to make him give up." She tells him.

"Does she know anything about him? Where he lives, what he's like."

"No, she has had no contact in eighteen years, she saw him when he was born and that's it, she never wanted any updates or contact, she just wanted to forget him and start a new life."

*

Walking across the terrace, Paul can see Nikki sitting with her feet over the edge, he can still hear her crying, and walking up behind her, he puts his hand on her shoulder. Surprised at his touch, she nearly jumps out of her skin.

"Sorry babe, I didn't mean to startle you, what's wrong?" Paul asks her, concern evident in his voice, he is starting to get worried now, thinking the worst, she's found someone else and is leaving him, she's got terminal cancer and doesn't know how to break it to him. He believes anything else and he can handle it. Sitting down next to her, both now looking out over Canary Wharf, The night sky lit up with a full moon, the sounds of London drifting across the water, the shimmering water of the Thames as the occasional boat sails by.

"I'm so sorry Paul, you were never supposed to find out." She blurts out without thinking about what she is saying. Not realising how this will sound to Paul's ears.

"Find out what? You're scaring me now." He says, a million thoughts going through his mind, the prominent, she's found someone else. "Have you met someone?" he asks, sorrow coming through in his voice. "God no, you're the only one for me, I would never leave you, I'm scared that you're going to leave me." She confesses.

"Why would I leave you?"

"You will when I tell you what I've got to tell you."

"We can work through anything"

"Not this we can't, you'll hate me, and I hate myself." Nikki wipes the back of her hand across her eyes, smearing the already streaked mascara. "Just promise me one thing—you'll hear me out, I'll tell you everything, then I'll go, you can carry on with your life and I'll leave you alone. I just want you to know the truth." She tells him.

"Babe, I am here for you, you're not going anywhere, whatever it is, and we can work through it together. I love you, always have and always will, nothing is going to change that." He tries to reassure her, not knowing himself if he means it. He loves her, he knows that, but he is scared of what she is about to tell him. He wants to be here for her, but he knows his own mind, and his hot headedness can get the better of him at times; it can take him a while to process information, especially when it comes to emotions. In some ways, he knows he's socially awkward, with Nikki though, they have always been very open with one another, and he has always been at ease around her. She makes people like her, he has never known anyone dislike her, and she has a personality that invites you in.

"When I was growing up, my mum and dad meant everything to me. My dad used to call me his princess, my mum and I would always be doing something together, baking, gardening and sewing. We were a very close family. They always wanted the best for me, and I always done my best to make them proud of me. Whether that was getting good grades at school, I was an 'A' Grade student all though school. I never had boyfriends; I would put studying before anything else because I knew it would please my parents. I remember when I was thirteen, my parents took me to Disneyworld in Florida, and we had such a good time, just the three of us. I suppose you could say I was spoiled, I never let it go to my head though, and I appreciated everything and every sacrifice my parents made for me. They never had loads of money, don't get me wrong they had money, but they would go without their luxuries to make sure I had whatever I wanted. I've had horse riding lessons, I've played the piano and violin, they even sent me for ballet lessons, all because it was what I wanted at the time. I love my parents, still do. They stopped loving me—not that I blame them, they have every right to hate me for what I put them through, the shame and humiliation they must have felt." She says, stopping to look out at the sky, and the light on in the building across the water, five minutes must have passed in complete silence, Paul not saying a word, worried that if he interrupts her she may not go on, and he needs to know what she is trying to tell him.

"I remember my dad telling me once that whatever I did, I could never disappoint him, and he would always love me. He said he only wanted what would make me happy. I can't believe what I put my parents through, they never deserved any of it. I still wonder today if they still hate me. My parents always loved me unconditionally, until that night I never had any doubts about the love of my parents. When I told them, I never thought they would react the way they did. For months they made my life a living hell." Nikki says, taking another pause.

The penny still hadn't dropped for Paul, he was still just sitting there listening, he wanted to take Nikki in his arms and tell her everything is going to be fine, but he can't. He can feel something building inside him that tells him he is not going to like what he hears. He can feel his heart rate quickening, the heat rising in his body, he hates himself for feeling like this, he should be supporting her, not condemning her before he's even heard the outcome.

"I remember going into the house the day I found out, my mum was home but my dad wasn't, I wanted to tell them both together. Mum took one look at me and asked what was wrong, she was concerned, I told her that I was fine and that nothing was wrong, she could see right through me. She made a pot of tea—after all that's what we British do in times of crisis, make a pot of tea—sitting at the kitchen table she poured us both a strong cup, plenty of sugar in mine. She then told me to tell her in my own time what the problem was, I'm sure she was thinking it was either a falling out I'd had with a friend, or maybe I wasn't feeling too well. I don't think she expected the bombshell I was about to lay at her doorstep—thinking back a bomb at the door would have been easier for her to handle. Sipping the tea, I can still taste that tea to this day, which is why I never touch the stuff, coffee for me all the way now." She says, letting out a nervous laugh, somehow trying to lighten the mood, not that anything was ever going to lighten the tension she could feel coming off

Paul in waves, sitting next to him, his body touching hers, she could feel his body tensing as the story progressed. "I started telling her that I had done something incredibly stupid, she just sat there listening, blowing her tea to cool it down. I explained there was a boy I fancied, then I went on to tell her about the party Becky and me had gone to at Leigh's house." Then without going into too much detail, "She just sat there in silence, I could see the colour rising in her cheeks, if she had held onto the cup she was holding any tighter it would have shattered. Then she uttered two words 'Get Out' that was it, just get out. I went up to my room, and just lay on my bed sobbing, knowing it would be a couple of hours before my dad came home from work. Within half an hour, I heard my dad pull up in the car outside; my mum had rung him and told him to come home. The next thing mum's at my door telling me to get downstairs, where my dad is sitting at the same table with a cup of tea.

He asks me to tell him what is so important that he had to leave work early, so I go through the story again, thinking that my dad—who has always thought the world of me—would be more understanding—I couldn't have been more wrong. The language that came from his mouth I would never have thought possible, I had never heard my dad use a bad word in sixteen years. He called me a common tart, and that if he got his hands on the little bastard that did it he would string him up by his balls and kill the fucker. Then in unison, they told me I couldn't keep the baby and that I would have to get rid of it. My mum's main concern was what the neighbours would think. I couldn't have an abortion, coming from a catholic background it was out of the question, it was decided that I would have the child adopted. They told me it was my problem and that I had to sort it, and once the abomination was out of my body, they wanted nothing more to do with me." She says, tears now streaming down her face. "I've hidden this from everyone until now, I received a letter from the baby I gave away eighteen years ago, wanting to meet me." She finishes, barely managing to get the words out, the last couple almost inaudible, beneath the sound of the sobs.

"I need time" Is all Paul can say, as he stands up and walks away, leaving Nikki sitting sobbing her heart out. He knows how hard that must have been for her to sit and admit to him, but inside his temper is raging, he doesn't want to say something that he will regret. Ten years they have been together, she should have told him, he could have handled it, now he learns she has an eighteen-year-old son, it's as though their life together has been a lie, all the time she has known one day her son would come looking for her. He has loved her, and shared everything with her, his childhood memories, his desires, everything, he thought she had done the same, but it turns out she has been selective with the truths she has shared with him.

He needs to get out of here, to be on his own for a while, to think. He wants to comfort her, he wants to hold her more than anything else, he just can't look at her at the moment. Walking down the stairs, he can feel his face getting redder and redder, his heart rate quickening. Walking through the door he vaguely hears someone ask if he's okay, he waves them away, walking straight to the front door and shutting it behind him. He heads down to the street, once out on the street, night sky above him; he heads directly across to the public gardens. At this time of night the gardens almost deserted, sitting on the nearest bench, the cool night air, causing the hairs on his arms to stand on end. Trying to calm down, he keeps telling himself to go back to her, tell her everything's fine, he can't.

Sitting there he sees a couple at the other ends of the gardens, stuck together at the lips, he remembers when Nikki and him used to come out here at night and sit on the bench, holding hands and kissing, not a care in the world. All the time she knew she had a son out in the world somewhere, knowing that one day he would come searching for her, looking for answers to questions he would surely have. Sitting watching the couple, their hands exploring each others bodies—they were certainly more daring than him and Nikki had ever been—even under the moonlight he could see him with his hand under her jumper, and her with her hand down the front of his trousers, oblivious to him sitting at the other end watching. He decides to get up, go for a walk, before they see him, and think he's some kind of pervert.

17

Sitting alone now, wiping the tears away, she hears his footsteps as he walks down the stairs. She had expected him to say more, scream, shout, call her names, but he hadn't, just three words 'I need time', does that mean there is still a chance for them, or that he needs time to decide the best way for them to split up. What is she going to do now, she can't go back inside and face Aimee and Steve, she's ruined their evening. At least now, it's all out in the open, whatever the consequences she doesn't have to run and hide any longer. She hears someone walking up the stairs, her heart skipping a beat hoping it's Paul returning, looking round, the disappointment visible on her face to see it's Aimee.

"Is everything okay? How did he take the news?" Aimee asks, knowing the answer, after seeing the way Paul stormed out of the place, she sent Steve out after Paul to make sure he was okay.

"Honestly I don't know, all he said was that he needed time, whatever that means, I know it must have come as a huge shock to him. After all, I've had eighteen years to get used to the idea that one day my son would come looking for me, I hoped it would never happen, but I think deep down I need to see him, I need to tell him how sorry I am." She says.

"He will come around, he just needs to get used to the idea."

"What if he can't, he didn't sign up for a wife with a child, why should I expect him to accept it. I've been trying to think how I would react if one day a kid showed up at our door saying he was Paul's son. I think I would hit the roof, there would be one subtle difference though, Paul would not necessarily know of the existence of his son, whereas I knew of mine, which I think is what is hurting him the most. I knew I had a son and didn't tell him, we've shared everything, the good memories and the bad from our past, but I have always held back when it comes to my family." She tells her.

"Do you want to stay here tonight, the guest room is made up, and I know Steve won't mind. I've filled Steve in on the basics, I haven't gone into any details, but he needed to know what was going on, I'm sorry." Aimee apologises.

"I didn't expect you to keep it from him; I thought you might have already told him before tonight. Thanks for the offer, but I'm gonna go home, see if Paul's there, and if he isn't then I'll wait." She says, giving her friend a hug, she gets up and makes her way across the terrace. "Thank you again—for everything."

"If you need anything, anything at all, give me a ring or just come up, the offer of the room is available whenever you need it, even if it's in the middle of the night." She offers.

*

Back in her own apartment, Nikki calls out to Paul, no answer; she wanders through in a daze, just in case Paul is here and doesn't want to talk to her, not that she would blame him. After checking the guest bedroom and finding nothing, she walks up the stairs to the mezzanine, still nothing, in the bathroom she catches a glimpse of herself in the mirror, what a sight, mascara streaked across her face, red blotches around the eyes. Her face is puffy. Filling the sink with water, she splashes her face, leaning on the edge of the sink; she can feel the tears welling up inside her again, her insides feel like they're curdling, determined not to start crying again, she goes into the bedroom, putting on her pyjamas, she goes back to the kitchen and pours a glass of wine. Sitting on the sofa, legs curled beneath her, she sips her wine keeping a constant watch on the door.

*

"I'm sorry to put on you like this." Paul apologises, "I know it's late and I've got you out of bed, I just can't go home yet, I'm scared that I'm going to say things I'm gonna regret. It's best that we're apart for now, I'm gonna go away for a few days, I thought a couple of days on a golf course in Scotland will do me good, give me a chance to think, I know Nikki isn't going to be happy but if it keeps us together it will be for the best." Paul tells his two best friends.

"I'm gonna leave you with Steve and I'll give Nikki a ring just to let her know you're here and that you're fine." Aimee says, getting up and going to the bedroom to make the phone call.

"Mate, whatever you need we're here for you, we're here for both of you. You can get through this. I don't suppose you want any company on this golf excursion of yours do you?" Steve says.

"Can you get the time off?"

"No problem, how long is the trip for?"

"I was going to come back Saturday morning, are you sure Aimee will be all right with you going?"

"She'll be fine, it's for a good cause. How are we getting there? We should be able to get a couple of flights from Heathrow tomorrow straight to Edinburgh."

"I'll get my stuff in the morning, explain to Nikki that I just need a break away to think things through, I don't know how she'll take it but I have to do it. When we sit down and talk, I don't want it to be a knee jerk reaction; I want to have thought everything through properly and calmly." Paul tells Steve.

18

Awakening from a deep sleep by a shrieking noise, it takes Nikki a few seconds to realise it's the phone ringing, getting up off the sofa where she must of fallen asleep, she goes to the table in the entrance lobby where the phone is, still ringing, she has no idea what time it is. Remembering the events of the evening, she thinks this could be Paul, is he all right? Has he had an accident? A thousand images scrolling through her mind, hesitating to pick up the receiver not wanting to hear bad news, eventually picking up, "Hello."

"Nikki, it's Aimee, Paul has just turned up here, he's asked to stay the rest of the night. I just wanted to let you know that there's no need to worry about him, he says he needs some time. I'm sorry it's so late and I'll pop down and see you tomorrow. Don't worry babe, everything is going to work itself out, now get some sleep and I'll talk to you in the morning." Aimee tells her.

"Can I talk to him?"

"Babe, let him be, he needs to work through this in his own time, Steve is going to try to talk to him tomorrow, now get some rest."

"How can I rest when he won't talk to me, I just want him to come home. I want him to hold me and tell me it's going to be all right. I need him." She pleads; Aimee can hear the tears in her voice and wants to take care of her.

"Do you want me to come down?" Aimee offers.

"No, I'll be fine, can you just tell Paul I love him and I'm sorry." Nikki asks, her sobbing now evident, the sound breaking Aimee's heart.

"Go to bed and we'll speak tomorrow."

"Thank you." She says, listening to the click as Aimee puts her phone down, still holding the receiver to her ear; she slumps down onto the floor, back to the cold wall, bringing her knees up to her chest, dropping the phone to the floor she hugs her legs with her arms, sobbing against the tops of her knees. She stays in this position for the next hour before tiredness and exhaustion take her to bed, her eyes red, her throat dry and sore, her body spent. Glancing at the clock as she drags herself up the stairs, four in the morning, she wonders what Paul is doing at this very minute. Getting into bed, the loneliest place in the world for her, the bed seeming impossibly large and empty, without Paul she doubts she will rest, she may sleep, her body unable to carry on any longer. She is asleep before her head hits the pillow.

*

"I suppose we'd better get some sleep." Steve says, as Aimee is coming down the stairs.

“How is she?” Paul asks Aimee.

“She’s cut up about it all, I could hear her crying, though she was trying to hide it.”

“Believe me I don’t want it to be like this, it’s just a lot to get my head around; what hurts most is that she didn’t trust me enough to share this with me earlier. I’ll leave you two to it, and I’ll see you in the morning, thanks again for everything.” Paul says, kissing Aimee on the cheek and shaking Steve’s hand. He heads of to one of the guest bedrooms.

“I’m gonna go with Paul tomorrow, you don’t mind do you, it’s only for a week.” Steve tells her, a pitiful look in his eye saying ‘he needs me’.

“You go babe, I think it would be better if he had someone with him, someone to talk things through with.” She says, then grabbing his hand with a cheeky grin on her face adds, “Well if I’m not going to see you for a week, I’ve got to have something to remember you bye, so get up to that bedroom now, you’ve got a lot of making up to do before you go tomorrow.”

“It will be my pleasure, whatever you want you shall have.”

19

July 29 2000

At eight on Saturday morning, Paul let's himself into their apartment, hoping Nikki is still asleep, carefully opening the door, he goes to the cupboard just inside the door where he keeps his golf clubs. Being as quiet as possible, he takes them out and leans them next to the front door, grabbing a holdall he makes his way up the stairs to get some clothes from the wardrobe. Reaching the bedroom, he sees Nikki in bed, the covers pulled up around her; he sees the tear stains on the pillow and feels a lump forming in his throat. Saying to himself 'this is for the best' trying to justify his actions and not succeeding, he has to do this, there is no other way for him to get past it, he knows that.

Creeping over to the wardrobe, he takes out the first items he comes to, he will make do with whatever he takes, just wanting to get out of there. Scared of waking Nikki, not wanting the confrontation with both their emotions supercharged as they are, he makes his way back down the stairs. Lingering to take one last look at her sleeping, watching the heave of her bosom beneath the sheets, longing to be next to her, blowing her a kiss before going down to the kitchen to leave her a note. Making his way silently out of the front door, feeling as guilty as hell for what he knows he is putting Nikki through but not able to see another way. Knowing it is cowardly, he should stay and work through this, he just can't with his head the way it is.

*

"Steve, where's Paul?" Aimee asks at just gone eight.

"He's just gone to get some things for the trip from the apartment; he said he wouldn't be long."

"Is he going to say bye to Nikki?"

"He didn't say, just said he'd be back in about fifteen minutes."

"Well I'll do you both some breakfast before you go." She offers.

With that the doorbell goes, Paul's obviously back, judging by the length of time he's been gone, Nikki is still asleep and unaware of her husband's plan. Steve gets the door and gives Paul a hand in with his stuff, setting them next to his own. He tells Paul that the taxi is booked for eight forty-five, and that Aimee is doing them something to eat.

"She doesn't have to do that; we could have got something at the airport. I feel bad that I've put you both out, I'm sorry." He apologises.

"You haven't put us out, besides we haven't been on a golfing trip for ages, it's long overdue." Steve reassures him as best he can.

"Well I appreciate it mate, if I can ever repay you just let me know."

"Now you come to mention it, I thought you could play golf left handed this week to give me a chance of winning for a change." Steve says with a laugh.

"Food's ready boys." Aimee shouts through to them. She's prepared croissants, jam and coffee, the best she could do at short notice.

"Thanks Aimee, you're a star. Will you take care of Nikki this week, hopefully when I get back we can sort this out properly?"

"Of course I will, do you still think this is the best way to sort it out, wouldn't it be better to stay and talk to her?" She asks.

"Yes, but I don't know what to say to her at the moment, and I don't want to say the wrong thing, this is the best solution I can come up with." He says tucking into the croissants and coffee.

At eight forty, the taxi driver buzzes to say he is there, and to ask if they needed any bags bringing down. Paul says goodbye to Aimee, giving her a peck on the cheek and asks her to tell Nikki that he loves her. Paul carries the golf clubs to the door, the taxi driver getting the two holdalls. "Meet you at the car Steve." He shouts.

"I'll be two minutes mate." Steve replies.

"Now don't have too much fun this week." Aimee warns Steve. "And remember just what you're missing on your lads' holiday." With that she opens her silk robe to reveal her naked body, with that Steve goes towards her, just as he reaches her she shuts the robe and ties the belt. "That's for when you get back and not before, besides you have a taxi waiting for you downstairs."

"That's mean; I can't wait to get back now." Giving her a long lingering kiss goodbye, not wanting to let her go, pulling her towards him, feeling her body against his. Pulling away, she tells him to go, and to try to talk some sense into Paul.

*

Waking at just after ten with a raging thirst, Nikki instinctively puts her arm across to the other side of the bed, the thoughts of the night before come flooding back. The ruined evening at Aimee and Steve's, telling Paul about Anthony on the roof terrace, Paul walking away from her telling her he needed time, then Aimee's phone call at some time in the early hours telling her that Paul is going away for a while. Burying her head in the pillow, tears no longer coming, having exhausted her supply of them last night, by the looks of it most of them ended up on the pillow.

Her first impulse is to ring Paul, but she knows that isn't what he wants, he wants time on his own, maybe he won't be gone long—a couple of days. Getting out of bed takes all her strength and willpower; she could quite happily stay where she is until Paul returns. Knowing that isn't an option, she heads down stairs to the kitchen, she may as well make some effort to function normally, and normal means putting a pot of coffee on. After switching the machine on, she spots the note left by Paul, opening it she sees Paul's handwritten note.

Nikki

> I'm going away for a few days with Steve, I just need some time to work through some things. I will be back on Saturday, I don't want you to worry, we will sit down and have a proper talk when I get back. The most important thing for you to remember is that I love you, I always

have and always will.

Paul

Saturday, he's going to be away for a whole week, Nikki's mind is struggling to cope with the prospect of him away for so long, why does he need a week? Pouring herself a coffee and sitting down to read the letter again, taking comfort from the fact that he still loves her, surely that means there is still hope for them. Or is she reading too much into it, just because he loves her doesn't mean he still wants her. With this thought, the tears start welling up again, unable to stem the flow she lets them roll down her cheeks and drip onto the kitchen counter, collecting in little pools.

20

Friday July 21 2000

Finding themselves on the roof once again, this is the first real chance they've had to talk since going to see Anthony's mum. Having finished their food, the time now getting on for seven, laying on the roof next to each other, Anthony in shorts and a long sleeved t-shirt once more—Anna name still clearly visible on his arm. Anna wearing cut off jean shorts and a bikini top, yellow and white polka dot.

"Aren't you warm in that long sleeved t-shirt?"

"A bit, but it was the first one I put my hands on." Lying but not knowing what else to say, he can't let Anna know the truth.

"We haven't had a chance to talk about Monday and seeing your mum, do you want to talk about it?"

"There's not a lot to say, I feel bad about spying on her. In some respects I wish I hadn't gone, knowing how unhappy it is making her is torture."

"You haven't made her unhappy, her not telling her husband before now is what's making her miserable. You have nothing to feel guilty about. She could've written back to you explaining the situation and asking you to be patient—but she didn't. You did what any normal person would've done, you went to see her, and other people in your position may not have been so restrained and would have confronted her." She says, almost getting angry at him for feeling guilty, trying to make him see that none of this is his fault, he didn't ask to be adopted, he has tried to make the best of his life in spite of it. She is proud of what he's accomplished considering the family he was bought up in, the lack of real love, he could have turned out a lot worse, resorting to alcohol, drugs or even suicide. She thinks he has managed miraculously well considering.

"I know you're right, but I can't help the way I feel, if I hadn't written the letter she would be going about her life without a care in the world—maybe I should write another letter telling her that I will back off."

"You'll do no such thing, why should your life be affected because she hasn't sorted hers out. No, we will give it a bit more time to see if she responds, after hearing her friends talking I think it is only a matter of time before she tells her husband, and once it's all out in the open there will be no reason not to contact you." She says with such force that he just closes his eyes, resigned to playing the waiting game a little longer.

"Aside from all that, what did you think of her from what little we saw?"

"I think she is very beautiful, you have her eyes definitely, and her skin. I wonder if there is another nationality in her family, maybe Italian or Spanish, because you both have that Mediterranean look about you, and the fact that you seem to tan so easily, it just isn't fair. I sit here for hours, go red and the following day I'm back to my normal colour—whereas you, you sit here for five minutes and it's as if someone's sprayed you with fake tan, it isn't fair." This brings a smile to his face, he looks over at her, with her pale skin, and he wouldn't have her any other way.

"I do hope she gets in touch, I don't know what I'll do if she doesn't. I need to talk to her, even if it has to be without her husband knowing, I don't need to be part of her life—although that would be nice—I just want to talk. Does that make sense to you?"

"Perfect sense, she'll be able to fill in any gaps in your life that no-one else can." Turning to face him, she puts her put her hand on his stomach, "She will be in touch."

21

Sunday July 23 2000

"How many holes are you winning by?" Steve asks Paul, knowing he hasn't won a hole yet, and as they are about to start the back nine, Paul is nine holes up. This is their first full day up here at Gleneagles, having arrived around midday yesterday, spending the afternoon settling in and having a few drinks, Steve tested the water and asked about the situation between him and Nikki. Paul told him that he was not ready yet, and he would let him know when he was. They had an early night wanting to ready for the eight o'clock tee slot the following day.

"You know full well I'm nine holes up, you need to win the next nine to tie." He says laughing, his tone changes, "I assume Aimee told you about Nikki and her son?"

"She did, how are you handling it, I can't imagine how I would feel if Aimee had told me she had a son."

"Believe it or not, it's not the fact that she has a son, or at least not entirely. I admit I never pictured myself with kids, saying that, if one had come along I would have been delighted and got used to the idea. What hurts, and what I am having trouble coming to terms with is that she knew this when we started dating, she knew when we got married, she has known for eighteen years. Not once has she trusted me enough to tell me the truth. It's not something she overlooked, it's something she made a conscious effort to keep secret from me. I'm sure she had her reasons, I understand that, but we are supposed to be a couple, we share everything, or we did until now." Paul says to Steve, trying to keep the hurt and bitterness from his voice.

"Now I'm not saying what she did is right, but looking at it from someone on the outside looking in, when should she have told you? Over a romantic meal in a restaurant, 'Oh by the way Paul I have a son', no, then what about when you proposed? What I'm trying to say is, there is no right time, maybe she wanted to tell you, but the time was never right. Then the longer she left it the harder it became for her to tell you, I'm not saying she's right, she's not, but I can sympathise with her." Steve counters, not wanting to appear to take sides, seeing it from both points of view he feels he can have an impartial perspective of things. In some ways, he feels that Paul is being unfair; at a time when Nikki needs his love and support, here they both are, on a golf course in Scotland playing a round of golf with not a care in the world. While Nikki is at home, probably out of her mind wondering what Paul is doing and thinking. He can imagine her thinking the worse that Paul has come away because he can't stand to be around her, and is going to leave her.

"I know you're right, in my head all I see is a son she should have told me about."

"Let me ask you one simple question—do you love her?"

"Of course I do." Paul answers, getting defensive now.

"Then that's all that matters, if you Love her you can work through it, I'm not saying it will be easy but you will get there. Look at that, it seems like I win this hole, we should have started talking earlier, and then I may have had a chance at winning." Steve says laughing, trying to relieve the tension that's beginning to build.

"I thought I'd let you have that one, I don't even know if she wants to meet him, I can't believe I didn't even ask her that. I'm ashamed that I just walked out on her Friday night, that was wrong. I was worried that I was going to say something I'd regret." He explains.

"I think you need to talk to her properly, listen to her reasons for not telling you, try to see it from her side, I know you're angry that she kept it from you, but you need to look forward. Does it bother you that she has a son, and he's not yours?" Steve asks.

"That isn't it at all, she had him years before we got together, I accept that she had a life before we met. I know we've all done things in our past that we're not happy with, I can live with that. As much as I hate to admit it, I think a lot of it has to do with my pride being hurt. Just the thought there is something about my wife that I didn't know, and she felt the need to keep me in the dark about it. As for her son, I think she should get to know him, it's isn't his fault for his circumstances, and I think Nikki needs to meet him. She would never forgive herself if she didn't. I think I know Nikki well enough to say that the guilt of giving him up for adoption must have been eating away at her since the second she let him go. And the thought of her having to let him go a second time would be too much for her, seeing the way she has been the last three weeks is testament enough to that. She has been on edge, short tempered, and I know a lot of that was the thought of telling me, but also the possibility that she would never get the chance to meet her son." Paul tells Steve. "I am sorry that we have dragged you and Aimee into this, do you know how long Aimee has known?"

"I can only tell you what Aimee has told me, apparently the letter arrived three weeks ago Friday, but Nikki didn't open it until the Monday and that was when she told Aimee. Aimee has tried to get her to tell you, she wanted her to tell you straight away, she felt it would be best out in the open, but Nikki was scared, scared of losing you, she told Aimee that you would leave as soon as you found out. I think Nikki is probably sitting at home now thinking that she was right, thinking her marriage is over, that isn't the case though is it?" Steve asks him outright.

"No, were not finished, I love her and always will, like I said I just needed time to get my head around it. It is a shock when your wife of ten years suddenly tells you that she has an eighteen-year-old son, how would you have handled it?" he asks rhetorically, "Now come on play your shot, if I win this hole then it's all over."

22

Sunday July 23 2000

Having shut herself away for the whole of Saturday, refusing even to speak to Aimee, Nikki realises that she needs her friend more than ever now. Getting out of bed, she takes a hot shower, getting dressed in a pair of grey sweat pants and a white t-shirt with a bright pair of red lips on, she grabs her keys and heads upstairs to Aimee's apartment. Standing outside, thinking do I? don't I? Eventually she rings the bell, now would be a good time to run she thinks, just run and keep on running away from this life, away from everything. But she doesn't, she stands her ground, she knows Aimee is going to be pissed at her for yesterday and Friday evening, she had refused to take Aimee's phone calls all day. And then, when Aimee had come knocking on her door, she had told her to go away, that she was fine and why wouldn't everyone just leave her the fuck alone. This was said after a couple of bottles of wine, she needs to apologise.

Aimee opens the door, seeing her friend she grabs her, pulling her close, “Don’t you ever do that again; I’ve been so worried about you, are you all right?”

“Aimee I’m fine, I am so sorry about yesterday, I just wanted to be on my own, the wine didn’t help, and you know me I never swear.” She apologise.

“That’s why I was so worried, it just wasn’t like you, now come inside, I think we need to have a chat.” Once inside they go to the hub of everyone’s home—the kitchen, Aimee going behind the breakfast bar, “What do you want to drink, I know it’s only lunch time but did you want a proper drink or is coffee okay?”

“Coffee will be fine; I may have a stronger drink later.” Nikki says, not sure if she could stomach alcohol at the moment. What she does need though is something to eat; not having eaten at all yesterday her stomach is letting her know it needs food. “I don’t suppose I could have a bit of toast?”

“Of course, did you see Paul yesterday morning when he picked his things up?”

“No I was asleep, he crept in, took what he needed and went, oh, he did leave me a note.” She tells Aimee, handing over the note. She waits for Aimee to read it.

“Reading that I would say he isn’t going to leave you, I think you just need to be patient and wait for him to get home, then the two of you can talk.” She offers her opinion to Paul’s note. Sitting there in silence, drinking their coffee, Nikki asks if they can go up to the roof terrace seeing as it's such a nice day. It's been a while since she has smelled fresh air, being cooped up all day yesterday; she wants the open space to breath.

Sitting on the rattan sofa set on the terrace, basking in the glorious sunshine, the temperature must be touching thirty. The view is astonishing from up here, looking out over the Thames and Canary Wharf. Aimee has come prepared, wearing skimpy shorts and a bikini top to make the most of the sun.

"Have you thought about what you want, forget Paul for now, what is it you want, do you want to meet Anthony?" Aimee asks, knowing this is probably the last thing Nikki is expecting her to ask.

"I don't know, I think so, but if Paul can't handle that..." She leaves the sentence half finished.

"I said forget about what Paul wants."

"Yes, yes I do want to meet him, I want to know everything about him. I don't have any right to want it, but I do. What if he meets me and doesn't like what he finds? What if I lose him all over again, what then? I can't go through that."

"I'm sure he will love you, he obviously wants to meet you, otherwise he wouldn't have got in touch, it will probably be awkward at first, although he's your son and you're his mum, you are strangers, it may take time to get past that."

"I've often thought about how his life turned out and what sort of a man he's become, has he got a girlfriend, has he got any kids. God no, then I'd be a grandmother." She says, laughing out loud, music to Aimee's ears, it's the first time in weeks since she has caught a glimpse of her old friend, she knew she was in there somewhere, and now she seems to be coming back.

"Granny Nikki, has a nice ring to it, we'll have to get you some cardigans and a knitted shawl." With this they're both laughing, tears rolling down both their cheeks, but for once tears of laughter, not sadness. Aimee just needs to keep her friends spirits high until Paul comes home on Saturday. "How do you picture him? Hold that thought, I think this calls for a proper drink, I'll get a bottle of wine, back in two minutes." While Aimee is getting the wine Nikki makes herself comfortable on one of the sun beds, removing her t-shirt to reveal a white sports bra, she relaxes on the bed, for the first time in weeks she feels almost human again. She can actually start to believe that she and Paul can get through this; she knows it's not going to be easy, she has to earn his trust back, but she will do whatever it takes. Although she doesn't want to lose Paul, she is going to see Anthony and if Paul can't handle that, then so be it. She has never thought of herself as assertive, but at this moment, she believes anything is possible; she is not going to ignore Anthony any longer, well not after Saturday. With that, Aimee is coming back with the wine and two glasses, pouring them and placing on the table between the beds, Aimee takes her place on the other and lays back.

"So, where were we? That's right you are going to tell me how you imagine Anthony."

"I thought of him as being quite tall, maybe not quite six foot, dark hair, olive skin like mine. I hope he doesn't have his dad's arrogance; his dad was good looking though, so he should have turned out handsome.

Apart from that, I have no idea; I used to think when he was growing up that it would have been nice to be able to watch him from a distance. Not to be part of his life, I gave that right up when I gave him away, although I wish now that I had asked for updates on his progress. I made it quite clear at the time I wanted no more to do with him, a decision I regret to this day. I just hope the family he went to live with have treated him well, treated him as their own. I wonder why he has sought me out so soon after his eighteenth, I mean he couldn't get the information until then, and that was less than three months ago, how has he tracked me down so quickly? I always thought it took years for an adopted child to find his birth parents. I'm glad I didn't put the fathers name on the birth certificate, I wouldn't want him to be the first person Anthony meets." She says, eyes still closed laying back, soaking up the sun, sweat beading on her chest and stomach.

"Will you tell him about his father?"

"Only if he asks, I won't lie to him, I won't go into detail about him, but if he asks a question I will try to give him as truthful an answer as possible. I'd rather he didn't meet his father, same as I'd hope he doesn't ask about my parents." She says.

"He's bound to ask about them, they are his grandparents after all, have you not had any contact with them since the birth?"

"None, I did write to them about a year after he was born, I never had any reply, in the letter I told them I was sorry for being such a disappointment to them, and asked for their forgiveness but I never heard anything back from them. Since that day I have been on my own, I decided that if they could not forgive then I was better off without them.

To this day I don't know if they are alive and well or if they're dead, assuming they haven't moved I still have their address and telephone number. If Anthony wants them I will be happy to pass them on, but I'll warn him not to expect a good reception. They called him a bastard before he was even born, what they are going to think of him now is anyone's guess." She says, finishing the last of her wine, and absently refilling their glasses. She feels good being able to talk, she has wanted to talk about Anthony for so long but didn't think she had anyone that would understand. Aimee has been amazing since that first day she was told and she can't thank her enough. Nothing she can do will ever repay her for the kindness and understanding she has shown her.

23

Friday July 28 2000

Sitting on the fire escape with his back to the door, Anthony looks a right state. He's smoking a Marlboro with one hand and a can of Carlsberg in the other, tears softly dripping off his chin, as he sobs quietly. At just gone six-thirty in the evening, he has been home from work now for nearly an hour. He has been in a funny mood most of the day, even snapping at Mike a couple of times. It has been playing on his mind more and more lately that he still has not heard from his mum, it has been nearly a month now. The more he thinks, the more scenarios he comes up with as to why she hasn't responded, he knows she has to tell her husband, but does she realise the agony she is putting him through. He can't understand what was wrong with him, he just has to be patient.

He's quite glad that Anna couldn't come round tonight; he hates himself when he's like this. He knows Anna cares for him, but he can't stand for her to see him like this. Putting out his cigarette, he instinctively pulls another from the packet and lights it. The night is warm for this time of year, so Anthony is out here in just a t-shirt and boxers, two empty cans already lined up against the railings, this being his third, which he finishes with one final gulp. Putting the cigarette in the ashtray he attempts to stand up—he doesn't handle alcohol very well—grabbing hold of the door handle, he hauls himself up. Going inside he heads to the fridge to grab another couple of cans, not noticing how loud he has the stereo. Making his way back to the fire escape and his own little slice of solitude, he doesn't hear the key turn in the lock. Passing through the door and closing it behind him, he again slumps down. Placing the two cans beside him, he immediately retrieves one of them back realising that his last can is empty, he opens this fresh can knowing he's had enough, but wanting this ache to go away, if only for a while.

He can feel the numbness washing over him, his mind becoming foggy; he welcomes the oblivion that the drink gives him. He is so glad Anna has never seen him like this, the fact that no one has ever seen him like this. He knows that for the next few hours he can be at peace with himself, stick two fingers up to the world, and tell it to go fuck itself.

Anna was supposed to be at home tonight as her Aunt and Uncle were coming over, and they were all supposed to have a family dinner. At six her Aunt rang and said they couldn't make it after all, something to do with car trouble, Anna knew they didn't like coming over. She liked her Aunt, her mothers' sister, she often wished that she had been born into her family instead as her Aunt is so much more fun.

Her mum told her about the cancellation, their plans had changed, they were now going out to dinner, and that she would have to get herself something to eat. She decided to grab a quick snack, then to go and surprise Anthony; she knew he had been disappointed when she had told him she couldn't come over for their usual Friday night ritual of pizza and DVD.

She got to Anthony's around six-thirty, grabbing the key from its usual hiding place she inserts it in the lock, she can hear loud music coming from inside, Miles Davis if she's not mistaken. Opening the door, she puts the key back under the mat before going in. Once inside she senses that something isn't right, she just glimpses Anthony heading out onto the fire escape with two cans of lager, and he is swaying quite a lot.

"It's only me" she calls out; there is no response, he just carries on, out through the door. Passing the stereo, she turns the volume down to a more reasonable level. It doesn't appear that Anthony has noticed her here, he's sat against the door, he didn't move when she turned the music down. Getting closer to the door, Anna is wondering whether she should just pretend she never came, and just leave. She decides to hang about for a bit longer just to make sure that he is all right. She sits on the floor with her back to his with just the glass between them.

Still unsure of what to do, she hears him light up a cigarette, and wishes she was that side of the glass, she would do anything at this moment for one. After a few more minutes of sitting there thinking that she should probably just go, she begins to hear Anthony talking. She can't think who he is talking to as there is no one near enough, then she realises that he is not talking to anybody, just himself.

"What was so wrong that you had to get rid of me?" he sobs, she can tell he is crying, she can hear his voice breaking up. "Why not just get rid of me before I was born, it would have been better for both of us—maybe I should do it now and save us all a lot of trouble" his voice is so soft as he talks, Anna can barely hear what he is saying. She hears him take a drink from the can, then hears it drop from his hand and can hear the contents running over the side of the stairs. She hadn't realised but she has tears running down her face, her heart is breaking for Anthony. She knew he had problems, but had never dreamt that it was this bad. Over the years, he has done a good job of protecting her from the real turmoil and hurt he's been feeling.

In that instant she knew there was never going to be anyone else for her. She loved him, this sudden realisation hit her full on, for ten years now all the emotions she had gone through had been building to this moment, she truly loved him. Tears were now free flowing down her cheeks, her chest is heaving as she tries to control the sobbing. All she wants to do is go out there and hold her Anthony. That's what he was now, whatever happened from now on, he was hers. Regardless of how damaged he thinks he is, she knows he needs her as much as she needs him. Getting up, she realises Anthony's no longer sitting by the door, there is a cigarette lying half burnt in the baked bean can, but no Anthony. For an instant, her mind is going ninety to the dozen—he wouldn't—no he can't—he wouldn't do it. Grabbing at the door handle, she pulls it open, rushing to the railing. She leans over looking down; she looks all around on the ground below. Nothing. Maybe he has gone down the stairs, no, he was only wearing his boxers and a t-shirt. Looking up she can see his legs hanging over the roof of the building. Grabbing the packet of cigarettes the climbs the stairs two at a time.

Anthony hears footsteps on the stairs below, the shock bringing him straight out of the daze he is in, a thousand thoughts rushing through his brain. Why won't they leave him in peace, all he wants is just to forget. Has someone reported seeing him on the roof? Do they think he is going to jump? Does anyone care if he jumps? At this point, he doesn't even think anyone would notice, with the possible exception of the people left to clear up the mess on the pavement. For them it is just another selfish bastard they have to scrape up. They'll be thinking, why can't people kill themselves during normal working hours.

When he sees Anna's head level with his knees, his heart sinks. Not Anna, what is she doing here, she said she couldn't come over tonight, Anna shouldn't be here. He puts his hands to his face to wipe away the tears, as if that is going to fool her. Then looking Anna in the face, he sees the tears streaming down her cheeks, her eyes red. In a fraction of a second his thoughts go from his own misery to Anna, what has happened to make her upset, if someone has done this to her he'll kill them. No one hurts Anna and gets away with it; it does not even occur to him that he is the cause of the tears. "What's wrong? What's happened? Are you all right?" all these questions seem to come out of his mouth at once, still he does not see that he is the cause of the pain she is feeling.

"I'm fine, it's you, I heard you talking to yourself. Why didn't you come to me?" She manages to blurt out through her sobbing.

Then it hits him, he obviously wasn't alone on the balcony, but he was, he would have noticed if Anna had been there. "Where were you?" he asks, confused now, the drink not helping, although he is beginning to sober up quickly, the dread building inside him. The thought that she had heard his ranting, and worse, his sobbing, how could he have missed her?

More composed now, knowing that he was alive and safe, she was never letting him out of her sight again. "I let myself in and saw you disappear out onto the balcony with the lager. I didn't want to disturb you, I was going to leave, but I thought I heard you crying" a lump catches in her throat; she stops herself from crying again. "I sat down with my back to you against the glass, that's when I heard you talking to yourself" a brief pause to compose herself once more. "Then when I turned round I saw that you had gone, I was scared Anthony, I thought..." she was struggling to bring herself to say the words, then with one deep breath "I thought you had jumped, I couldn't get out here quick enough. When I didn't see you squashed on the floor I could breathe again"

Laughing now, not out of malice or to make fun of her, it was just the way she said squashed, he couldn't stop it.

"Don't laugh at me," she says.

"Sorry, I'm not laughing at you" seeing the hurt in her eyes, he quickly adds "It is just the way you said squashed, I'd never thought of myself as squashed before" a brief pause before he continues, this time taking her hand in his. "I am so sorry that you have to see me like this, I never wanted anyone to see me in this mess, especially you" not able to maintain eye contact, he looks away at nothing in particular. He knows she is judging him, he can't bear it. "I would never kill myself, I might think about it a lot, but I could never do it, I don't ever want you thinking that one day you are going to come here and find me dead, you won't" he tries to reassure her as much as himself. He honestly doesn't know if he could do it or not. What he does know is that if he did no one would ever find him.

Still holding her hand, he pulls her closer and hugs her tight to him, tears again starting to roll down his cheeks. They stay like this for what seems like an eternity, neither wanting to break apart, as neither wants the other to see their tears. Anna eventually pulls away, desperate now for that cigarette. Opening the packet, she pulls two out, lighting one, she hands it to Anthony. Then lighting the other, she draws heavily on it getting the smoke deep into her lungs, both now sitting there with legs hanging over the edge, staring out at the sun, hands still clasped together. After they have smoked their cigarettes, and both lit another, Anthony asks "What are you thinking?" not sure if he wants to know the answer, but asking nevertheless. Is she going to tell him that she can't handle this, deserting him, like everyone else seems to do. Not that he would blame her, if he was in her shoes, he wouldn't put up with him.

"Not much, I wish you would talk to me though," she says, hoping he doesn't know she isn't telling him everything. How can she, does she just sit here and tell him that she loves him, she thinks that she has always loved him. He wouldn't be able to handle that right now. So instead, she'll just have to make do with being there for him.

"What do you want me to say, for as long as I can remember I've had thoughts of killing myself? I haven't, yes I get times when I think it would have been better if I hadn't been born. I think that if your mum doesn't want you, why should anyone else" he stops to smoke his cigarette.

Anna notices his use of the word 'mum', in all the years she has known him he never once heard him call his adoptive Mother 'mum'. She is beginning to get a real sense of the hurt and betrayal his adoption has on his life.

"I always get the sense that people don't understand what it means to be adopted. They see it that just because your parents didn't conceive you, it makes no difference. They're your parents and they love you, what they don't see is the doubt in the child. For as long as I can remember, I used to think when I was younger, that the day would come when they would send me back. Not back to my real mum, but to a building where there are rows of shelves with children sitting on them, a bit like a shop, where prospective parents go to pick their chosen child. They would walk along the aisles, scrutinising the children, this ones too old, this one has the wrong colour eyes. Asking questions of the shop assistant, is this one well behaved? Is this one going to be clever? Because we don't want a stupid one. I think this goes back to the day, when I was about five or six."

A brief hesitation while he recollects the story. "That's right; it was after we had finished the evening meal. My parents had a rule that you had to ask to get down before you left the table. I was being stubborn and wouldn't ask, so they told me I would stay there until I did.

At seven o'clock they told me to go to bed, this was the usual time. I thought I had won, even though I was going to bed I hadn't asked to leave the table. Then the next morning when I got up, it was a Saturday, my Mother dragged me back to the table and made me sit there until I asked to get down. She finally gave in mid-afternoon, she told me to get out of her sight and that if I ever did it again they were going to take me back to the shop and demand a refund." The recollection starts the tears again; Anna puts her arm around his shoulder and pulls him closer. She kisses the top of his head.

"Why haven't you ever told me that story before?" She asks, not expecting an answer. "How often do you get like this?"

"It depends" he can't look her in the eye, he just looks down into his lap. "I can go weeks without it getting to me, but a comment overheard, a smell, can get me thinking, there is nothing I can do to stop it. I know it's irrational to think the way I do, I know I should just get on with living my own life. Something inside won't let me, it eats away at me, I'm scared it will eat away until there is nothing left. I want to live my life, I want to get married, I want to have children. But until I know who I am and where I come from I don't feel that I can".

"So what happens if she won't talk to you?" Anna asks reluctantly.

The truth, I don't know—I need another cigarette," he says, offering Anna another and lighting up again. "Say I forget all about her. Live my life. Have a family. What do I tell my children when they ask about my family, their grandparents? What if I'm carrying a genetic disease that I pass on to my children? Just so many things need answering before I can think about settling down and having my own family." Anthony replies.

"Well I'm here for you, whatever you need, just please don't shut me out. I want to help." She pleads. "I do like it up here," she says trying to lighten the mood.

"I come up here quite a lot; it's like my own little sanctuary. It's beautiful late at night; I'll often come and lie up here, just looking up at the stars. The peace is amazing in the early hours. A couple of times I have come up here when I can't sleep and watch the sun rise. I love seeing the world transform from the blackness of the night, the gradual addition of colour, bit by bit, second by second." He reminisces, talking to no one in particular.

Anna is just staring at him, as if it's the first time she has seen him. Watching his mouth move as he talks, listening to his melodic voice. Things she never noticed before. How did she not realise that she is in love with him? For ten years, they have been best of friends, occasionally flirting with each other. Ten years, in which time neither of them becoming close with anyone else, she had never been attracted to anyone. Anna had no idea if Anthony had ever fallen for anyone; he had never indicated to her that he fancied someone. Where does she go from here? Does she tell him how she feels and risk their relationship? For the time being, she decides to keep quiet.

"You've gone very quiet, which is so unlike you," Anthony says.

"Just enjoying the peace and quiet, enjoying the company," she truthfully admits.

"Have you eaten? Do you want me to make you something?" Anthony realises he's starving; he should have eaten before drinking.

"I had something before I came over, but I'll go and make you something. Beans on toast alright?"

"I don't deserve you" he says, "Why do you put up with me?"

"It's a hard job, but somebody's got to do it" Anna jokes, when all she wants to say is 'because I love you'. "Come on, we'll come back up here after you've eaten".

They both head back down the fire escape stairs, back through the door into the flat. "Go and have a shower while I make you dinner" Anna tells him.

"Yes boss" he salutes as he says it. Heading off to jump in the shower, "Come and join me if you want..."

"You wish," she taunts, then under her breath with Anthony out of earshot "Or should that be I wish", thinking, how did things get this bad this quickly. Making her way to the kitchen, she starts to make dinner for Anthony.

Standing in front of the mirror, Anthony realises how bad he looks. He has dark streaks snaking their way down from the corners of his eyes, across his cheeks and ending at his chin. His eyes are red and swollen, he feels so embarrassed that Anna has seen him like this. He can barely look her in the eye, what must she think of him. Stepping out of his clothes, and into the steaming shower, the tears come again, leaning with his hands on the wall behind the shower, his head directly under the powerful jets of water in the hope that the noise will drown out his sobs. He just stands there, thoughts just running round his head. How can he possibly tell Anna the thoughts that go through his head, she'll have him committed. He knows some of his thoughts aren't rational, he knows most of his problems are of his own making, he wishes he could just move on.

Wrapping a towel around his waist, he heads back to where Anna is waiting with a plate of beans on toast. "That looks great" he thanks her. Sitting down, tucking into the food, he hadn't realised how hungry he was. He is still struggling to look her in the eyes; he can feel her eyes on him.

"Do you remember when we first met?" Anna asks, completely changing the tone of the conversation, instantly it is as it normally is.

"How could I forget?" he says between mouthfuls. "I remember the removal van pulling up a couple of doors from our house, my parents had been talking for days, wondering who the new neighbours were going to be. I overheard my mother talking to Betty next-door one day; she was saying that she hoped it wasn't another Indian family moving in." he puts the last forkful of food in his mouth before continuing. "Just behind the removal van, a car pulled up, I had been riding up and down the road on my bike—not really my bike at all, it was Tracey's old one, because she had got a new one the previous Christmas. I stopped when people started getting out of the car, I remember my parents talking later about the posh family that had moved in. All I remember thinking when I saw your mum and dad get out of the car was, aren't they smart? Then this vision of beauty got out of the back seat, wearing a yellow summer dress, golden hair blowing about in the wind—well maybe that bit was in my head. I remember you looking over at me sitting on my bike, all I could think at that moment was I was in love, and I was going to marry this angel sent from heaven. I think that day changed my life." Anthony finishes, starting to blush, he doesn't know why he just told her all that. He can feel the heat building in his cheeks.

"Are you blushing?" She asks in a childish voice. "You've never told me that before, did you really think we would get married?"

"I was only eight" he laughs, "Besides, you are beautiful, why wouldn't I?" he realises now that it is the drink talking, he would never be saying these things if he was sober. He wouldn't have the nerve to be this honest and open normally. He can feel his cheeks getting redder and redder, and the room is getting warmer. He doesn't appear to be the only one who is blushing. Anna's cheeks have gone scarlet, and she can't look at him.

"Don't be stupid, I'm not beautiful" she barely manages to get the words out, she can feel her cheeks positively glowing.

"You don't know how beautiful you are, do you?" he asks; while he has his nerve, he may as well carry on being honest. She'll just think it's the drink.

"I need a drink, do you want one?" She asks, "Or have you had enough".

"No, I'll have another one, and don't change the subject" he says.

With her back to him as she is walking to the fridge, she says, "I'm not beautiful, you're just drunk" still with her back to him tentatively waiting to hear his response. Her heart is hammering in her chest, wondering if it is just the drink, they do say people tell the truth when their drunk. She knows she shouldn't be getting her hopes up, he might not even remember any of this in the morning.

"I know I've had a few drinks, but you are stunning, you should take a good long look in the mirror. You are definitely way out of my league," he answers. She brings the drinks, not able to look at him, he watches her as she walks onto the balcony. He stays where he is, watching as she begins to climb up the stairs to the roof. After a few minutes, still wearing just a towel, he grabs the cigarettes and heads up after her. He hopes he hasn't upset her. Reaching the roof he sits down next to her, giving her a nudge, he says, "You okay".

"Fine, I just needed a bit of fresh air," she answers.

"Here, this will help" he says handing her a cigarette and laughing.

"Thanks" she takes the proffered cigarette and lights it. "We will reach your mum, whatever it takes, we will get you your answers." She says this with such force, and conviction that he believes every word.

He puts his arm around her shoulder, pulls her closer, kissing the top of her head he says, "I love you".

24

Saturday 29 July 2000

"Right, are you all set Paul?" Steve asks as he's loading the bags into the back of the taxi, the week has flown by, he thinks he has got through to Paul about Nikki.

"Ready, I can't wait to get back home now and see Nikki; I just hope she can forgive me for just leaving the way I did. I'm going to support her in anything she wants to do, if she wants to meet him I'll be there for her. Now come on let's get home." Paul says with conviction. They should be home just after lunch, Steve called Aimee to let her know and asked her to tell Nikki, he also told her to tell her that things were going to be okay.

After an uneventful forty-five minute flight between Edinburgh and Heathrow, they touch down at twelve-fifteen, they should be home by one-thirty depending on traffic.

25

Saturday July 29 2000

"Come on Anthony, we can catch the nine o'clock train if you hurry" Anna tells him.

"I'm coming" he tells her, coming out of the bedroom, dressed in stonewashed jeans and a white t-shirt, Anna's wearing jeans and Anthony's Miami Dolphins football jersey again, looking more like a dress on her. He grabs his keys from the side and his wallet, neither bothering with a jacket as the forecast is for a warm, dry day. Slamming the door behind them, Anthony grabs hold of Anna's hand and running down the stairs two at time, almost pulling her off her feet.

"Careful, I nearly went over then" she yells at him, catching her footing at the last minute to stop herself falling.

"Sorry, but like you said if we hurry we can catch the nine o'clock train," he laughs.

At the bottom of the stairs they both start laughing, walking now at a slightly less frantic pace, they have fifteen minutes before the train is due, the station is only at the end of the high street, a couple of minutes away even at a slow pace.

They reach the station with more than enough time to spare, going over to one of the automatic ticket machines; Anthony puts the money in for two one-day travel cards. This will allow them to travel anywhere in London all day, and then home again when they've had enough, not that Anthony or Anna ever get fed up with going to London. Waiting for the tickets to be dispensed from the machine, Anthony looks over at the drunk sitting in the corner with his bottle of whatever in a brown paper bag. The smell of piss and vomit in the train station is overpowering, they just want their tickets, and to get up to the platform for the cleaner, fresher air that awaits them. Not that it is cleaner or fresher, with all the diesel fumes, but at least it's not piss and vomit.

As the tickets spill from the ticket machine, once again Anthony grabs hold of Anna's hand and drags her up the nearest flight of stairs out into the bright sunlight, both taking an exaggerated gasp of air, walking along the platform still hand in hand, they start people watching. A game they play whenever they go into London, it helps kill the time waiting for trains, and while on the train.

"So what's the story with the old man over there, with his pin striped suit, leather briefcase and umbrella" Anna asks, the idea is not to be boring, but to come up with a feasible assessment of the person.

"Well for starters, the briefcase isn't what it appears, he works for MI5 or one of the government agencies, in his briefcase is a file for his next assassination target, concealed in the briefcase is a tracking device, a suicide pill, should he be captured. If he presses the button on the side of the case, a knife pops out of the end allowing him to use the case as a weapon. The case is armoured allowing him to use it to stop attacks. The umbrella isn't an umbrella, it's a rifle—who would need an umbrella on a day like this—I ask you. So there you have it my dear Watson, he's a government assassin" this last he says in his best Sherlock Holmes impression.

"You watch too many James Bond movies" Anna comments.

"Your turn now, the young woman on the other platform, sitting on the bench" he asks. The woman in question is dressed in a flowery summer dress, bright yellows and whites, carrying a small purse; she keeps looking up at the clock suspended from the platform roof.

"She's waiting for the train, but she isn't going anywhere. She bought a ticket so that she could be as close to the train when it arrives as possible. She's waiting for her sweetheart; he's been serving in the military overseas. It has been a year since she waved him off from this very platform. He is coming home to propose to her—notice no wedding or engagement ring—when he gets off the train he will be dressed in his best naval uniform, he will have his duffel bag slung over his shoulder. Then she'll jump into his arms, he'll pick her up and twirl her around" she says, finishes with a bow from the waist, as if addressing her adoring fans.

With that, the train approaches on their side of the tracks, as it pulls past them drawing to a slow stop, they can see that the train is pretty much empty, one of the benefits of being nearly at the end of the line.

There's only a couple of rural stations it passes through before reaching them. As the train comes to a complete stop, the noise of the brakes being applied making a screeching sound, Anthony opens the carriage door, helping Anna get on before he follows closely behind. They pick out two seats facing each other by the window. Sitting down, they notice that their carriage is empty, and no one seems to be getting on either.

After a couple of minutes, the train starts up once more and begins slowly chugging out of the station. As the world begins to pass them by Anthony leans over to Anna, and taking both of her hands in his he says, not looking into her eyes but down at his hands "I'm sorry about last night, I didn't want you to see me like that." It almost comes out as a whisper.

Knowing how hard that had been for Anthony to say she puts her hand under his chin and raising his head up to look him straight in the eyes, "You don't have to apologise to me, I just wish you had talked to me sooner" she says.

"You know I find it hard to talk to people, I don't know what's wrong with me," he says, thankful that they're the only people in this carriage; the last thing he wants is an audience.

Anthony's trouble with communication stems back to his upbringing by his adoptive parents, in their home they expected him to be seen and not heard. Going hours on end not speaking unless spoken to, even when spoken to he knew no one cared about what he had to say. His parents would ask him something, then before he had a chance to answer they would be off doing something else, he believed at times that he must have been invisible. His sister on the other hand, the household seemed to revolve around her, what daddies little princess wanted she got. If daddies little princess said tell Anthony to shut up, then Anthony got told to shut up, usually with a smack across the legs with the bamboo cane, the cane with split ends, kept on top of the kitchen cabinet.

Anna had seen first-hand how Anthony's life had been and sympathised with how he had turned out. But life is short, she needed to bring him out of himself and help him move on, in her opinion the best thing that ever happened in Anthony's life is the night his parents were killed in a car crash—she hated having these thoughts. Since the accident Anthony's personality is beginning to shine through, he is smarter than his parents had ever given him credit for, he is also extremely funny, with a wry sense of humour.

As the train trundles along the track, Anna stares into his eyes, "What are you thinking about, right at this moment, don't think, just say," she says somewhat unexpectedly.

"You" he blurts out, not realising until the words are out of his mouth that he has said anything, he's hearing them as if they're coming from someone else's mouth. His mind now working overtime, knowing what her next question is likely to be, trying to come up with a satisfactory response, not wanting to tell her the truth, he is in love with her. She knows he loves her, but not that he is in love with her.

"What do you mean me?" she wants to know. The question he knew she was going to ask.

"That I don't deserve you," he says going slightly red in the face.

"I don't believe you," she responds, "Tell me what you are really thinking?" she demands.

Anthony thinks about his response carefully, he wants her to know how he feels, but is scared that if he tells her, then they can't be friends anymore. So, in his usual style he tries to make light of it, "You want the truth, you can't handle the truth" he roars in his best Jack Nicholson impression—a line from one of their favourite films A Few Good Men—then bursts out laughing. Hoping he has diverted her questions for the time being, Anna follows suit and joins in with the laughter. She knows not to push him too hard, when he resorts to jokes or impersonations it means the discussion is over.

"Can I ask you a question?" She asks after sitting quietly for the last ten minutes.

"Of course." Nervous now, she never asks, she always just blurts questions out.

"Last night when we were up on the roof, I noticed some marks on your arm."

His worst nightmare, his mind buzzing with questions, did she see what they were? Does she know it was her name? What does he tell her? "There nothing, just burns." He hopes that will be the end of it.

"They didn't look like normal burns. They looked like straight lines." She points out, "You don't have to tell me." She quickly adds, seeing the look of embarrassment on his face. She wishes she hadn't bought the subject up.

He looks down at his hands as he picks at the skin at the side of his nails, his mind deciding how much to tell her, thinking that a degree of honesty maybe his best course of action, not the whole truth, just a portion of it. "Sometimes when I think about my mum, I go into a different place, a place I don't want to be in." He tries to explain, but the words aren't saying what he wants them too, unable to look at her, he tries to carry on, feeling her eyes upon him. "The pain helps me cope with the pain of not having her in my life. I'm not making much sense, it's hard to explain." He knows he is rambling, but if he doesn't try now he never will. "Sometimes when I think about her I burn myself." There, it's out there, I've said it, no going back now. He hasn't realised that he's crying, it's only the tears beginning to sting and her arm around his shoulder that bring him back—when did she sit next to me? She pulls him closer, gently kissing the top of his head, his unruly curly hair tickling her chin. They stay like this for the remainder of the journey, not another word spoken of his confession.

Arriving at Baker Street, they disembark the train, making their way along a myriad of tunnels, down escalators into the bowels of London—the last fifteen minutes seeming not to have happened, he realises now more than ever how much he loves her. Advertising boards everywhere you look, advertising everything from theatre tickets to haemorrhoid cream, the tube network is always so busy, Anthony and Anna hold hands believing safety in numbers, as they battle their way down yet another escalator, the temperature dropping the deeper they go, the number of people increasing. London really is a multi-cultural society, everywhere they look, there's a different nationality, all creeds and colours. As they round the last corner, a train is just entering the platform; there are always plenty of trains on the underground. Jumping on the train as the doors slide open, already overcrowded, somehow more people still seem to fit.

The heat in the train is stifling, this close to other people Anthony can't help notice that some people should wash more frequently. Still it's only three stops before they get off, with his arm protectively around Anna's waist, she snakes hers around his. Feelings stirring in both of them, neither knowing how the other feels. At the first stop, some people get off and only a few get on, leaving them with a bit more breathing space, though Anthony keeps Anna close to him. Then at Oxford Circus more people seem to join the train than leave, only one more stop and they can get out into the fresh air of Piccadilly Circus.

Stepping out into the warm air right in the heart of London, Anthony and Anna just stand there looking around, they're always amazed at the sights and sounds of this wonderful city.

"Where should we go first?" Anna asks.

"I don't know about you but I could kill for a cappuccino," Anthony says pointing at a coffee shop over the other side of the road. Somehow, they make it across the busy streets to the coffee shop; it's like one of them computer games where you try to get across the road without being squashed.

Sitting down at the sole remaining table, Anthony goes up to the counter to place their order, he orders them both a cappuccino with a maple and pecan Danish. Anna is staring out the window when he returns with breakfast, "Can I ask you another personal question?" she asks without looking away from the window, then before he can answer, "Do you think your adoptive parents loved you? And did you love them?"

"The truth, I don't know, I think they loved me in the way that they cared enough to take in a child that's not their own. Nevertheless, there's a definite difference in the way they loved me to the way they loved Tracey. It's in the eyes, whenever they told me they loved me, there was no sparkle in their eyes, I don't think they were bad people. It is just a fact that they didn't receive what they thought they would when they decided to adopt me, I don't blame them, I really don't." he says, taking a bite of his Danish, and a mouthful of his coffee before continuing. "Did I love my parents? Not in the way I should, I think it is more gratitude than love. It was when they died I realised that it wasn't love as it should be. I never cried once, not when I heard, or when they buried them. As you know, I didn't go to their funeral, thanks to Tracey and the fact she's a bitch. The worst part is, I don't regret the decision. Maybe they would have loved me if I had loved them back." He finishes with a touch of resignation in his voice.

"Sorry I didn't mean to pry, and I don't want to ruin our day," Anna apologises.

"It felt good to admit it," Anthony confesses, "Come on, finish your coffee, and let's go and have some fun."

Anna is pleased that she hasn't upset Anthony, but she wants to get him talking about things and opening up to her. She wants to get him prepared in case things with his birth mother don't go as planned. She worries about him bottling all these feelings up, worried that for eighteen years he hasn't spoken to anyone about how he feels. He tells her some things, but nothing compared to what she has found out the last two days. She's always known he's troubled, she never realised how much he was hurting. Just listening to him speak, she could hear it in his voice, although he tries his best to hide it, the sadness and regret comes through.

Heading left out of the coffee shop, they head along Shaftesbury Avenue, walking along, Anthony with his arm around her shoulder, Anna with her arm around his waist and her hand in the back pocket of his jeans. Anyone seeing them together would believe they were a couple; they have the look of two young people in love. “Do you fancy a look round Soho?” Anna asks.

“Why not, could be fun,” Anthony says. Sun beating down on their backs, they head up down one of the side roads heading up towards Brewer Street, taking in all the sights and smells of the urban streets. With the chic boutiques, and myriad of restaurants, suddenly turning onto Brewer Street the real Soho comes alive, with its shops and their blacked out windows promising untold ecstasy should you choose to enter. From the lap-dancing bars to the sex shops, mixed in with the exclusive restaurants and bars, Soho has it all. Anthony and Anna look on as they watch men coming and going from the lap-dancing bars and sex shops, “Have you ever been in a sex shop?” Anna asks Anthony.

“No, have you.”

“No, do you want to go in and have a look, I’m curious about what’s in there, aren’t you?” Anna says.

“Come on then, after you,” he says guiding Anna through the door of the nearest shop, windows simply stating, XXX Adult Shop, with its white windows not giving a hint of what to expect on entering. Anthony imagines a smoked filled dark seedy place, old men standing around looking at magazines. He couldn’t have been more wrong, after almost pushing Anna through the door, they find themselves in a light airy space, just like a proper shop. He was wrong about the old men too, instead they saw several couples, and many of them middle aged. The shop was set out in sections, magazine and DVD on one wall, costumes in another area, and sex toys in a small side room. Then another door where you could find bondage gear beyond, Anna instinctively heads over to the costume section, girls and their clothes!

"Ooh, look at this," Anna is holding a nurse uniform, bright white short dress, barely long enough to cover anything, with red crosses on it, and a name badge on it declaring that the nurse was 'Anita Lay'.

"I never saw you as a nurse," Anthony jokes.

"Well what do you see me as?" Anna asks, tongue in cheek.

"Maybe a busty wench," he says, holding up a wenches outfit. "No, that's not it, what about a sexy cheerleader?" he says, grabbing a red, white and blue outfit, complete with pom-poms and panties which resemble a piece of string with a triangle attached.

"So, that's what turns you on," Anna says, winking at him.

"I didn't say that" his face getting a rosy glow to it, "Is it hot in here?" he asks, knowing he's blushing.

"Let's go over there," she says pointing at the racks of toys and potions. Making their way across the shop they over hear a couple discussing which lingerie to buy, to Anthony it sounded like the lingerie was for the husband, not the wife. He looks round to see Anna standing next to an array of lifelike penises, going over to join her.

"So which one's it going to be?" he asks.

Grabbing the biggest and thickest one, she waves it about in front of her, and then pokes him with it.

"I think you're going to be very disappointed in life," he says, both now laughing, trying to keep the noise down so as not to draw attention to themselves.

"Are you telling me they're not all like this?" she says with a sad, bewildered look on her face, it's this look from Anna that melts Anthony's heart, an innocent little girl with high expectations. The way she cocks her head to one side, fluttering her eyelashes and pouting, Anthony doesn't understand how he has not acted on his attraction to Anna for all these years, he has the sudden realisation that he never loved his parents, for what he feels for Anna is stronger than anything he ever felt for them. Still confused about his love for Anna or is it something else, he doesn't know, all he knows is that of all places to make the discovery it has to be a sex shop in Soho, he always knew he had feelings for Anna, but what he is feeling at this precise moment is stronger than anything he has ever felt. He decides then and there that he is going to tell her how he feels, not exactly at this moment, as he doesn't feel it would be appropriate with her standing there waving a giant dildo at him.

"So, which one of these is like yours?" Anna asks, waving her arm across the display, "now don't be shy, you can tell me" she laughs.

Going beetroot red, Anthony says, "I think it's time we left." Grabbing her hand, he guides her towards the door, "I can't take you anywhere can I?"

"You're no fun anymore," Anna says, attracting attention now from the guy behind the counter, looking at them as if they've stolen half the shop. Bursting through the door into the busy street, attracting even more stares from passers-by, they're both now roaring with laughter. "I forgot to get the cheerleaders outfit, you know I would've looked good in it," Anna says, prompting even more laughter from the pair of them.

Walking along now aimlessly, neither of them knowing where they are heading, just enjoying the warmth of the sun, hand in hand Anna gives a slight squeeze, turning to look at Anthony, "Are you happy?" she asks.

"Yes, at this precise moment I couldn't be happier" he answers honestly, "I'm happy most of the time, I just have these dark times that I don't seem to be able to control, they're not as frequent as when I was younger. When they come I'm best left on my own, it's not fair on anyone to be around me." He adds.

"I know I've already told you this, but I'm here for whatever you need."

Anthony leans over and kisses the top of her head, "Thanks".

"We have to go there one night," Anna says getting all excited, pointing over at a building, much like the other buildings in the street. The difference with this one is, it's the legendary Ronnie Scott's Jazz Club. Their idols have all played here, they would love to spend an evening there.

"We will, one night, I promise you," Anthony assures her.

After getting lunch at one of the many back street cafes, Anthony suggests going to St. James's Park to do a spot of sunbathing and relaxing. What he is hoping is to test the waters to see if Anna has any feelings towards him. After walking down to Trafalgar square and admiring Nelson's Column, Anna once again amusing him with her innuendoes about the size of Nelson's column. With all the tourists sitting around the steps feeding the pigeons, the results visible on the lion statues and Nelson himself in the form of the silver grey bird crap. Turning right onto The Mall, a fantastic view of Buckingham Palace in the distance, heading towards the palace they soon come upon one of the many entrances to St James's park, the lush green grass between their feet, not what you expect from the sprawling urban jungle that is London.

Anna stops, putting her hand on Anthony's shoulder while she removes her trainers and socks. Stuffing the socks into the trainers, she's enjoying the feel of the cool grass through her toes. Anthony's offer to carry her shoes is gratefully accepted, walking beneath the canopy of the trees, alternating between the warm sun beating through in contrast with the cooler shade directly beneath. Reaching the lake, they find a spot on the bank, away from the other tourists. Sitting down Anthony removes his shoes and socks, while Anna rolls up her trouser legs, and lies back on the ground, pulling up her top revealing her taut flat stomach. Anthony lies next to her, their arms touching, relishing the touch of her skin on his, the closeness of her, not just her physical presence, but spiritually as well. Feeling the hairs on his arm standing on end at the thought of what he is about to do. The hammering in his chest is now so loud to his ears; he hopes Anna can't hear it. "We've been friends a long time, haven't we?" Anthony asks, not knowing where he is going with this conversation, distracted by the undulation of her breasts with every breath she takes.

“Yeh, years,” She says, eyes closed.

“We’ve been through a lot together haven’t we,” he says.

“Some stuff better than others,” she remembers.

“I’ve never quite understood how we became friends, I know at first it was because you moved in, but we were only eight at the time, and yet we’ve stayed friends ever since. What made you want to be friends with me?” he asks.

“Who said I wanted to be friends with you” she says laughing, “seriously though, at first you were the only person I knew when we first moved in that was my age. Then it wasn’t long after that, I think we were nine, we were round at your house, your mum had just made us cream crackers with cheese. I can still smell the house; it always had a hospital, antiseptic type smell. Then your sister came in shouting that you had broken her doll, she was crying but there weren’t any tears, and that was when your mum said ‘that’s what happens when you adopt a child, you don’t know what they’ll be like’. I remember thinking at the time what is adopt, so when I went home I asked my mum what it meant, and she explained it to me. From that moment I thought, I’m going to be his friend for life, he needs someone on his side—don’t you think that’s pretty profound for a nine-year-old, I’ve always been way beyond my years,” she laughs nervously.

“So what you’re telling me, you’re my friend out of pity,” he puts on his best sounding hurt voice.

“No, that’s not what I’m saying,” she nudges him playfully. “I care about you, I always have.” She adds.

Lying back looking up at the sky, Anthony decides it’s now or never, his heart feels like it's about to burst from his chest, his mouth is drier than the Sahara. His palms are sweating profusely, trying to find the words, knowing this could be the end of a beautiful friendship. Plucking up all the courage he can, he gets enough spit in his mouth to get the words out, "Have you ever thought of us as more than friends?"

Silence—this is not a good sign he's thinking. Anna's mind is spinning; before she answers, she needs to process what she thinks he has just said. Her heart is racing, she has butterflies in her stomach, she's hoping it's what she's been waiting for. "Before I answer, things don't have to change between us after what I say" She starts, His heart sinks, he knows he shouldn't have said anything. "But to answer your question, yes I have. I always knew I felt more for you than just a friend, then last night I realised that I love you. That doesn't mean we can't be friends, but I'm glad you know how I feel." She finishes, thinking that this is not perfect timing but he is the one that bought the subject up.

"You don't know what a relief that is, I've been dreading telling you how I feel, I was worried I'd lose you as a friend" he says, turning over onto his side, facing her, taking her hand in his, "I can't believe it's taken ten years to tell you I love you, but Anna I do, I love you."

Anna turns to lie on her side to face Anthony, her butterflies beginning to calm down, a single tear rolling down her cheek.

"You are so beautiful," he says, wiping away the tear, oblivious to anything going on around them, world war three could be breaking out and he wouldn't notice, or care. This is the happiest he thinks he has ever been.

"How long have you loved me?" Anna is curious now.

"I don't know, but I've been thinking more and more about you over the last few weeks. I know what you're thinking, it's because I'm a mess at the moment, with all this birth mum stuff, but I think I have always loved you, I just didn't know what love was. Even before I found out that I was adopted, I don't believe I ever loved my parents or sister, I always thought it was weird when growing up that I wasn't very close to my parents. I used to see the other kids' parents pick them up from school, you could see the love in their eyes for their children, I never saw that in my parents' eyes, it might as well have been a stranger picking me up. I often wondered when I was growing up what love felt like, I always knew that what I felt for my family wasn't love, then there was you, you were complicated. What I felt for you when we were growing up was like family love, I loved you as if you were my family. Then I remember it changing when we were fifteen or so, I started to notice things about you, things you shouldn't notice in family members. There were times when I would look at you and think, I feel more than just friendship, but because we were friends, I didn't think you felt the same way, I couldn't bear losing you as a friend." He confesses.

"So why tell me now?" She carries on probing.

"I thought it was worth the risk, I could've been way off the mark, but I've felt lately that you were feeling more for me than just friendship. Something Mike said the other day prompted me into action too, he said something about you being snapped up by some lucky man, and the thought of you with someone else made me realise I was jealous, something else I've never felt before. All the time Tracey received love from our parents, I never once felt jealous; I just accepted it as life." He tells her. Not knowing what to do next, he places his hand on her waist, leaning in and giving her a kiss on the lips, the first time he's kissed a girl in eighteen years, hoping it won't be the last. The scent of almond and apricot soap and the sweetness of her kiss making him realise how lucky he is. Her lips pressing onto his, he can feel tears running down his face, for once with happiness. Pulling away, he sees that Anna is crying too, the relief that after ten years they have at last found each other. He wipes away her tears, the two of them just gazing into each other's eyes, the realisation that if they died now, they had each other.

26

Saturday July 29 2000

Walking through the apartment door, he'd half expected Nikki to be there waiting, no sign of her, the place looked deserted. Putting his golf clubs back in the cupboard, still no movement, maybe she was out, although he knows Steve had told Aimee what time they would be back and you can bet she had told Nikki, so where is she. Walking across the expanse of the living area he sees the door open to the veranda, a small metal balcony which juts out about six foot from the building, it gives them a small outside area to sit. As he reaches the door he sees a sight that warms his heart as well as other parts of his body, Nikki is reclining on a sun lounger, wearing the briefest of bikinis, she suddenly realises she is being watched, seeing it is Paul she is up and off in one fluid movement, wrapping her arms around him.

"I'm so glad you're home, I'm so sorry." She manages to get out between tears.

"It's me who should be sorry babe, not you; I should never have left you here." He says brushing the tears away, gazing into her deep green eyes, he realises he could never have left her, her eyes would always have bought him back, well that and the body he sees in front of him, bronzed, beaded in sweat, she looks amazing.

"Come and sit down, we need to talk." Nikki pulls him by his hand and sits back down; Paul sits on the chair opposite, now beginning to look worried. "While you were away I've had a lot of time to think, I don't blame you for going away, I wanted to tell you so many times over the years. The longer I left it the harder it got, until I just hoped it would never become an issue. I have decided though that I would like to meet him." Having got the words out the relief floods in, more than relief, exhilaration at the realisation that she is going to see her son, whatever Paul has to say she is now telling him she is seeing Anthony. "You don't have to be involved, I will keep him away from here, and he doesn't have to interfere with our lives." Rushing to get that last sentence out, to soften the blow of her resolve.

Paul, taken aback with the assertiveness of his wife; he has never seen her like this, a pleasant surprise at this turn of events. "Babe, slow down, it's fine, that's what I want to tell you. This last week I have been thinking what you must have been going through, keeping this secret all these years knowing that one day your son could come knocking on our door. I agree, I think you should meet him, at least to hear what he has to say, and if it's okay with you I would like you to involve me. Although I think the first time you meet it should be on neutral ground and somewhere public, just the two of you talking, I can be there for you, but at a distance. I'm not saying this to scare you but there are a lot of strange people about and I would feel better knowing you weren't alone. You need to be sure that this is what you want; I'll support you no matter what you decide. What are you hoping to get from meeting him?"

"More than anything I want to explain, I don't want him thinking I didn't want him, I couldn't keep him. He needs to know that what I did, I did out of love for him; I thought it would give him a better chance in life. Better than I could have given him, what did I have to offer? I need him to understand that I love him." As the words leave her mouth the thought hits her like a thunderbolt, she loves him, this is the first time she has thought about him in this way, she can see it now, she loved him from the moment she knew he was growing inside her. She loves Paul, but this is different, this is the love a mother gives her child, not wanting or expecting anything in return. Unconditional love. The purest form of love there is. Leaning over to Paul and putting her arms around his waist and head on his shoulder she whispers "I love him." Tasting the saltiness as the tears run down her cheek into her mouth, for once she welcomes the tears.

Paul puts his arms around her, kissing the top of her head and whispers back "I know you do, I haven't been here for you when I should have been and for that I'm sorry. I've been a jerk; I should've been more understanding. So what's the next step?"

"He has given me ways to contact him, I thought about writing him a letter, but I'd rather meet him face to face, would you call him and arrange the meeting for me, I know it's a lot to ask."

"Of course I will, do you want me to call now?" He offers.

"Are you sure you don't mind? I was thinking if he agrees to meeting, then we could meet at Rico's next Saturday around eleven, what do you think?" She says.

"I think that's perfect, I can sit at another table, he doesn't even need to know I'm there. If you get me the number, I can give him a call now."

"Thank you, I don't deserve you." She says, getting up and going inside to retrieve the number. Paul watches her as she goes, the sweat glistening on her back, he still can't believe that she has an eighteen-year-old son. She returns a moment later with the letter from Anthony, he can clearly see the tear stains on the paper, in places the ink has run, a couple of words illegible, though he is sure that if he asked Nikki what those words are she could quote them without a problem. He imagines she has memorised the letter verbatim. Taking the letter, reading it himself once more, hoping that this is not some sick joke and is not just someone trying to get money from her. He hasn't expressed this concern to Nikki, he did mention it to Steve, and it was he who suggested a public place for the meeting and that Paul should be in the vicinity. The last thing Nikki needs is for someone to try to con her, especially in the vulnerable state she's in. Dialling the number on the paper, a couple of seconds and he can hear it ringing, two rings—three rings—nothing, letting it ring for nearly a minute he cuts the call. "I'll try again later; he could be at work or just out. The look of disappointment on her face is evident, we'll get hold of him don't worry." They are both now sitting next to each other on the lounger, Paul has his arm around her shoulder, she has her arm across his stomach, "Have you thought about trying to reach out to your parents again?" he asks her, now seems like a good time to bring the subject up, while everything is out in the open.

"No, I've managed for the last eighteen years without them, I don't see what is to gain by getting to know them again, besides I don't think I can ever forgive them for what they put me through, if Anthony wants to contact them, that's entirely up to him. I wish you could have met my parents when they were nice, I loved my parents up until the day they threw me to the wolves, I couldn't have wished for better parents. I never dreamed that when I told them I was pregnant that they would react the way they did. It was as if I didn't know them, they became complete strangers overnight, going from the most loving parents a child could wish for to being the devil incarnate. I'm not sure what was worse, my mum berating me and being generally unpleasant, or my dad's utter refusal to have anything to do with me. I think my dad hurt me the most, I was always his little princess, I could do no wrong in his eyes, and we were so close. I sometimes think that if maybe it had just been me and my dad then things may have been different, I think my mum's influence was a lot to do with his attitude towards me, the silence was sort of his way of saying 'I'm not getting involved', he would never go against her. When she decided that I would not be allowed back into the house once the baby was born, that was my fate sealed. I know I had been stupid and probably got what I deserved, but I thought when I contacted them after a year things might have calmed down." She tells him.

"No one deserves what they did to you, it is despicable and they should be ashamed of themselves, everyone makes mistakes, but they are your parents, they should have stood by you no matter what. Which is partly why I'm so sorry for the way I reacted, I'm no better than they are." He apologises once again.

"You had every right to react the way you did, I kept a secret from you and we always agreed that we would never have secrets, I don't blame you for the way you reacted, I blame myself for not telling you everything sooner, even when I knew the inevitable was about to happen, I waited three weeks to confess."

"Well, what do you say we call it quits, start as equals again and move forward?" Paul offers, with his arm still around her shoulders he runs his finger up and down the inside of her forearm.

She in turn snuggles tighter into his chest, "That sounds like a plan, now what do you say?"

For the next thirty minutes they explore each other's bodies like never before, making love in the open air, not caring who sees, unashamed of the love they have for each other.

"God, I love you babe, that was amazing." Paul whispers into her ear, "Do you think we scared the wildlife?" He says taking a look around suddenly realising how exposed they are.

"I love you too, more than you can imagine." She responds, also aware of their current position, out in the open on their balcony for all the world to see. Paul puts his boxers back on and Nikki puts her bikini back on after retrieving the top from where Paul had tossed it. Lying back on the lounger, Nikki lying between his legs, her back to his chest, soaking up the early afternoon warmth of the sun, both dripping with perspiration, their bodies slipping against one another as if coated in oil, "Do you think he'll like me?"

"What's not to like babe?"

"What if he only wants to meet to tell me he hates me for ruining his life?"

"I'm sure that isn't why he is doing it, I've read the letter, it sounds as if he just wants to get to know you, so stop worrying." He tries reassuring her.

"Part of me thinks I should never have given him away, but then the other part tells me that his life would have been worse with me."

"Hopefully you'll get the chance to explain all of this to him."

"What do you think it will be like when I first meet him?"

"Probably awkward at first, at the moment you are complete strangers, you've got to get to know each other, I'd imagine it is going to be just as hard for him."

"My stomach already feels funny at the thought of meeting him, what am I going to be like on the day?" She says, starting to panic at the prospect of meeting her son. The stress of the previous week, the not knowing what Paul is thinking, have all but passed now, her only reservations now are for the meeting. They have eighteen years to talk through, that's without going into the reason for her doing what she did all those years ago. What if he asks about his dad, what should she tell him, should she lie? No, if she has learnt anything, it is that lies get you nowhere and hurt everyone involved. If he asks about him, she will tell him the truth, a watered down version of the truth, but the truth nonetheless.

"Remember I'll be there, a couple of tables away, but I'll be there, he may even bring someone himself."

"Like who? A friend? What if he brings his parents?" She suddenly realises that he could possibly bring his parents, which would be awkward. Up until now, she had assumed it would just be Anthony turning up to meet her, she hadn't considered anyone coming with him. The more she thinks about it the more she realises how much sense it makes that he would not turn up on his own, of course he will have someone with him. More reasons to be nervous, the meeting hasn't even been arranged yet, and already she's as nervous as hell.

"If you're getting stressed now, what are you going to be like on the day?" Paul says laughing, not to be cruel, but knowing that Nikki can have a tendency to worry over the stupidest things. Big things don't bother her, the house could burn down around their ears and she would be the one with the calmest head and the most rational, but given a small problem, say she forgets to pick something up for dinner, she will worry like hell about it. It's just the way she is—and he loves her for it.

"I wonder what his parents think about him trying to contact me? Maybe they encouraged him, or maybe they don't know. I wonder if he has any brothers or sisters." The questions now just rolling off her tongue, the more she thinks about him the more questions seem to pop into her head.

"With a bit of luck, in a week you will be able to ask him yourself."

"Are you sure you're all right about all of this, I don't want you to feel left out, and I meant what I said you, you can stay completely out of it if you want to, it doesn't have to change things between us."

"Like I told you before, we're in this together. Believe it or not, now that I have had a chance to get my head around the fact you have an eighteen-year-old son, I'm actually looking forward to eventually meeting him. He'll hopefully be better on the Playstation than you, unless he's inherited the 'I'm no good at computer games gene'". He Jokes.

With that she thrusts her elbow back into his ribs, "Don't think the two of you are going to gang up on me, otherwise I'll be sending you both to bed without any supper." For the first time in a long time Paul witnesses her laughing out loud, a laugh that he knows comes from deep within, the relief of all the stress she has kept pent up inside her now dissipating. He doesn't think he has ever heard a more genuine sounding laugh from her, in all their years together he now realises the effort and energy it must have taken her to keep this secret. To bear the knowledge of her son, thinking about him and not being able to talk to anybody, knowing that one day it would all have to come out and she would have to deal with the aftermath. Juggling her life with him, with the life she left many years before, but having the baggage to carry around with her, never able to off load any of it, until now with everything out in the open it is like being with a new woman. The change in her is nothing short of miraculous.

"I forgot to ask, how was the golf trip?" She suddenly remembers where he has been for the last week, she feels guilty for not asking sooner, so far it has all been about her.

"Too easy, Steve lost every round; he should get some lessons. We had a chance to catch up, we talked about our situation a couple of times, and just so you know both he and Aimee said I was an idiot for leaving." He tells her, not wanting her to think they were talking about her behind her back. Steve wanted us to come home early, but I insisted we stay the week, I just had to get my head right before I came home, I was wrong, I'm sorry."

"I think you were right, I think the break did us the world of good, if you had stayed we would both have said things that we regret, things that may not have been easy to come back from. At least this way, we both came to our own conclusions and expectations and luckily we agree. If we had of come to a difference of opinion, I think we would now be in a better position to resolve them, I think we would be able to talk about it more rationally. That night on the terrace, I was far too emotional to discuss anything, if you had said the wrong thing I would have had a meltdown, I know I would. The three weeks leading up to it were torture, I pushed you away, I thought it would make it easier for both of us if you decided to walk away. I thought if I kept pushing, when you left it wouldn't hurt as much. Then when you left, I realised it didn't matter how much I pushed you away it still hurt because I love you, and nothing will ever change that." She confesses to him.

Putting his arms around her, he kisses the top of her head, "I will never leave you, I'm assuming all the skeletons are out of the closet now."

"Well, mine are out, the closet is now officially empty, what about yours?"

"Mine has been empty for years, there were never any in there, maybe a few ex-girlfriends had bodies like skeletons, I went through a thin faze, a couple of them I could pick up with one hand, now I prefer a bit more meat on the bone." He says while giving her a squeeze.

27

Sunday July 30 2000

Feeling a light brush against his lips, Anthony is awakened to a sight which brings a smile to his face, standing over him is Anna, fresh out of the shower, towel wrapped around her body with a second for her hair. Grabbing her around the waist he pulls her to him, pressing his lips firmly to hers, Anna responds by parting her lips, offering her mouth to his, kissing passionately, eventually pulling away. “Did you sleep well?” She asks.

“Not bad actually, this couch can get a bit uncomfortable at times.” He says. They have agreed to take things slowly after yesterday, for although they have known each other for ten years, what they are now is different. After revealing to each other how they feel, they are now officially a couple. Anthony wants them to take it slowly, to get to know each other properly, without skipping the first flushes of a new relationship. Rather than just sleeping with each other, which would be acceptable considering how well they know each other, they don't want to miss out on the bit where they get to know each other's bodies. The long sessions of kissing, the first touch of their hands on each other's bodies, all leading up to the most intimate union between two people. In essence, they want to date each other like any two normal people that find they have an attraction to one another.

"If you want to have a shower, I'll rustle us up something for breakfast."

"Can't we just stay here for another few minutes?" He begs, pulling her close once more, kissing her neck enjoying the freshness of her skin, the tropical coconut smell of her shampoo is intoxicating. If he died now, he would die happy, something he can never remember feeling in eighteen years. Coming to the realisation that this is what life is about, not who you are or where you come from—though important, especially for someone that has no idea of either—but love, the love between two people can conquer all, he knows it's a cliché but it's true. Owning up to Anna about his feelings and his deep love for her has put his life into perspective, he still needs to know about his mum and about himself, but for the first time in his life, he sees that it is worth living for other reasons.

"Now go and have your shower." She demands, smiling at him, letting him know that in time they will get to the good stuff.

*

All morning Nikki keeps going on at Paul to try ringing Anthony, each time he has to tell her it is too early, the first time she woke him up at seven to ask him if he thought it would be too early to try. Paul knows how much meeting Anthony means to her, he has never seen her like this, he has always thought of her as complete, their life together, her work, everything about their existence seemed to be perfect—until Anthony—since the skeleton has been let out of the closet, she is different. Different in a good way, there's a serenity about her, a completeness not present before, even the way she is badgering him to ring, there is no real sense of urgency, although implied he knows just the thought that he wants to meet her is enough. The thought that he is out there in the wide world somewhere thinking about her, thinking about his mum, that's what she is now—a mum. A mum without the messiness, without the sleepless nights, without the stress of taking care of another living soul, she has become a mum by default—but a mum nonetheless. At just past eleven Paul comes over to his wife, she's sitting outside on the terrace reading a Patricia Cornwell novel, she thought it would take her mind off asking Paul every five minutes if he would ring Anthony.

"I'll give him a try, hopefully he's in now, I know I don't need to ask but are you sure about this?" Paul asks her.

"Positive, he should be up shouldn't he, it has gone eleven."

"He definitely wouldn't have been up when you wanted me to call at seven o'clock this morning." He says laughing. "Right here goes." Dialling the number, which he knows from heart after the number of times he rang it yesterday with no luck. It starts ringing, after the tenth ring he hears the distinctive sound of the other end picking up.

"Hello" Anthony answers.

"Hi is that Anthony Allen?"

"Yes, who's this?" His tone guarded, his phone hardly ever rings and when it does it's either Anna or Mike.

"My name is Paul Pope, you wrote to my wife a few weeks ago—Nicola Anderson."

With the mention of the name, Anthony's pulse quickens, his heart races, he can feel a lump forming in his throat, telling himself to stay calm, impossible with the amount of adrenaline now coursing through his veins. Surely, this amount of adrenaline is not good for you. Anna looking over at Anthony from the kitchen, he'd just got out of the shower, so his hair is wet, he's wearing a towel and his face is losing its colour, and is now ashen white. Trying to get his attention, she ends up throwing a tea towel at him, barely missing him but having the desired effect. Looking over at her he sees her mouthing the words 'who is it?' his response is to cover the mouthpiece and whisper to her 'It's Nicola's husband', with that she lets out a squeal of delight, she knows how much Anthony has dreamt of this moment his entire life. She hopes it is good news.

"I'm ringing to hopefully arrange a meeting for you and my wife; she didn't ring herself because she wants the first time to be face to face. He explains, "We were hoping that this Saturday would be good for you." Nikki is now standing next to her husband hoping to catch the sound of Anthony's voice, barely able to hear a thing, getting frustrated at only hearing one side of the conversation.

"Saturday would be good, where does she want to meet, will you be with her?" Anthony asks.

"There's a coffee shop not far from where we live, it's called Rico's." he then proceeds to give Anthony the full address of the location, Anthony giving no indication that he already knows the coffee shop. "I will be there but I won't be at the table with you, you can understand my concern I'm sure, after all we don't know you do we?" Paul tries to get across that it's not that they don't trust him, they just want to be careful.

"That's fine, I understand, will it be okay if I bring my girlfriend?" Anthony can't believe how calm his voice sounds, his insides are churning away, he feels sick, palms are sweating, it's a wonder the phone hasn't slipped through them, he can't believe that his mum has agreed to meet him. He looks over at Anna, who is standing there still in her towel, the one on her head has now gone, her blonde hair trailing down her back, she has a look in her eye he has not seem before and her smile radiates. He can't decide what the look implies, it almost looks as if she is proud of something, just what that is, he has no idea.

"What time do you want to do Saturday?"

"We could probably get there for around eleven o'clock"

"We'll see you on Saturday then." Paul Finishes.

"We'll be there, and I look forward to meeting you both." Anthony says before hanging up the phone. Anna comes running over to him, she'd been unable to move, rooted to the spot while he had been on the phone, scared of interrupting or putting him off. She jumps up at him, wrapping her arms around his neck and her legs around his waist, how they both never went flying is anyone's guess. Giving him a kiss on the cheek he says to her, "What was with that weird look you had on your face when I was on the phone?"

"You called me your girlfriend, your mum's the first person you've told." Now he understands, she has a look of excitement on her face at the prospect of being his girlfriend; he always knew she was weird. Putting her down, she almost loses the towel, holding on to it just before it begins to unravel, she's glad it's a big one.

"What do you want to do today?" He asks her.

"I thought we could just laze about if that's okay with you, maybe go and sunbathe on the roof for a bit."

"In that case I'll put a pair of shorts on." He heads to the bedroom to get dressed, Anna just stares at him walking away, she can't believe how lucky she is, she never thought her and Anthony would ever be an item, she had given up on that idea long ago, now she has everything she ever wanted. Anthony returns wearing just a pair of Ben Sherman tartan shorts, his toned body sending shivers down Anna's spine. "Go and get dressed and I'll meet you up there."

Up on the roof Anthony has laid a couple of large towels out, he's bought a bottle of water, a couple of glasses and the cigarettes. There isn't a cloud in sight today, the sun is high in the sky, and the temperature must be close to thirty. As he's relaxing back on his elbows, he sees Anna's head appear over the roof, he doesn't expect what follows, as she becomes more visible he sees she is wearing her bra and knickers. Conscious of only wearing shorts himself he tries to concentrate his thoughts on mundane things, washing up, cooking, anything but what he sees in front of him.

"Before you ask, I haven't got a bikini here, and this isn't much different is it?" She says, knowing the effect this is having on Anthony, she knows she can be a tease when she wants to be. "You don't mind do you?"

"Not at all, you'll have to bring more of your things over." He says lighting up a cigarette for Anna and one for himself.

Laying down next to him and taking the proffered cigarette, inhaling, before reclining on her elbows, "Are you asking me to live in sin with you?"

"You spend most of your time here; why not move in if you want, I know Mike won't mind."

"So tell me exactly what your mum's husband said to you." Anna wants to know.

Anthony fills her in pretty much word for word, he doesn't think he will ever forget the conversation; surreal doesn't even begin to sum up what it felt like. How many people can say they have buried there parents and then have a conversation with the husband of their mum. They have a laugh about the meeting place, the same coffee shop they were at not two weeks ago.

"I feel guilty now about spying on her." He confesses.

"I know what you mean, but we didn't do anything wrong, we went for a coffee, it just happened to be opposite where she works." Anna tries to rationalise, leaving out that they sat outside her apartment and the following of her to the coffee shop, one small detail conveniently omitted. "Why did you ask if you could take me?"

"I want you to be there, if you want to come that is. Paul—that's Nicola's husband's—said he will be there on Saturday but that he will sit at a different table to give us a chance to talk, so you may have to sit with him at first, I'll understand if you'd rather not come." He adds at the end, he doesn't want to pressure her into anything.

"Of course I'm coming, do you think I am going to miss out on meeting your mum. Besides, I wouldn't let you go on your own?"

"I'm glad you'll be there, I didn't want to go alone." Staring at her, with her head back, eyes closed, the contours of her body beginning to make things stir within him, he hopes she doesn't want him to get up to get her anything at the moment.

*

After Paul hangs up the phone, Nikki wants to know exactly what he said.

"Did he sound pleased that you had phoned?" She wants to know.

"I think so, he's very polite, I will say that." He tells her.

"Come on, what else did he say?" She says, beginning to get agitated with him now. Paul knows this, which is why he is dragging it out.

"He said they would be there about eleven o'clock Saturday, I gave him the address, that was pretty much it, you heard most of it." He tells her.

"You said 'they' would be there, who are 'they'?"

"Didn't I say? He's bringing his girlfriend." Paul knows he hasn't mentioned this little fact, he just likes seeing the look on her face. He didn't expect the punch on the arm though. "Ouch, what was that for?"

"For being a jerk, you should have told me straight away that he had a girlfriend, did he mention anything about his parents?"

"No, but then you'll have time to ask him Saturday all the questions you want." He tells her, "You've got almost a week to think of what you want to say to him, and what you want to ask."

"I've had eighteen years to think, there's so much I want to know, and so much I want to tell him, starting with an apology and explanation."

"From what you've told me, you don't need to apologise, you did what you thought was in his best interest, you loved him and wanted to give him the best chance of a decent life."

With that she hugs him tightly, not wanting to let him go, and putting her mouth up to his ear she whispers "Thank you, I love you so much.

28

Saturday August 5 2000—8:55 am

"Are you sure I look smart enough?" Anthony asks Anna for the tenth time this morning. He's already changed clothes twice, he's now wearing a stone coloured pair of Chino's with a white polo shirt, the polo shirt having long sleeves to cover up what's left of the makeshift tattoo he burned into his arm. The plan is to get the nine-fifteen train into London, to arrive at their destination in plenty of time. It's usually the women that take the time to get ready, yet this morning Anna was ready in about ten minutes, and it's Anthony that is having the wardrobe crisis. His nerves are on edge, although exhilarated at the prospect of meeting his mum in a few hours, doubts are creeping in. What if she doesn't like him, what if she takes one look through the window and decides to go home, that's why he's paranoid about his outfit, he can't afford to get it wrong.

Standing there at a fraction over six feet, his Romany features, with the olive skin and short dark curly hair, like a young David Essex, he creates quite an imposing figure.

"You look great, now we really need to get going, are you nervous?" She asks, they are both still enjoying the first flush of young love, and have been inseparable for the past week, spending as much time together a possible, with Anna pretty much moving into the flat—with Mike's blessing, his only worry was what had taken them so long—though Anthony is still sleeping on the couch. As much as they both want to be together in every sense of the word, so far they have the resolve to resist temptation.

"A bit, I'll just go to the loo again before we head off." This will be the third time he's been in the last half an hour; nerves are definitely getting the better of him. Who wouldn't be nervous, meeting his mum after eighteen years is going to be no walk in the park for either of them. Returning from the toilet he looks at Anna, he still can't believe she's his girlfriend. Wearing a pale blue summer dress with thin over the shoulder straps, and finishing just above the knee, flaring out just at the bottom, she looks gorgeous. Her blue eyes coming alive with the colour of the dress, and her hair is immaculate, Anthony has never known anyone that can look this good with so little effort, and yet Anna still doesn't think she's attractive.

"Now are you ready?"

"Yes, let's go before I need the toilet again." He says with a nervous laugh.

Heading out to the station, Anthony checks that they have everything,

"Do you think I should have sorted out some photo's to take of when I was younger?"

"You can do that next time you meet her, I am sure this time will be questions and learning about each other." She says, pulling the door closed before he can find another excuse to delay things.

"So you think there will be other meetings?"

"Definitely, she would not have agreed to meet you and then say goodbye, never to see you again, would she. I get the impression this has been quite hard on her and her husband, you heard what I heard at the coffee shop when we were listening to her friends. It sounded like her husband had no idea you existed until the last couple of weeks.

"He sounded all right about it on the phone when I spoke to him, I got the impression though that he is a bit... what's the word I'm looking for? Suspicious isn't quite it, but close enough, I don't know if he thinks I'm after something, but he seems very protective of his wife."

"That's natural, I'm protective of you, and you're protective of me, he's only looking out for her, trying to minimise the possibility of her being hurt. You've got to remember, I know it's different but she has been going through this with you for the last eighteen years, neither of you knowing what the other is feeling, but you've both been on the same journey in some strange way, don't you think?"

"I suppose you're right, like you always are." Holding hands now as they walk down the stairs. They have trouble keeping their hands off of each other these days, they have always been touchy-feely even as friends, but since becoming boyfriend-girlfriend they don't miss an opportunity to press flesh to flesh.

*

8:55 am

"Do you think they'll turn up?" Nikki asks Paul, both sitting at the breakfast bar enjoying their morning coffee, Paul with his toast and marmalade, Nikki saying she couldn't possibly eat anything this morning. She's been up for nearly two hours now, unable to sleep, a mixture of excitement and apprehension, this is here third cup of coffee, if she's not careful she'll be so high on caffeine come the time for the meeting.

"They'll turn up, I'd imagine he's thought of this day for a long time, he's not going to let it pass him by. I'd imagine he's as nervous as you if not more so. Now stop worrying, everything will be fine, I'll be there, remember we can leave at any time, for whatever reason, it's a lot to go through for both of you."

"Have I told you just how much I love you?"

"I love you too babe, I'm gonna take a shower when I've finished this, unless you want to go first."

"No you go ahead, I'm just gonna sit outside for a bit, it looks like it's going to be a scorcher of a day."

Finishing the last of his toast and draining his coffee, Paul gets up and heads for the shower, leaving Nikki alone with her thoughts. She takes the rest of her coffee out to the terrace, sitting down on one of the chairs; she takes a folded piece of paper out of the pocket of her satin robe. Carefully unfolding it, someone watching her would think it was a rare document seeing the care taken, reading Anthony's letter once again, wondering if she has missed anything, knowing she hasn't. For the last two hours she has been going over in her mind what she is going to say to him. The stumbling block she has is how you tell someone that you had to give them away, how do you try to make them understand that what you did, you did with their best interests in mind.

She has tried to put herself in his shoes, how would she feel if her mum had given her away, would she be able to forgive her. Unfortunately she keeps coming up with the same answer and that is what is scaring her, she knows in her heart that she would not be able to forgive the woman that had given her away. Irrespective of the reason for her doing so, she doesn't think there is a good enough reason for a mother to give her child away. She wishes that she knew then what she knows now, if she had she would never have given him away, she would have struggled to keep the baby and bring it up. But she didn't, and there is nothing she can do about it now.

She doesn't know what she will do if this is the one and only meeting, she has to make the most of it, starting with a grovelling apology—for what good that will do. In her heart she is hoping for an ongoing relationship with her son, her son, does she have the right to call him that, or did she give that privilege away with him to his new parents. She has a lot to thank them for; just for the fact he is still here and wants to meet her. She wonders if she will ever get the chance to thank them for that small mercy. Less than two hours to go now before she meets up with Anthony, how should she introduce herself, 'Hi I'm your mum' no that would be too pretentious, 'Hi I'm Nikki, I gave birth to you eighteen years ago and then gave you away'. Now she is just being ridiculous, she'll just introduce herself as Nikki and ask him how he is. Stick with simple questions at first, how was the trip here? Did you find the place okay? Boring stuff like that, at least it may help lighten the mood. Her heart tells her though that there is nothing light about this meeting, this will be the second toughest day of her life, the first is the day she gave him away, so it is ironic that the second worst should be when she has to explain her actions to the person it affected the most. Whether he will thank her for what she did or tell her it was the worst decision she could possibly have made, she is about to find out.

29

10:00 am

“You’re very quiet.” Anna remarks, not needing an answer, just trying to get him to interact with her, she has seen him like this in the past where he becomes introverted. She worries about what’s going on in that head of his, even more so on a day like today. He has built this moment up in his head for as long as she can remember, some days hating his mum for giving him away, others feeling guilty for being born and having to put his mum in the intolerable position of having to make that kind of decision. At its worst is the hatred and anger that she knows is boiling inside, she hopes it is not one of those days today.

“Sorry, It’s just I’ve built this day up in my mind for eighteen years, and now it’s finally here, I don’t know what I’m expecting from this meeting, some sort of miracle cure, some assurance that I am loved by her, or is it just curiosity to make sense of why I'm here. All I know is I'm nervous as hell, what if she doesn't like me?"

"She will love you, what's not to love; after all I fell for your charms, didn't I?"

"I know, but it did take you ten years to realise it." He breaks into a smile, he knows what Anna is up to, she is trying to get his head in a happy place because she knows when he's like this it's hard not to like him.

"Right, it's just gone ten, we should be there in about half an hour, assuming to tube goes in our favour, then a ten minute walk. So we should be at the coffee shop about quarter to eleven." Anna informs him, efficient as ever.

"Come on then, last one to the platform pays for coffee." He shouts as she runs down the escalator, not giving her a chance. Not that it matters too much, he knows he'll be paying for the coffee anyway. He believes it should be the man that pays, Anna hates that about him, as she likes to pay her own way, after all she earns more than Anthony, but he will always insist on paying when they go out.

Having navigated the tube system, they come out into bright sunshine, having to accustom their eyes to the brightness. Anthony used the restroom before leaving the station; he's discovered that nerves make his bladder weak. They walk the familiar road, familiar in that they have walked it once before, though the sights and smells are imprinted on Anthony's mind from the last time, the combined smells from the numerous takeaways littered along the road, mixed with the exhaust fumes of the traffic. Although on a Saturday things are considerably quieter, not nearly as much traffic, and at just gone ten-thirty they are still on track to get there for quarter to eleven. Anna with her arm around his waist and her hand in his back pocket, Anthony with his arm around her shoulder, looking like what they are—a young couple in love.

*

10:00

"What time do you want to leave, it will take us no more than five minutes to get there, but if you wanted to get there early it's up to you?" Paul shouts up to Nikki, who's changing for the second time. He understands that she wants to make a good impression, but he's sure that Anthony is not going to care if she's wearing jeans or a dress by Versace. He himself is just wearing jeans and a plain white t-shirt. Even in this he looks smart, the t-shirt showing off his defined muscular body.

"We'll leave when I've got dressed; I'd rather be there early, get a couple of tables. I don't want to miss them. Do you think this is okay?" she asks from the top of the stairs.

Paul looks up to where she is standing, "You look great." He notices that she has gone back to wearing the jeans she had on first but this time with a flowery summer blouse with three quarter length sleeves.

"Are you sure?"

"Yes, now come on or we'll be late" At not quite ten past ten, there is no way they will be late, but Paul knows without pushing her she will change again and again and again, always ending with the first outfit she tried on. Coming down the stairs, he thinks he has got through to her.

They leave the apartment heading towards the coffee shop, holding hands, he gives her a kiss on the top of her head, "How are you feeling?"

"Good, I think, what's the worst that can happen? I still don't know what I'm going to say to him."

"Just talk to him as if he's one of your customers, don't try to force it, the conversation will progress naturally, after all there is so much you can talk about, if you get stuck ask about his family, ask about his life, what his ambitions are, ask about his girlfriend." Paul tries to put her at ease.

"Do you think we'll recognise them when they come in, or maybe they're already there? Do you think he will look at all like me?"

"There are bound to be similarities between the two of you, that's inevitable, how much? Who knows?" He points out.

Getting to the coffee shop, they make small talk with Rico, who tells them that he has reserved a table for them. Nikki had told him that she was meeting up with a family member when she was in here yesterday; they never expected him to go out of his way and reserve the table. They order their coffee, Paul with his double shot of espresso and Nikki with her latte. Sitting down by the window, they have a great view up the street in the direction Anthony will be coming. With not much foot traffic and even less vehicles they should spot them a good three or four minutes before they reach there.

"When they get here I'll say hello, then I'll leave you two to talk, I'll try to get his girlfriend to talk to me, so that you can talk to Anthony on his own, is that okay?" Paul asks.

"At the beginning yes, then depending on how it goes, we can all sit together. If his girlfriend doesn't want to leave him, then she can stay, I don't want to make him uncomfortable, as it is they have had to come somewhere they don't know. If I'd have thought, we should have gone to meet them at a place of their choice, not dictate to them where the meeting is going to happen."

"Just remember, we can leave at any time, just let me know and we will leave, no questions." He notices that even while she is speaking to him, she can't take her eyes off the window and almost straining her neck to see as far up the street as possible.

After finishing their coffees, Paul gets up to get refills, It's now almost quarter to eleven.

*

10:41 am

As they pass the apartment building where his mum lives, they take a quick look to see if there is anyone leaving the building, there isn't so they carry on walking, now hand in hand. Anna can feel his palm sweating, once again he has gone quiet, he's been very chatty up until reaching the apartment. Coming around the bend, that takes them to the street the coffee shop is on, they should be there in a couple of minutes. Anna swears she can hear the beating of his heart in his chest, giving his hand a squeeze, she stops and stands in front of him, planting a kiss on his lips, "We can turn around at any time, whatever you want we will do, remember that." She says, staring straight into his eyes, She would love to be able to see into his mind to see exactly what is going on in there right now.

"No, I'm ready; it's now or never, let's do this. Will you be all right sitting with her husband Paul at first, I'll introduce you, but then I think she wants it to be just the two of us."

"We've already discussed this and it's fine, this is about you and her today, no one else matters, just forget we are there." He doesn't know how he has ended up with someone as good as Anna in his life, considering what a screwed up home life he has had, it's a miracle she has stayed around this long. They carry on walking towards the coffee shop, they can see the salon on the other side of the road about two hundred yards away, and they know that Rico's is opposite. As the yards dwindle between them and his mum, Anthony can feel his heart beating in his chest, any minute it will burst, the sound of it in his ears is deafening, he can vaguely hear Anna trying to say something to him, 'Anthony, Anthony, Anthony'.

"Sorry, were you saying something?" He enquires.

"You were in a world of your own, do you want to stop and take a breather?"

"No, I'll be fine, we're nearly there now, let's keep going, It'll be fine when we've met them, then I will probably relax a little, I think it's the not knowing that's making me like this. I've played this out a million times in my head, and never been this nervous."

A hundred yards to go now, they can begin to make out Rico's.

*

"Paul, there's a couple coming down the road, do you see them? He's in pale trousers; she's in a pale blue dress. Do you think that could be them?" Nikki asks, her excitement building, she hadn't been sure if they would turn up or not, and these are the first people that could possibly be them. Paul once again sees the young woman he fell in love with all those years ago, his Nikki is back,

"I see them; he's got dark curly hair." Even as they're talking the pair are getting closer, they can see that they are holding hands, Paul can see that the girl seems to be very protective of Anthony, they keep stopping, with the girl turning to face him, almost as if she is telling him everything is going to be all right.

"Do they look familiar to you?" Nikki asks with a strange look on her face. Her mind whizzing round in circles trying to place them, she knows she has seen them before.

"You can probably see yourself in him, that's why he looks familiar." Paul rationalises.

"But the girl looks familiar too; I know where I've seen them!" The realisation hits her like a tonne of bricks, a couple of weeks ago, Aimee and her were leaving the apartment, and she commented to Nikki that she thought the couple in the gardens had been looking at her, then she saw the same couple walk past the coffee shop on the opposite side of the road. Quickly relaying this to Paul, as the couple are about to enter the coffee shop. This turn of events have certainly thrown her, the idea that her son had already seen her, and that she had seen him without realising it was her son. She always thought that when she saw her son she would know instinctively that he is hers. In fairness to her she did point the couple out to Aimee, so something inside of her was stirred; now she knows why.

*

"We're here, last chance to change your mind." Anna tells him, she has never seen him this pale and nervous before.

"Come on let's do it, I'm as ready as I'll ever be."

30

Entering they see his mum sitting at a table with, they presume her husband, she looks as pale and nervous as he does, the man is standing up and coming towards them. Anna squeezes his hand tighter, trying to reassure him, or is it that she is feeling his nervousness by proxy. They can't help but notice how good looking and fit this guy is, he has Italian and European features, for some random reason Anthony's first thought is 'this could be my new stepfather' for whatever reason he thinks this it seems to work wonders. He has to stop himself from smiling, even laughing out loud; his heart rate is beginning to decrease, along with the noise in his ears. Anna notices him visibly relax, and can't work out why. As Paul reaches them he extends his hand.

"You must be Anthony?" Looking straight into his eyes, "I'm Paul, Nikki's husband, we spoke on the phone, and I'm sorry I don't know your name." this directed at Anna.

Taking the proffered hand and shaking with a firm grip, "It's nice to meet you, and this is Anna, my girlfriend." He says the pride evident in his voice for all of them to hear.

"Hi Paul, it's a pleasure to meet you." Anna says shaking his hand.

"We're sat over here," Gesturing towards the table where Nikki is sitting alone. Both now follow Paul.

"This is my wife, Nikki. Nikki this is Anthony and the young lady is Anna, his girlfriend."

After all the introductions are out of the way, Paul asks if they would like a drink and something to eat, both opting for just a drink—cappuccinos. Anthony offers to help him, not knowing what to do or say, and both heading to the counter. Anna takes a seat at the table opposite Nikki, neither of them knowing whether they should talk or wait until everyone is there, eventually Nikki breaks the ice.

"How long have you two been together?" She asks, thinking it's a fairly neutral question, she is also captivated by her beauty, she always thought that Aimee her friend was beautiful, but something about Anna, exudes more than just attractiveness, she can't pick one thing about her, it's just everything and nothing.

With a slight laugh, not meaning to be rude she says, "Since last Saturday." The shock is evident on Nikki's face, Anna quickly goes on to say, "But we've been friends since we were eight, it's just taken us a long time to realise we are perfect for each other."

The candidness with which Anna tells her this endears her to her, she is glad her son has had someone like this in his life.

"Let me get these." Anthony says to Paul.

"No, it's alright I've got it, besides, we made you travel down here, I'm sorry we didn't even think about arranging it somewhere close to you." Paul apologises.

"That's fine; it's not that far on the train."

After paying for the coffee, Paul says to Anthony that they had better get back to the table, as he is sure the girls are talking about them, Anthony knows he's just trying to break the tension.

Back at the table, Paul looks over at Anna, "So, Anna would you like to join me and keep me out of trouble while these two talk?"

"Of course." She says, getting up from her seat, she gives Anthony a kiss and wishes him luck. "It was nice to meet you Nikki."

"Likewise, we'll all sit together again in a bit hopefully." Nikki assures her. With that, Paul and Anna go to sit at a table two away from where they are.

Sitting down opposite his mum for the very first time, Anthony's mind goes blank, although he knew what she looked like, he knows her age, he had always assumed his mum would be older, he hadn't realised just how attractive she was when they saw her a couple of weeks ago. Up close as he is now he can see himself in her, most noticeable her eyes, it's as if he is looking in a mirror when he looks into hers, both of them sharing the same deep green eyes.

"Before we start can I just ask one thing?" Nikki tentatively asks.

"Sure go ahead."

"Have you ever been here before? I know it's a strange question, but when I saw you walking down the road, I could have sworn I had seen the two of you before."

"Guilty, I should apologise for that, after I didn't hear anything from you I decided to come and see where you lived, Anna just came along for the ride. I'm sorry; I thought that if you weren't going to reply to my letter, then I at least wanted to see you, to see what you looked like. I would never have just knocked on your door though." He can feel the redness in his cheeks; it feels like he's been caught doing something he isn't supposed to be doing.

"That's fine, I just didn't want to think I was imagining things," She says with a laugh, helping to relax both of them, before getting serious again, "Besides I'm the one that should be apologising, I should have written sooner, but my husband had no idea about you, I had to sort that out first. But you have to know I always wanted to meet you." She says, looking down at her hands, not able to meet his eyes.

"I know we both probably have so many questions to ask, where do you want to start, I thought we could take it in turns to ask a question, rather than one of us doing all the talking, does that sound okay?" Anthony asks, he had never thought of it going like this, but now that he was here sat in front of her, he thought that she must have as many questions about him as he has of her, he had never properly thought about her side before now.

"That sounds good; you can go first if you want." Nikki tells him, relieved that it isn't going to be an interrogation, this way they get to learn small things about each other, instead of everything in one go.

"The first question is why? I have the basics from social services, but I would like to hear it from your side, the limited details I've been provided with tell me that your parents wouldn't have me or you back in their house after I was born." He asks the one question that he has wanted the answer to all his life, or at least the portion of his life once he knew he was adopted.

"Can I start by saying that I am going to be candid with you, I'm not going to gloss over anything, if that means you may get hurt by some of the things I tell you, then I'll apologise in advance, that isn't my intention, but I feel you are entitled to know the truth."

"That's fine by me, it can't be worse than some of the scenarios that have gone through my mind over the years, at times I hated you for what you did, at others I felt deep sympathy for having put you in that situation, and yes you did hear right I have blamed myself over the years. Rationally I know it has absolutely nothing to do with me, but I always thought that if I hadn't been born or even conceived then you would not have had to make the decisions you did. I know it makes no sense but in my head at times it was all my fault for how things turned out." He says, himself being candid in a way he had not thought he was capable of, something about sitting in front of the woman who gave birth to him lets him open up fully to her. He can see that she has a tear on her cheek, "Sorry I didn't mean to upset you, are you okay."

"Please don't blame yourself for any of this, this was down to me and me alone, you have nothing, and I mean nothing to feel guilty about. You'll make me feel worse if I know you blame yourself for any of this." She wipes away the tears, trying to compose herself, she sees Paul looking over at her, mouthing the words 'Are you okay', she gives a smile in response, and a slight nod of the head. This isn't lost on

Anthony; he's glad that she has someone watching out for her. "Now where were we, that's right—Why? A big part of me wanted to keep you, you have to know that, but I was young, I was sixteen when I found out I was pregnant. I had been stupid, it was the first time I had been with a boy, and I regret it to this day. I don't regret that you were born as a result, and I'm glad you're sitting here now. When I told my parents that I was pregnant I didn't expect the reaction I got, I was always very close to them, especially my dad, in his eyes I could do no wrong—until the day I announced I was going to have a baby. Then everything changed, neither of them would speak to me, during the nine months I was pregnant with you, I think my dad said half a dozen words to me. My mum slightly more but usually of the derogatory kind, I was called all the names under the sun, I think they were more concerned with what the neighbours would think than the fact I was carrying their grandchild. I had various discussions with the social worker, and my best friends mum, and they all said that I would not be able to cope with a baby without the support of my parents. Being only sixteen, I took their word for it, never believing that I would be capable and strong enough to bring you up on my own. I know differently now, and I wish I had made different decisions. Looking back, maybe I should have kept you, and if couldn't have coped then I could have put you up for adoption. The social worker told me that they had a loving family lined up that was looking for a baby boy. A family that already had a two-year-old daughter and that unfortunately they couldn't have any more children so were looking to adopt. It sounded perfect, a family that desperately wanted you. Not that I didn't want you, I was incapable of caring for you in the way that you deserved or needed." She says with more tears beginning to form in her eyes.

Anthony can see how much that had hurt to tell him, and he's grateful for the honesty, he truly believes every word she has just told him. For once in his life he is beginning to make sense of why what happened did and the circumstances that conspired to put him where he ended up, with a family he always felt never wanted or needed him. A family that constantly made excuses for his existence to anyone that would listen, excuses for why he behaved the way he did, excuses for his temper when it reared its ugly head, excuses for his stubbornness. When in reality many of these traits are not bred into him they are environmental traits. His anger would only come to the surface when in his parents company and only then when it was clear that they didn't want him in their family unit. His stubbornness is borne out of a need for them to notice him; it was his way of getting his families attention. When he was good and no bother to anyone, they simply pretended as if he didn't exist.

"I am sorry that you were left with such a tough choice, purely from my point of view I would have preferred you to have given it a try looking after me. I would rather have had a tougher life with you than the life I have had, don't get me wrong there are some things I am grateful for from the life I have, especially and most importantly Anna. I think without Anna I wouldn't be here now." He can feel the tears welling up in his eyes, he promised himself that he wouldn't cry today, rubbing his eye to clear the moisture, making out he has something in it isn't fooling her. She reaches across the table and takes his hand in hers.

“I am so sorry, I honestly thought that giving you to a loving family was in your best interest, If I could have seen into the future I would never have given you up.” She tells him.

*

“Do you think everything’s okay?” Anna asks Paul, they can both see that Anthony is upset, and Nikki isn’t fairing much better. Anna just wants to go over and comfort him, but Paul puts his arm out to hers as she begins to get up from her chair.

“They need to work this out between them, let’s just see how it goes.” He wants to go over there as much as she does but his resolve is obviously much stronger than hers. “Now you were telling me about how it took you and Anthony so long to become boyfriend and girlfriend.” Paul has taken quite a shine to Anna, she is friendly, easy going and intelligent for her age, he’s met a lot of youngsters and many of them have trouble stringing a coherent sentence together, but much to his surprise he has found himself liking the both of them. Although he has only had a fleeting conversation with Anthony, his politeness goes a long way to showing his character.

*

“Right I think it’s your turn now to ask a question.” Anthony says, wiping away the last of the tears.

“Do your parents know you’ve made contact with me, and if they do, how have they taken it?” Thinking it’s a fairly straightforward question.

“My parents died when I was sixteen.”

“I’m so sorry, I didn’t know. What a stupid question to ask.” She’s embarrassed that she has asked such a question.

"It's okay, we weren't close." He then tells her about not going to the funeral and his sister. "You can ask another question, that one doesn't really count."

"Did you think about me while you were growing up?"

"Yes, a lot. I didn't find out I was adopted until I was about nine, although I knew from much younger that something wasn't right. I didn't look like my parents, friends at school would be picked up by theirs and they would resemble them in some way. My parents looked nothing like me. As soon as I found out about the adoption, Anna and me used to make up stories about where I had come from. Rarely a day went by that I didn't think of you in some way, sometimes with a deep love, others with extreme anger and hurt that you had given me away. I've struggled for years to come to terms with who I am, not knowing where I come from is one of my biggest stumbling blocks, something I hope this meeting is going to help with. Even just sitting here with you, I can see parts of me in you. For instance, I can see that I have your eyes, and obviously your colouring. Do you see anything familiar in me, Is any of it from my dad?" He's not sure whether to ask about his dad, he's been agonising over this since the meeting had been arranged. Should he ask about his dad or not, he doesn't want to upset her and put her off meeting him again, but on the other hand surely he has a right to know. At least asking the question this way, it leaves it open for her to talk about him, and if she doesn't then he will leave it for now and pursue it at a later date, assuming there is going to be a later.

"Yes a lot, like you say you have my colouring, and eyes—it's like looking into my own when I stare at you. Your build you get from your dad, but do you mind if we don't discuss him today? I know you must have questions about him, but I was hoping we could leave that chat for another time. Sorry I'm assuming that we will meet again, that should have been my first question—what are your expectations from meeting me, is it just for information?" the tone of her voice tells Anthony that she is hoping for more than that. There is a certain desperation letting him know that she wants more than a question and answer session.

"Honestly? I don't know, definitely more than questions and answers, I would like to get to know you, learn about your life with Paul—he seems nice by the way—other than that I thought we could take it from there if that's okay with you."

"That sounds perfect, I don't want to lose you now that you've found me, I want to know all about your life, good and bad, and I would like to get to know Anna as well, she seems to be a major part of your life. I want to hear about your parents, as long as you don't mind talking about them, basically I want to know everything. Listen to me demanding what I want." She laughs nervously hoping she hasn't overstepped the mark. Seeing the smile light up Anthony's face, she knows he wants the same.

"I feel bad that Paul and Anna are sitting separately, would you mind if we included them now, I have no secrets from Anna, and I'm more than happy for Paul to hear anything I've got to say. Tell me if you'd rather keep it like this for now."

"I'm more than happy." Catching Paul's eye, she gestures for him and Anna to come and join them.

"So how's it all going?" Paul asks. Anna sits down next to Anthony and takes hold of his hand.

“Great.” Anthony answers. He gives Anna’s hand a squeeze to reassure her that everything is okay. He is extremely pleased with how things have worked out so far, he had only ever dreamed that his first meeting with his mum would go this well. Most of the resentment he has held onto for all these years is finally dissipating. He thinks there will always be moments when he will think back to the times where he detested her and what she did, but he believes he can get past it and not let it affect his life the way it has dominated him for eighteen years. He feels a genuine bond to Nikki, the kind he never felt for his parents or sister, he believes he can imagine what it is like to be a part of a family. He would not have thought the bond would be something that could hit him as hard as it is, he just hopes that Nikki is feeling the same.

After making some small talk, about what everyone does for a living, discussing each other’s general well-being Paul suggests taking Anthony and Anna back to the apartment as it is such a nice day, they can have a drink and sit outside.

31

Walking back the way they had come, Anthony with his arm around Anna's shoulder, and Paul and Nikki holding hands, anyone seeing them would not believe that Nikki and Anthony were mother and son. They could easily be mistaken for brother and sister, with Anthony looking older than his eighteen years, and Nikki looking considerably younger than her thirty-four. Back at the apartment, Nikki gives the two of them a tour while Paul gets some drinks together.

"This place is incredible; it's such a gorgeous space." Anna says, awestruck at the sheer size of the place, this is without seeing the view across the Thames to Canary Wharf. "Do you have good neighbours?"

"Upstairs is Aimee and Steve, Steve is the architect that designed them, he's also Paul's best friend. And I'm Aimee's business partner in the salon. Then downstairs is Hayley, she's been my best friend for as long as I can remember."

"Did either of them know about Anthony?" Once again opening her mouth without thinking, "Sorry I shouldn't have asked that."

"No, neither of them knew, up until I received the letter I had never told anyone, I think because I was ashamed of what I had done. You hear so many stories of women who can't have children and there's me giving one away. You don't need to apologise for asking questions Anna, if it's something I don't want to talk about I'll let you know, but don't be afraid to ask anything."

"What did you think when you received the letter?"

"To be honest I was devastated, not because Anthony had got in touch, but because I had been stupid enough not to have told Paul. We've been married ten years and all I could think about after reading the letter was how I was going to break the news to him, how do you explain to someone that supposedly knows all there is to know that suddenly you have an eighteen-year-old son. I thought I was going to lose him, he actually went away for a week straight after I told him, he said he 'needed to think'. The night I told him, he walked out, he didn't come home and then Aimee told me the next day that Paul and Steve were going away that morning. I don't think I have ever cried so much as I have the last few weeks. With the possible exception of when Anthony was born, then I cried for weeks after wondering if I had just made the biggest mistake of my life. I don't know what would have happened if I had decided to keep him, where would we be now, would he have resented me for not being able to provide him with a good life. There are a lot of 'what ifs' in my life." She notices that Anthony has wandered off, and she can see him talking to Paul out on the terrace, she knows everything is going to be good from here on out. "Can I ask you something about Anthony?"

"Sure."

"You've known him a long time, how has he handled it really?"

"I don't want to talk behind his back, but I always thought he handles it pretty well, we used to sit and make up stories of what his real family may have been like, sometimes stupid ones. Recently I saw the side he kept hidden from the world, a darker side, and for some reason that endeared me to him more, not that I ever thought it possible. Seeing the vulnerable side to him made me want him more, I think I loved him from the first moment I saw him, but something happened over the last few weeks that made me realise he is the one, the only one for me. I think if you want to know more about what he has gone through you need to ask him. You understand that I don't want to break his confidence don't you?"

"Of course, I wouldn't expect you too, I think at the moment we just need to get to know each other better before I start asking the personal questions. Shall we go and join the boys?"

Out on the terrace, Anna and Anthony have wandered to the other end to admire the different views, also giving them a chance to talk and likewise Nikki and Paul.

*

"What do you think of them?" Nikki asks Paul, concern in her voice, she hopes Paul has taken to them the way she has. She has been pleasantly surprised how well-mannered they both are, how respectful.

Not that she had been expecting louts, not actually knowing what to expect, but pleased nonetheless. She's looking at Paul intently to see what he is thinking, getting the impression that he likes them too.

"I like them, I'll be honest, when I set up the meeting I had expected it to be a one-time deal, I thought he would ask his questions, his curiosity satisfied, then they would go off and live their lives and we would carry on with ours. What I didn't expect is that I would genuinely like them so much. They're friendly, intelligent and despite the upbringing Anthony has had he's turned out remarkably well. As a couple, they are perfect together. You should be proud of him."

"Why should I be proud, I had nothing to do with his upbringing, It's his parents that would be proud were they still with us, I get the impression from Anthony that they wouldn't have been, if they ever noticed him at all. I think they missed a great opportunity, never realising what they had in Anthony. It still feels odd thinking of him as Anthony, when all these years he was Mark to me, I'm sure I'll get used to it."

"Like you said, his parents weren't interested in him, so to me that means his genes are the reason he's turned out so well. Half those genes being yours, makes you responsible for what he is today."

Leaning into him Nikki gives him a kiss on the lips, "Thank you for everything."

*

"Are you glad you've met her?" Anna asks, both of then looking out over the London Skyline, out of earshot from Nikki and Paul. Anna wants to know the truth now of what Anthony thinks of his mum.

"Yes, it wasn't exactly what I expected, but in a good way. Over the years I have envisaged the moment I meet her. There were things I wanted to tell her when we came face to face. How hurt and betrayed I had felt my whole life, not to hurt her like she hurt me but to make her realise just what she had done when she gave me away. I swore that no matter what she said I was going to make it clear how I felt, but seeing her today in the coffee shop, I couldn't. No, that's not quite right, I didn't want to, just because she hurt me, that doesn't give me the right to hurt her back. When she started talking about how my adoption came about, I felt sorry for her, I could see the sorrow in her eyes at the mistake she knew she made all those years ago. Looking back at all the events eighteen years ago, I can't help feeling that maybe it had been for the best. What life would she have had, a baby at sixteen trying to cope on her own, wondering where the next meal was coming from, who knows where either of us would have ended up? I'm not saying I'm glad I was adopted, but at least it gave her a chance at a normal life, at the sacrifice of her child I grant you, but that is something she has lived with all these years. It has probably been just as hard for her, if not harder. I've had you to whine to all these years, she's had nobody. Can you imagine how that must have eaten her up inside, the knowledge that her son was out there and could turn up at any time? I know I can't. Despite all of that, she runs a successful business, has a loving husband and a lovely home, and until my letter turned up they seem to have had a happy life. I just hope I haven't ruined all that for them."

"I'm sure you haven't, just look at them, they seem happy don't they?" Both now looking over at Nikki and Paul, she just gave him a kiss on the lips.

"They do."

*

All back together again, they chat for another few hours, about how Anthony is doing in the patisserie, he promises to make them something for the next time they meet. They talk briefly about his family and his sister. Nikki notices that when he talks about them, he's on edge, he doesn't like speaking badly of them, but at the same time finds it very hard to say anything positive, leaving just the mundane facts of their life to discuss. What Nikki wants to know is did he love them, but she is afraid of the answer, she has no right to expect loyalty from the son she gave away. She understands that his allegiance would be with them, but she gets the impression that—and she feels bad for thinking it—he has no emotional attachment to them whatsoever. She has seen that his emotions can be strong at times; she witnessed it in the coffee shop only a few hours ago.

She can't help wondering if his parents picked up on this and that's why they didn't take to him. Not that she's defending them, any mother that can tell her son that she's taking him back for a refund doesn't deserve the love of her child, for sixteen years that's what he was, he was their child. She can see the love in his eyes when he looks at Anna, a more powerful love she has never seen, wondering how it took them so long to decide they are meant to be together. Anna has it too, that longing look whenever they look at each other.

"Anthony, can I ask you a personal question, you don't have to answer, and I'll even understand if you tell me to get lost." She can see a worried look cross his face, his brow furrows, worried that it's going to be something awful, something maybe about his burning fetish, he is not ready to confront that particular demon just yet. He will at some point, he managed it with Anna, but he doesn't want his mum to think he's some kind of freak.

"Sure, go ahead."

"Did you love your parents?" She's pleased to see the look of relief on his face.

"Funny you should ask that particular question; Anna wanted to know the exact same thing a while ago. The simple answer is no, I cared about them, and I was grateful to them, but did I love them, no." He has it clear in his mind now, whereas before he thought he loved them in some way, now he can say with some certainty that he didn't. He feels more love towards Nikki than he ever felt for his parents. And the love he feels for Anna is incomparable to anything he has felt for any other living soul.

"I hope you didn't mind me asking?"

"No, that was an easy one to answer."

"Would you two like to stay for dinner?" This from Paul, who has just been sitting absorbing the conversation for a while, not feeling left out but realising this is their time, the most important time probably in both their lives when they need to bond. Or more to the point they need to increase the natural bond that already exists between the two of them.

"We'd love too, but we don't really want to travel back too late, there are a lot of weirdo's on the trains at night." Anna, always the sensible one points out this simple fact, she doesn't want to drag Anthony away from here, but she has at least given him an out should he feel he needs a breather from it all. She knows today must have taken it out on him. She looks at him to let him know she is happy either way—they have their own way of communicating things to each other, a certain look and the other knows what's going through the others mind.

"You're more than welcome to stay over, we have a guest bedroom or bedrooms if you prefer." He looks over at Nikki to make sure he hasn't crossed a line, clearly seeing that the line doesn't exist concerning Anthony, evident by her radiant smile, she's back to the young woman he fell in love with all those years ago once more.

"If you're sure it's no trouble, and one room will be fine." Anthony gets an approving look from Anna, both knowing this will be their first night of sleeping in the same bed. He just wants the closeness of her body tonight, nothing more. He wants to hold her and make sure she knows he's not going anywhere, ever. He's aware that she's been worried about him for a long time, more so after the night she found him drunk and sobbing, and then again when she found out about his self-mutilation. Admitting though that she felt flattered he would put himself through so much pain, while all the time thinking of her and only her (He had eventually admitted what the marks spelled out). She still had a go at him though for being so stupid, pointing out that he could have got an infection, or anything.

"We'll get a takeaway tonight, but one night you will have to come round and sample your mum's cooking, you can't beat it." Suddenly realising what he has said, he quickly apologises, his face reddening, and his cheeks flushing, and then noticing that everybody else seems to be grinning like Cheshire cats. "Have I missed something?" Suddenly confused by everyone's reaction to him calling Nikki 'mum'.

"I think it's because we've all been avoiding the white elephant in the room all day, no one knowing whether they should point out the fact that, yes, Nikki is Anthony's mum. And yes Paul that technically makes you his step-dad." With Anna's comment, they are now all laughing hard, the look of realisation on Paul's face that without having to do anything he has suddenly inherited a stepson. As the tears of laughter begin to subside, so as not to leave Anna out.

"Just so you don't feel left out Anna, could that mean someday soon I would be your mother-in-law." More laughter ensues before Paul asks the all-important question about which takeaway they should get. The consensus is for Indian, Paul places the order for an assortment of dishes, and they can all have some of each.

Nikki shows them to their room, it's beautifully decorated in shades of whites and a deep damson colour for the bed linen. Nikki hands them some towels and tells them that if they would like they would have time for a shower before the food arrives, and that if there is anything else they need she will be in the kitchen.

Completely alone now for the first time since they walked into the coffee shop this morning, Anthony pulls Anna to him and gives her the tightest hug imaginable.

"Have you seen the size of the bed?" Anna pulls away from him and launches herself on to the super king-sized four-poster bed. Anthony joins her a bit more serenely, lying next to her, face to face.

"Are you sure it was okay for me to say that we would stay over, and that one room is enough. I can ask her if we could have the other room if you'd prefer." His words getting tongue-tied, feeling guilty now for assuming Anna would be happy sharing a bed with him.

"It's perfect; I think it's been a perfect day. Did it go as well as you had expected?"

"Better." One word is all he needs to say.

"Your mum isn't what I expected; I can't believe she's as normal as she is. Sorry that came out wrong, what I mean is, I thought that after what she has gone through she may have been guarded towards you. Afraid to let you see the real her, I was worried you'd be the same, but I think both of you have been very open with each other. Right I'm gonna have my shower first if you don't mind."

"You go ahead." He lays back on the bed watching Anna go through into the bathroom, closing his eyes and thinking back to the day's events. He never in a million years thought they would still be here now, getting ready to share a meal with his mum and her husband—or should that be stepfather. The more he thinks about them the more they don't fit the image of what he expected. They were young, trendy—you only had to look round the apartment to see that, they are not the sort of people you would expect to have an eighteen-year-old son. In all fairness though, Paul had no idea his wife had a child, let alone one that can legally drink and get married. He's surprised at how well Paul has taken to both him and Anna, it's as if they have all known each other for far longer than the past few hours. How much of that is because him and Nikki have a natural bond, regardless of only just meeting, there definitely seems to be some kind of force which joins them and has done since he was born. An unbreakable link that would have remained had they never met, if

Anthony's curiosity and need to see and meet her had not been so strong he believes that the bond would still be there. In some respects, he's known her all his life, for she is a part of him, half his D.N.A. after all comes from her. But what he can't figure out is why he has no burning desire to know anything about or even meet his dad, and yet he should share the same link to him—he just doesn't—and he can't explain it. He goes back to his child hood, thinking of the times, and there were numerous, when he dreamed of this precise moment, and there was never a single time when things went this well. Even in his most optimistic states of mind, he couldn't envisage the meeting with his mum going like this. The strangest pert of it all is he doesn't see Nikki and Paul as mum and step dad but as friends, the age difference is irrelevant, if you enjoy each other's company then that should be enough. In the back of his mind there is a part telling him to take things slowly, don't get carried away, this could yet be a one off meeting, maybe they're just being polite and don't want them travelling back on the train too late. Maybe they just want more information before saying a final goodbye.

These thoughts wrenched from his mind as a completely new vision fills his head, that of Anna who has just stepped from the bathroom, wearing only her bra and knickers.

"The shower's all yours."

"Couldn't you be bothered to get dressed, not that I'm complaining?"

"I thought I'd let them air for a bit, seeing as we didn't bring a change of clothes."

Getting off the bed, he moves towards her, embracing as they meet halfway between the bed and bathroom. A long lingering kiss, Anna can feel him getting aroused; he's running his fingers down her spine stopping just short of her knicker line.

"Don't go getting any funny ideas mister."

"Spoilsport."

"We'll get to the good stuff soon enough, and besides I do believe it was your idea to do this properly."

"I know, but when you're standing there in front of me looking like that." Stepping away from her and indicating with his arms as if presenting her at an auction 'and here we have this fine specimen of a woman'. "What do you expect; after all I'm just a man." His parting shot as he leaves her to get in the shower.

*

Nikki gets the plates for dinner, Paul the cutlery, laying the table for four.

"They aren't what I expected; your son is the spitting image of you though. I didn't think I would like them so much, I thought that would come with time and getting to know them. You must be pleased with the way he's turned out."

"He's perfect." The pride evident in the tone of her voice and the smile creeping into the corners of her mouth, "They make a lovely couple don't you think, I think Anna has more to do with the way he's developed than anyone. She should take credit for the way he's turned out. I do regret though not being there for him when he was growing up. All the questions that went unanswered, the pain he must have gone through." Seeing the tears forming in her eyes, that glassy look that tells him they're imminent, taking hold of her and hugging her tight.

"It's not your fault, you did what you thought was best for him." Wiping away the tears with his thumbs as they leave her eyes, "I think today means more to him than anything else in his life, and the two of you have the next god knows how many years to be a family."

"I know, but you don't want a family, and here I am thrusting one upon you whether you want it or not. It's not fair on you." The last sentence catches in her throat, not wanting to lose Paul and at the same time wanting Anthony in their lives.

"This isn't the same, he's a grown man, we haven't got to take care of him, he will just become part of our life. Besides, I genuinely like him, and Anna, they're both welcome here whenever they want."

"Thank you; you don't know how much that means. I couldn't bear the thought of losing him all over again, I know I've missed the first eighteen years, but I would like to make it up to him somehow, does that make any sense to you?"

"Of course it does, I know you feel bad about having to give him up for adoption, but he's found you now, and I will do anything to make sure you are happy."

Epilogue

Sunday January 7 2001

"You're the one that said you were happy to make the phone call." Paul reminds her.

"I know." She resigns herself to the fact that yes, she is the one that told Anthony she would make the phone call. She's put it off for too long, she always said it was the one thing she wouldn't do for Anthony, she was happy to give him the phone number to him so he could make the call. For some reason, she still can't recall exactly how it happened, but over the Christmas festivities Anthony asked if she would call her parents and tell them that he would like to meet them. Whether it was too much wine, the overwhelming happiness of spending her first Christmas with her son and his girlfriend, she doesn't know. All that matters is she agreed to phone her parents.

"Do you want me to call them?"

"No this is something I have to do, besides, what's the worst that can happen—they slam the phone down on me—best case is they agree to meet with Anthony." Telling herself this makes no difference, the thought of speaking to her parents after all these years terrifies her. As much as she misses the closeness she shared with her mum and dad, her lasting impression of them is seeing their car drive off after dumping her at the hospital all those years ago. She can still recall seeing their taillight come on as her dad stopped about a hundred yards from where she stood. Inside the sudden sense of hope that they regretted leaving her like that and they were coming back to be with their daughter. All she wanted was for them to come back and tell her that they loved her and everything was going to be all right. But they didn't, as she watched the car, instead of turning around to come back to her, it turned left back onto the main road towards home—home meaning nothing to her now, home the place she used to live, home a place she's never going back to.

She remembers the sadness and sense of loneliness like it was yesterday and the thought of speaking to her parents causes a lump to form in the back of her throat. What if when they answer she can't talk? What if her voice seizes up and nothing comes out? What if whoever answers the phone hears her voice and puts the phone down? All these 'what ifs', would it be better if they no longer live there, if they've moved away to start a new life, at least then she can tell Anthony she has tried, will that be enough to placate him and stop his longing to meet his maternal grandparents. She is still grateful that he seems to have no interest in meeting his father—a loose term for what Neil is, father is a stretch of anyone's imagination—the correct term for him is the man that

fucked her and planted a seed in her belly. So far all he knows about him is a brief description of what he looks like, she explained to Anthony that it was a one-night stand, a mistake, and no more. She hasn't told him how he humiliated her and left her all alone in that bedroom. Or how he had made her lay on the carrier bags in case she got blood on the bed linen, she left out the part about how rough he was with her and that it was all over in a matter of minutes, he doesn't need to hear any of that. It was bad enough going over it all with Paul, she certainly couldn't tell Anthony the truth about his biological father.

With the phone still gripped in her hand, she wanders out onto the terrace, letting the warm sun embrace her, she sits on the lounger, it's now or never, punching in each number in turn, it's funny how she has never forgotten the number even after all these years. Hitting the last number, there is a slight delay before she can hear the familiar tone of the phone ringing at the other end. Almost as soon as she hears it she cuts the call, she can't do this, she feels a tear running down her cheek, not realising she had started crying. She doesn't know why she still lets her parents get to her like this, they are the ones that should feel ashamed, not her. They abandoned her, not the other way round, she has nothing to feel guilty about, but no matter how much she tells herself, she still blames herself for the breakdown in her family. Do they care so little that they couldn't even pick up the phone to her or write over the years, the smallest communication from them would have meant so much to her, but they were even incapable of that.

She tried reaching out to them before with no joy, what makes her think it will be any different now, this times it isn't for her, it's for her

son. The very same son that started all this in the first place, the reason they banished her from their home and life. Although after meeting Anthony, she realises all the sacrifices from that part of her life have been worth it. Given the chance she would do it all again, with the exception this time she would keep him and make a life for the both of them together, not farm him out to another family to take responsibility for her son.

"Are you okay? What did they say? Why are you crying?" She hadn't realised Paul had come out and sat beside her. He's wiping away the tears as he's asking the questions.

"I haven't done it yet, I dialled and as soon as it started ringing I put the phone down, will you stay with me while I try again." He puts his arm around her and kisses the side of her head to reassure her that it's going to be fine, everything is going to work out.

Dialling the numbers again, she hears the familiar tone once again, her free hand entwined with Paul's, two rings, three rings, four rings, her heart is pounding in her chest knowing that at any second she could be hearing the familiar voice of either her mum or dad. Nine rings, ten rings, how many more should she give it before she puts the phone down, in her head she tells herself two more rings and that's it, I've tried. On the twelfth rings she hears the unmistakable click of the phone on the other end picking up, a male voice on the other end reciting the telephone number back, a tear escaping from her eye at the sound of her dad's voice.

"Hello, who am I speaking to?"

"Hello dad, it's Nicola, your grandson would like to meet you."

About the Author

Craig was born in Luton in 1971. He is a trained chef and worked in the industry for nearly twenty years before various career changes including web designer, and cleaning company owner, however he is back in the kitchen and currently works as a Chef Manager, although would like to write full time should the opportunity arise.

He lives with his wife Tina and their cat—Tia Maria—in Norfolk, since moving there in 2003 from Hertfordshire. His hobbies include writing and painting, along with various other crafts.

He also enjoys music and reading, invariably listening to Jazz while writes.

Printed in Great Britain
by Amazon